DEATH
OF A DAMN
YANKEE

Books by Toni L.P. Kelner

DOWN HOME MURDER

DEAD RINGER

TROUBLE LOOKING FOR A PLACE TO HAPPEN

COUNTRY COMES TO TOWN

TIGHT AS A TICK

DEATH OF A DAMN YANKEE

Published by Kensington Publishing Corp.

A LAURA FLEMING MYSTERY

DEATH
OF A DAMN
YANKEE

Toni L.P. Kelner

KENSINGTON BOOKS
Kensington Publishing Corp.
http://www.kensingtonbooks.com

KENSINGTON BOOKS are published by

Kensington Publishing Corp.
850 Third Avenue
New York, NY 10022

Library of Congress Card Catalogue Number: 98-075557
ISBN 1-57566-431-3

First Printing: August, 1999
10 9 8 7 6 5 4 3 2 1

Printed in the United States of America

To my sister,
Connie Perry Spencer:

"I hold you as a thing enskied and sainted."

—*Measure for Measure*
Act I, Scene 4

Acknowledgments

I want to thank:

- My husband Stephen P. Kelner, Jr., for his able assistance, constant support, unfailing respect, and eternal patience.
- My daughter, Magdalene Kelner, for taking long naps.
- My new daughter, Valerie Kelner, for not arriving early.
- Signe Spencer, for supplying Marshall Saunders.
- Max Levine, for inspiring Max Wilder.
- Eric Bergemann, for teaching me that passwords aren't always safe.
- Elizabeth Shaw, for proofreading the manuscript in record time.
- Amy Solano, Anne Solano, Rachael Solano, and Victoria Walker, for keeping Maggie happy so I could work.

Chapter 1

I didn't want to drive by the old warehouse, but I couldn't seem to help myself, and from the amount of traffic on that dusty back road, I wasn't the only one. Normally, the only ones who go that way are the handful of folks who live around Walters Lake or optimistic fishermen. Today, there were two cars ahead of us and three more behind us.

"The vultures are circling," I muttered to Richard.

"We're not vultures," my husband said. "We can go back if you want to."

"We may as well keep going," I said, as if it didn't matter to me. "There's not a good place to turn around until we get to the lake anyway." It was a lousy excuse, but Richard didn't argue.

After a few more yards, we passed the last of the scraggly pine trees and could see what was left of the warehouse. There was actually more of it still there than I'd expected. Aunt Maggie had told me the place had burned down to the ground, and I'd never realized how much wreckage remains after a building "burns down." Misshapen beams reached up toward the roof that wasn't there anymore while timbers tilted against the remnants of the wooden floor.

The stink of the place sneaked into the car, despite the

rolled-up windows. It wasn't the clean smell of burnt wood, and even though I tried to convince myself that it was from the paint on the walls or maybe asphalt shingles from the roof, my imagination supplied a more gruesome reason for the stench.

The fire had leached the color away, leaving nothing but black. The only bright spot was the yellow police tape flapping in the breeze. Police Chief Junior Norton must have put that up as soon as she realized that the building wasn't the only thing to burn. There'd been a man's body inside.

I'd only met Marshall Saunders two days before, but I'd liked him, despite the furor he'd caused in town. Though I wasn't convinced his motives for coming to town had been pure, I was sure that he hadn't deserved this.

"He should never have come to Byerly," I said softly to Richard. "And we shouldn't have come back."

"Laura, you know this wasn't our fault."

I nodded, but it was going to take a lot more than that to convince me that Marshall's death had nothing to do with the reason Richard and I were in Byerly. How could I be sure that I wasn't responsible for a murder?

Chapter 2

It was Tuesday evening not quite a week before when we were talked into going to Byerly. When the doorbell rang, I was sprawled on the couch reading the newspaper while Richard looked through the mail. We weren't expecting company, but our apartment is in Boston's Back Bay, meaning that friends on the way to Symphony Hall or shopping on Newbury Street sometimes drop by. I got up, pressed the intercom button, and said, "Hello?"

"Laurie Anne?"

I certainly didn't expect that. My friends up North call me Laura—only my family and the other people in Byerly call me Laurie Anne. The thing was, I didn't recognize the voice, and I sure as heck hadn't been expecting anybody from Byerly to drop by. "Yes?" I said hesitantly.

"Laurie Anne, this is Burt Walters. I was wondering if I might speak to you and your husband."

I was so surprised you could have knocked me over with a feather, but I pushed the buzzer, and said, "Come on in." Richard looked just as mystified as I was as I opened the door to our apartment so Burt would know to climb up to the second floor.

I just couldn't imagine why Burt Walters would be in

Boston, any more than I could imagine Byerly without the Walters. They owned the mill and the bank, and had a finger in every pie in Byerly that included money. With Burt's daddy Big Bill Walters in charge of the city council, they came close to running the town, and their social life reflected that. Though they occasionally received guests at their pseudo-antebellum mansion, complete with columns and a veranda, I'd never known them to visit normal people like my family.

My first thought was that something awful had happened. Aunt Nora's last letter had mentioned the spate of accidents at Walters Mill. Could one or more of my cousins have been hurt? But Aunt Nora or one of her sisters would have called me if that were true.

What about that fire she'd written about? Could there have been another—one so bad that all of my aunts, uncles, and cousins had been injured, leaving only Burt able to give me the news? No, that was even more ridiculous. Burt would have called or sent a telegram, not hopped on a plane to Boston. Besides, I've got too much family—you'd have to burn down the entire state of North Carolina to get them all.

There was no time for any other crazy ideas before Burt got upstairs, which was just as well.

Burt said, "Good to see y'all," and shook Richard's hand and then mine. I waved him inside and onto the couch, and offered him a glass of iced tea, the way I'd been taught, when what I wanted to do was to ask him what in the Sam Hill he was doing there. But people from Byerly don't rush into explanations until the proprieties have been observed.

Burt Walters was a small man, getting thick around the middle, but still keeping his hair carefully dyed black. In

Byerly, he spent the spring and summer in seersucker suits, but his wife must have warned him that a navy blue Brooks Brothers blazer would be more appropriate for Massachusetts weather.

He took a swallow of his iced tea. "At least somebody up here knows how to make tea. Most of the places I've been don't serve it, and the ones that do don't put the first speck of sugar in it."

I had to smile. "I ran into that problem when I first moved up here. It's easier to find after Memorial Day, but even then, no restaurants sweeten their tea." I paused, hoping he'd get on with it, but when he didn't, I said, "Have you been in town long?"

"About a week," he said. "We were supposed to head back home this morning, but I told Daddy that he shouldn't miss a chance to see Opening Day at Fenway Park tomorrow, so we changed our reservations."

"That's right—Big Bill is a baseball fan. I bet he's really looking forward to it," I said. I paused again, still waiting for Burt to tell us why he'd come. When all he did was swallow more iced tea, I finally asked, "Is there a problem with my family?"

"No, of course not." He squared his shoulders, and said, "I'm sorry. It's not like me to dilly-dally, but this has been a tough decision for me to make. We Walters have always kept our business to ourselves, but I'm going to have to take you two into my confidence. If y'all don't mind keeping what I'm about to say to yourselves, that is."

I looked at Richard, who nodded. "All right," I said.

"My father wants to sell Walters Mill," he said.

I'm sure the shock showed on my face—Walters Mill without the Walters was unthinkable. Big Bill had founded the place as a young man, and ruled with an iron hand until stepping down for Burt to take his place. Despite the family's other business interests, the mill remained the most important part of their domain.

Burt went on. "That's why he and I are up here. We've been meeting with the people who are planning to buy us out."

"You mean you're selling to Northerners?" If anything, that shocked me even more. Not that Byerly was prejudiced against any one Northerner—most folks liked Richard, even if he did talk funny—but there are still plenty of people who warn darkly of carpetbaggers, as if Reconstruction weren't quite finished. "How did this all happen?"

"It seems that Daddy put out some feelers, looking for people who might be interested."

It seems that? "He didn't tell you beforehand, did he?" I guessed.

Burt didn't say anything, but the look on his face told me I was right. "A friend of a friend put him in touch with a couple named Marshall and Grace Saunders, and they've been talking to Daddy for a while now."

I wasn't sure how to go about asking my next question. "If they buy the mill, then what . . . ?"

"Then what happens to me? Oh, our other holdings would keep me occupied."

Burt didn't look happy at the prospect, and Richard said, "You don't want to sell, do you?"

"No, I don't, and I've got plenty of reasons not to. You know I'm Daddy's only heir, and Dorcas and I aren't likely to have any children." I'd heard that Burt's wife Dorcas had miscarried more than once trying to continue the Walters line. "Daddy's worried about what would happen to the mill after I'm gone, and that's part of why he wants to sell now."

"But there is another heir," I said.

Burt nodded. "Y'all know that, but Daddy doesn't."

It was an odd story. Burt's older brother, Small Bill, had been revered as a hero after his death in Vietnam. Only he didn't die in Vietnam. He traded dog tags with a dead man named Leonard Cooper, and while Cooper was buried in Byerly with much pomp and circumstance, Small Bill started a new life that didn't include living under his father's thumb. Though Small Bill was murdered in Byerly years later, Big Bill had never found out about his son's deception, and didn't know about Small Bill's son, Michael. Burt was the only one of the Walters to know the truth.

Richard and I had found out by accident when trying to help my aunt Daphine get out from under a blackmailer. That blackmailer, who was also Small Bill's murderer, had committed suicide, which was how we'd been able to keep Aunt Daphine's secret, and we'd agreed to keep Small Bill's secret, too.

Burt said, "The mill was supposed to go to Small Bill, and it's only right that it go to his son someday. I swore on my brother's grave—his real grave—that I'd tell Michael the truth and make sure that he gets what he's entitled to, but I just can't do it while Daddy is still living. It would break his heart."

Though touched by Burt's depth of feeling, I was also skeptical. "What about your other reasons?" I asked.

Burt looked sheepish. "I don't know if you realize it, but the mill hasn't been doing real well these past few years."

That was hardly a surprise—anybody who knew Byerly knew that. Some folks traced the bad times to Burt's first day in charge, while others blamed changes in the garment industry's growing reliance on foreign factories, and a small minority blamed the unions for enforcing unreasonable contracts. Part of the problem had to be the aging equipment, which was causing all kinds of maintenance problems. Whatever it was, the mill was definitely not doing as well as it had during Big Bill's reign.

"It's not that I haven't tried to fix the problems," Burt said. "We've had productivity issues before—all I have to do is track where the work is slowing down. And it's not my fault that the equipment isn't lasting the way it used to. The maintenance schedules have worked up until now. If the supervisors would follow them properly, we wouldn't have all those breakdowns." Then, as if realizing he'd told us more than he meant to, he said, "I'm sure I can turn things around in time, so there's no need to rush into anything, but Daddy just won't listen."

I tried hard not to let my skepticism show, but probably some of what I was thinking came through, because Burt hurried on. "Besides, I don't trust Saunders or his wife. I think they're union busters."

Considering the number of times Burt and Big Bill had done their best to earn that title themselves, that was the pot calling the kettle black. "Do they have a history of doing that kind of thing?" I asked.

"That's the problem. This is their first big business venture. Saunders started out in your field, Laurie Anne—computers—which he says is how he learned what kinds of management techniques work, so he switched to management consulting a few years ago. He seems smart enough, and some of his ideas are quite intriguing, but I just can't believe that an outsider would have the same concern for the welfare of Byerly that we Walters have."

Burt was on shaky ground there. As far as I could tell, the only welfare the Walters had ever been concerned with was their own. Sure, they'd done a lot for Byerly, but never without benefiting as much or more than the town did. Not that that was wrong, but I didn't think Burt should blame the Saunders for their lack of altruism until he displayed some selflessness himself.

Knowing that Burt usually has his own best interest at heart, I started wondering just why it was he was telling us all of this. "This is going to be a big change," I said.

"Not if I can help it," Burt said determinedly. "I intend to stall just as long as I can."

"Then it's not a done deal?" Richard said.

"Not quite. These things take quite a bit of negotiation, and you can be sure I'll be doing my best to slow those negotiations down."

"Does your father know about your objections?" Richard asked.

"He knows I'm reluctant," Burt said, "but under the circumstances, I thought it best not to let him know how strongly I feel."

In other words, Burt was afraid to go against his father openly. It sounded silly for a grown man to behave that way, but then again, Big Bill wasn't the first man I'd want to cross, either. "Does he know you're talking to us?" I asked.

"Of course not," Burt said, scandalized. "He thinks I'm out shopping for my wife. His knowing that I'm here would defeat the whole purpose of my enlisting y'all."

"Enlisting us for what?"

"I want you two to come back to Byerly and see what you can find out about Saunders and his wife. I just know there's something fishy about them, something I can use to convince my father not to sell to him."

I'd suspected that was where he was heading, so I wasn't as taken aback as I might have been. After helping various aunts, uncles, and cousins out of various jams, Richard and I had developed a reputation.

"Don't you think a private investigator would be more helpful?" Richard asked.

Burt waved the idea away. "My father already hired an agency to do the usual background checks, and they said everything looked fine."

"Then why do you think Laura and I could find anything they missed?"

"Because no outside investigator would ever be able to understand the whole situation."

That sounded suspiciously like a snow job, and having survived several Boston winters, snow didn't affect me the way it used to. I said, "What you're saying is that your father might find out if you hired a real investigator, whereas he's used to me and Richard nosing around."

"There's some truth in that," he admitted, "but I honestly believe that you two are the best qualified for the job."

I looked at Richard, who raised one eyebrow, and knew exactly what he was thinking. I was thinking the same thing. "No offense, Mr. Walters, but why should we want to stop the deal?"

He made a steeple of his fingers. "I assumed that you'd want to help, considering how many members of your family work at the mill. Let's see now, there's your uncle, Buddy Crawford, and his boys, Thaddeous and Willis. And your cousin, Linwood Randolph. And of course your cousins, Idelle, Odelle, and Carlelle Holt. You wouldn't want any of them to lose their jobs, would you?"

I took a deep breath before I spoke. "You wouldn't be threatening my family, would you?"

"Of course not. Your family's jobs are safe forever as far as I'm concerned. What I meant is that I can't make that assurance on behalf of a new owner. In my experience, reengineering frequently leads to layoffs."

He had a point. Burt, despite his failings, didn't lay people off unless he had to. Somebody who wasn't so attached to Byerly might not be so squeamish about downsizing. On the other hand, the mill's going bankrupt wouldn't do my family any good, either. If the mill closed down, not only would they lose their jobs, but most of them would have to leave town to find work elsewhere. I didn't want them forced out, ending up Lord knows where. Maybe the Saunders were what the mill needed to save my family's jobs and homes.

This wasn't a decision we could make on the spur of the moment. Too much was at stake. "Richard and I have to think about this," I said.

"I should tell you that we don't have much time. Daddy wants to settle things quickly—he's talking about signing an agreement by the end of next week." Almost to himself, he added, "Though I've got an idea that might buy me more time . . ." Then he stood up. "We'll be staying at the Park Plaza through the day after tomorrow, so you can reach me there. Though if my father should answer the phone—"

"Don't worry," I said. "We'll keep what you said confidential, no matter what we decide."

"I appreciate that." He shook both our hands again, and left.

Richard and I talked it out all that night, and first thing the next morning, we called Burt to tell him that we'd do it.

We did set some conditions. One, we offered no guarantees—there was a good chance that we wouldn't find anything bad about the Saunders, and we weren't going to make anything up just to suit him. Two, he had to pay our expenses whether or not we succeeded. Three, we could stay in town no longer than a week. Luckily, the next week was spring break at Boston College, where Richard taught, but he had to be back in town for the start of classes, no matter what. And four, there was something we wanted in return if we did manage to find out something that would stop the sale. Burt quickly agreed to our stipulations, which I knew from a short stint of flea market dealing meant that we hadn't set our price high enough.

But as Richard quoted from *Two Gentlemen of Verona*, " 'Words are bonds.' " Or as I would have put it, we'd made our bed, now we were going to have to lie in it.

Chapter 3

▼○▼○▼○▼○▼

The next Sunday, we flew into Hickory Regional Airport, the closest airport to Byerly. The plane was running a few minutes late, so I wasn't surprised to see Aunt Nora anxiously scanning the passengers getting off the plane as if afraid Richard and I had gotten lost in mid-flight. Then she saw us, and her whole face lit up. As soon as we got within reach, she pulled both of us toward her and hugged us to within an inch of our lives.

"It's *so* good to see you two," she said, her eyes misting. One of Aunt Nora's charms is the way she cries when she's happy. "I didn't expect y'all to be back this way before summer at the earliest."

"It was kind of a last-minute thing," I said. "I finished a huge project right when Richard's spring break started, and since we couldn't think of anyplace we'd rather go, here we are. You don't mind, do you?"

"Mind?" She hugged me again, harder than before.

Though I really had just finished a big project, and it really was spring break, I still felt guilty about not telling her the real reason we'd come.

Thaddeous, a taller version of his mother, was waiting his turn for hugs, and we cheerfully obliged him. Then I handed him the thick letter that his girlfriend, Michelle, had asked me to deliver, and he was so intent on reading it as we went to claim our luggage, that he nearly ran into the wall.

April in Boston is hit-or-miss as far as the weather is concerned—you're as likely to get snow as sunshine. North Carolina's April is rarely so wishy-washy, and this year, it was glorious. Flowers were blooming, birds were singing, and the sky was the bright color University of North Carolina alumni call Carolina blue.

"I better drive," Aunt Nora said. "There's no way I'm going to let Thaddeous behind the wheel, not with his nose in that letter."

Thaddeous grinned, but once our luggage was loaded into the trunk, he eagerly climbed into the backseat of the Buick and pulled out the envelope again. I couldn't blame him. He and Michelle had been involved long-distance for over a year now, and though she'd done her darnedest to find a job in Byerly, she just wasn't having any luck. If she hadn't been such a good secretary, she would have settled for one of the less interesting jobs my relatives could have arranged for her, but she didn't want to take a step down. So they were stuck with letters and phone calls.

I pushed Richard toward the front seat with Aunt Nora, saying, "You need the leg room more than I do." My husband is considerably taller than my own five-foot-two, but that wasn't the only reason. The fact was, I was pretty sure I knew what Aunt Nora was going to talk about, and I didn't want her to see my face while she spoke. Richard did some acting in college, so I knew he could be counted on to keep his thoughts to himself. It went without saying that Thaddeous wasn't going to notice anything that Michelle hadn't written.

So nobody would be able to tell that Richard and I already knew about Aunt Nora's big announcement.

Sure enough, before we got out of the parking lot she said, "You two will not believe what's been happening in the past few days. It was supposed to be a secret, but Hank Parker at the *Gazette* found out and he put it in Wednesday's paper."

I could see the side of Richard's face, so knew he was showing her his interested-but-concerned expression, but Aunt Nora let the suspense build as she pulled out onto the highway toward Byerly. Then she said, "The Walters are selling the mill!"

Richard's drama coach would have been proud of him as he made all the right sounds of surprise. I tried to echo him, but knew I wasn't very convincing. Fortunately Aunt Nora was too caught up in her story to notice.

"Would you believe that they're selling the place to Yankees?" Then, remembering she was talking to my Massachusetts-bred husband, she reached out and patted his leg. "Not that there's anything wrong with that, of course, but it's just such a surprise that they'd even think of selling, let alone to— To people from out of town."

Byerly hasn't got much in the way of industry, just the mill, so of course the ramifications of the buyout were endless, but since most of them had already occurred to me, I quit listening. Instead I stared out the car window, waiting for us to pass the piece of the highway that offers a quick glimpse of Walters Mill.

It wasn't hard to spot. It's the biggest building in town, and made of mud brown bricks that make it the ugliest, too. The Walters don't waste money on landscaping, so it's surrounded by asphalt parking lots and fences. Generations of my family have worked at the mill, and since the other businesses in town would dry up and blow away without the mill workers, even the relatives who don't work there depend on it indirectly. Folks tend either to love the mill for taking care of them, or despise it for controlling their lives.

I'd always been on the despising side. It isn't just the brown lung that claimed so many mill workers—the Burnettes missed the worst of that. It isn't just that Burt Walters is a petty tyrant—I've seen and heard of worse bosses. It's the inevitability of the place, knowing that if nothing else works out, you can always work at the mill. Some people find that a comfort, but I've always considered it a threat.

I've sometimes wondered if I would have stayed in Byerly if it hadn't been for the prospect of working there. I decided early on that I wanted to run a computer, not a loom, and when I went up North for college, I knew I didn't want to come back. I had other reasons for staying in Boston after graduation, first and foremost Richard, but avoiding the mill was a big part of it. That made my coming back home to help decide the mill's fate more than a little ironic.

Aunt Nora finished telling us what she'd heard about the buyout just as we pulled up in front of the Burnette home place, currently owned by my great-aunt Maggie. The house is never going to make it onto a list of stately homes of North Carolina. The original structure was a simple white clapboard farmhouse, but as the family got bigger, so did the house. The problem was that some of the Burnettes were better builders than others, which made it a perfect example of a house built by a committee. I'd spent countless hours there before my parents died, and afterward, moved in with Paw so he could take care of me. Maybe it isn't beautiful, but to me it was home.

"I thought you two might want to change before the cookout," Aunt Nora said.

"Cookout?" I said.

"The one the Walters and the Saunders are throwing to try to smooth over some of the objections to the buyout," Richard explained.

"Oh, right," I said, thinking that I should have paid more attention to what Aunt Nora was saying.

Thaddeous helped Richard and me unload our luggage and carry it to the door, but then started back toward the car, and I realized that Aunt Nora was still sitting behind the wheel.

"Aren't y'all coming in?" I asked.

"We'd better not," Thaddeous said. "Aunt Maggie is none too happy with us right now."

Richard nodded as if he knew what Thaddeous was talking about, which made me wonder what else I'd missed on that ride.

I rang the bell, and a minute later, Aunt Maggie opened the door. My late grandfather may have been the last to know exactly how old his sister was, because she hadn't bothered to enlighten the rest of us after he died. Though her hair had gone gray early, she was still a vigorous woman, but she may have given that impression by personality rather than by actual appearance. The T-shirts she usually wore left no doubt as to her opinions, and today's was no exception. In bold red, white, and blue letters, it said, "Look for the union label." Even Aunt Maggie's dog, Bobbin—a mix of German shepherd, chow, and golden retriever—was wearing a collar with a union label.

I started to give Aunt Maggie a hug, but she glared beyond me at Aunt Nora's car, and said, "What are *they* doing here?" while Bobbin kept watch suspiciously.

"They picked us up at the airport," I explained, "but they thought it would be better if they stayed put while Richard and I change for the cookout."

"There's no need for them to hang around out there. I'll take y'all to the cookout myself."

I was about to suggest that we all ride together, but decided that until I could get Richard alone and find out what I'd missed, I'd better be careful to avoid stirring things up worse than they already were. So while Richard carried in our bags, I scooted back out to the car to thank Aunt Nora for picking us up and tell her that we'd see her later.

As usual, Aunt Maggie was putting me and Richard in my old bedroom. The maple bed, dresser, chest, and nightstand were the same as ever, with the maps I used to dream over still stuck on the wall with thumbtacks marking both the places I wanted to visit and those I had been to. Even the bedspread was the same as I'd used, but it was looking a bit threadbare, and the maps were yellowed and curling.

Richard was changing from his good pants to a pair of blue jeans, and I stopped just for a second to enjoy the view. Though my husband's dark hair rarely looks combed, he always has a terrific rear end.

I was already wearing jeans, but I exchanged my sweater for a short-sleeved blouse, ran a brush through my light brown hair, and put on makeup to disguise the fact that Boston hadn't had enough warm weather that year for me to get any sun. Then I said, "Okay, what did Aunt Nora say in the car?"

"I should just let you catch up on your own," he said loftily. "If you'd paid attention—"

I stuck my tongue out at him. "So tell me, why a cookout?"

"With the buyout cat out of the bag, so to speak, Big Bill has invited everybody in town to a cookout to officially introduce Marshall and Grace Saunders."

"Okay, now why didn't Aunt Nora and Thaddeous want to come inside? And why didn't Aunt Maggie want them to?"

"They're not on speaking terms."

"Because of the buyout?"

He nodded. "Apparently, the entire family is split down the middle. Aunt Nora and Thaddeous are for it, but Aunt Maggie is enthusiastically against it." I was going to ask for more details, but he said, "We'd better go. I think I hear Aunt Maggie's subtle signal."

I heard the pointed jingling of her car keys, too, so I grabbed my pocketbook and followed Richard down the stairs even though I wasn't much in the mood for a cookout. The situation was worse than I'd expected. I'd realized that the buyout was likely to set folks against each other, but I hadn't thought about how much the Burnettes would be affected. I should have known better. If the mill buyout had set Burt Walters against his own father, why should the Burnettes be immune?

I hoped Richard and I were doing the right thing. What right did we have to interfere? Whether or not selling the mill was best, shouldn't it be the people involved who decided? Finally, we'd decided that it could only help for Walters to know what kind of people he was dealing with. If the Saunders were on the up and up, then we'd tell Burt, and if not, then the sale should be stopped. Richard and I wouldn't be making any actual decisions ourselves, and Byerly and the Burnettes could only benefit from knowing whatever there was to know.

Still, I felt ill at ease as we climbed into Aunt Maggie's Dodge Caravan. Worse than that, I felt like a spy for Burt Walters, which was the last thing a member of the Burnette family should be.

Chapter 4

▼◊▼◊▼◊▼

The cookout was being held at Byerly's ball field, which had been paid for by and named after the Walters. This early in the spring, the grass was still green, the bleachers and fence were freshly painted for Little League season, and the red clay parking lot wasn't too dusty yet. A slew of people were there ahead of us, and we could smell the charcoal and lighter fluid from the grills as soon as we got out of the car.

"Should we have brought something?" I asked Aunt Maggie.

"Nope. Big Bill's paying for everything."

"He really does want to sell the mill," I said. I'd never heard of him spending a penny he didn't have to.

"He should know better than to think he can impress us with a bunch of hamburgers and hot dogs," Aunt Maggie said with a sniff. "This is nothing but an excuse for those Yankees to try and convince us that they're just plain folks."

"Then why did you come?"

"I like hamburgers as much as the next person, and if Big Bill Walters is fool enough to waste his money, I'd just as soon he wasted it on me as anybody else."

"Aren't you going to try to sway his opinion?" Richard said. " 'When a world of men could not prevail with all their oratory, yet hath a woman's kindness overruled.' *Henry VI, Part One*, Act II, Scene 2."

I didn't know about kindness, but there'd been talk in the family about Aunt Maggie and Big Bill ever since the time they went out dancing, especially after he was spotted visiting the flea market where she did business.

But Aunt Maggie said, "That man wouldn't know good advice if it walked up and bit him."

In other words, she'd already tried to change his mind and hadn't had any luck.

The field was enclosed by a chain-link fence, and as we got to the gate, we saw a cluster of people stopped there.

"Lord love a duck," Aunt Maggie said in disgust. "They've set up a receiving line. 'Just plain folks,' my tail end!"

Aunt Maggie grumbled as we waited to be greeted by Big Bill Walters, Burt, and a couple that had to be the Saunders, but after all the buildup, I was glad for the chance to meet the prospective buyers. I'm afraid I stared openly at them, trying to get a feel for what they were like. It looked as if Aunt Maggie was right about them not being "just plain folks," at least not by Byerly definitions. For one thing, though the tailored red suit Grace Saunders was wearing was very chic, it was way too formal for a cookout. Besides, one look at her was enough to tell me that she wasn't really interested in polite chitchat. There was something about the precise cut of her jet-black hair, and the firm handshake she was giving the man she'd just been introduced to. Maybe it was just the look in her eye—I've seen that look on plenty of businesswomen in Boston. It wasn't ruthless or cruel necessarily, but it was the look of somebody out to make the best deal possible.

Marshall Saunders looked more friendly, but I think he felt less comfortable than his wife did, even though his khakis and polo shirt were far more appropriate for a cookout. The way he stood and held his hands, and the way he kept looking around and tugging at his sandy blond beard were oddly familiar, but it took me a minute to put my finger on it. Then I whispered to Richard, "He's a computer geek."

"How can you tell?"

"He just looks like a computer geek. Can't you picture him working at my office?"

"You might be right," Richard said.

Then Burt saw the three of us. "Why if it isn't Miz Burnette! And you've brought Laurie Anne and Richard! I didn't know y'all were in town."

I thought he was overplaying it, but nobody else seemed to notice.

"Hello, Burt," Aunt Maggie said. "Y'all picked a nice day for this shindig."

"Didn't we though?" he said, beaming as though he'd arranged it himself. "A bright beginning, wouldn't you say?"

"We'll see," Aunt Maggie said, and moved on to Big Bill.

"Hey, Mr. Walters," I said to Burt. "I hope y'all don't mind Richard and me crashing your party."

"Not at all," he said cheerfully, and I had a hunch he was resisting the temptation to slip us a sly wink as he gave me a social peck on the cheek and shook Richard's hand. Aunt Maggie had Big Bill tied up, so Burt bypassed them to go to the Saunders. "Marshall, Grace, let me introduce two members of one of our most prominent families: Laurie Anne and Richard Fleming. Laurie Anne's late mama was one of the Burnette girls."

Marshall murmured, "Pleased to meet you," as Grace

put out her hand for shaking. I'm never sure how hard to shake another woman's hand. Some prefer a light clasp, while others must work on their grip the way men do. Grace fell somewhere in between, no doubt appropriate for a businesswoman. "Do you both work at the mill?" she asked.

"We don't live in Byerly," I explained "We're visiting from Boston. Didn't I hear that you two were from up our way?"

She looked surprised, and I could almost see her recalculating our place in her plans. "Wellesley, actually."

That figured. Wellesley was a lovely town, but it had a reputation for being highfalutin, and since some people moved there to be highfalutin themselves, the reputation stuck. "We're in the Back Bay," I said.

"So you're not in the hosiery business?"

"No, Richard teaches at Boston College."

"Economics? Business?" she asked hopefully.

"Shakespeare," he said.

"Oh," she said, and I could tell she was mentally filing him as someone she didn't need to know. "And you, Laurie Anne?"

"Just Laura. I'm a programmer."

She nodded politely, probably thinking that I wouldn't be useful to her either, but Marshall perked up.

"What kind of programming do you do?" he asked.

"PC-based, mostly database management software. I work at GBS in Cambridge."

"I've heard of you guys."

"You do consulting, don't you?"

He nodded. "I can't seem to stick with one product— once it's developed, I get bored."

"What Marshall means is that his talents are wasted on

day-to-day maintenance," Grace said hurriedly, obviously trying to put a more positive spin on it for the Walters' benefit.

Aunt Maggie broke in long enough to say, "I'll catch up with you two later on," and then wandered onto the field. Grace turned her attention to a mill supervisor who'd come up to speak to the Walters, and I could see that Richard was listening to their conversation.

"Have you been at GBS long?" Marshall asked me.

"Ever since college," I said.

"Harvard?"

"No, that's my husband's alma mater. I went to the technical school across town."

"M.I.T.," he said approvingly. "I went to Harvard for computer science, but I would have loved to go to M.I.T."

"Why didn't you?" If his grades had been good enough to get him into Harvard, surely he could have gotten into M.I.T.

"Saunders men always go to Harvard," he said wistfully.

"So how did you go from computers to management consultant?" I asked, hoping the question sounded light.

"My wife's idea, actually," he said, which didn't surprise me. "I enjoyed the programming, but she saw that it wasn't giving me enough scope, and that I could better apply what I'd learned as a consultant."

"And now you're an up-and-coming industrialist."

"Grace's idea again. She heard about Walters Mill, and saw it as an opportunity for both of us. I'd probably have been happy to stay a consultant, but now that I'm here, I see a lot of room for modernization and applying new techniques."

"Really?" If he'd announced that to the rank and file, it

was no wonder people were upset. Nobody likes an outsider telling them how to do their jobs.

"You wouldn't believe how primitive the mill's inventory system is, not to mention billing. They actually use index cards—I didn't know they still made index cards."

Being in favor of computerizing that kind of thing myself, I had to laugh.

"And their record-keeping. All the data are there, but there's no system to it. No graphs, no statistics—no attempt has ever been made to compile the kind of performance data that can help pinpoint areas for change. I've spent all week entering in data, and only have the start of a reasonable database. Grace and I really have our work cut out for us."

"You sound pretty confident that the sale will go through."

"I don't see why it shouldn't. Walters wants to sell, we want to buy. The rest is just details."

"You're not worried about labor opposition?"

He looked blank. "That's Grace's department."

I had to keep myself from wincing. Marshall was a nice guy, but from the way he talked, he was like a lot of computer types I'd met. His expertise was numbers and technology— he was completely oblivious to the people involved. I wondered if he had the slightest idea why they were having a cookout.

Next he went into a description of the technical details of what he was doing, but even I had trouble following him. Eventually he noticed that my eyes were glazing over, and said, "Let me run out to the car and get my laptop so I can show you what I'm talking about."

Grace must have heard him, because she said, "Can you

hold that thought, Marshall? There are some people I want
you to meet."

He reluctantly moved to her side, and Richard and I took
that as an opportunity to leave.

"What do you think?" Richard asked, once we were out
of earshot.

"Maybe they can help the mill," I said.

"None of that," he said, wagging a finger at me. "We're
not supposed to make that kind of judgment, remember?
Our only job is to determine whether or not the Saunders
are trustworthy."

"You're right," I said. "It's just hard to separate the
issues." I thought about what I'd seen of the couple. "Marshall seemed honest enough. He was talking pretty openly
about what he'd been doing, and even wanted to show me
his graphs."

"Show you his graphs?" Richard said in horror. "I'm
shocked that he'd even make such a suggestion."

I poked him in the side. "Anyway, he sure didn't act as
if he had anything to hide. Grace, on the other hand . . . She
strikes me as somebody looking for the main chance. Not
that that makes her dishonest, but she sure is focused."

"She has a lean and hungry look," Richard said, "if you'll
excuse the adaptation of *Julius Caesar*, Act I, Scene 2."

"Just this once," I said. "Did your eavesdropping confirm
my impression?"

"It did, and it was fascinating to watch. When Grace met
a person, she immediately determined how important he or
she is and acted accordingly. With city leaders, she was
perfectly charming, but with mill workers, her charm was
directly proportional to rank. She fawned over supervisors
and union representatives, but was merely polite to anybody

else. She's focused, all right, and I think she'd do a lot to get her way."

Of course, all businesspeople want to make the best deal possible. The question was, would Grace merely cut a few corners to get that deal, or would she do something actively unethical? "They're kind of a mismatched couple, aren't they? A computer geek and a yuppie from Hell."

"Almost as bad as a Southern computer programmer and a Yankee English professor," Richard said.

"Touché. I guess opposites really do attract." I gave him a thorough kiss to remind him that our attraction was still alive and well.

Chapter 5

By then, we'd reached the outskirts of where people were gathering. There weren't any of the usual cookout activities, like softball or horseshoes. Instead animated conversations were going on everywhere, and after a moment, I realized there was a split in the crowd, complete with an aisle of empty space down the middle of the field. Not even the kids around were crossing the invisible barrier.

Aunt Maggie was close by on the right side, drinking a Coke and listening as an older man talked and gestured furiously.

"They're union busters, Miz Burnette!" he declared. "We've got to make a stand, draw a line in the sand, fight them until the bitter end."

Aunt Maggie seemed glad to see us, maybe as a way to stem the flood of clichés. "Floyd, this is my great-niece, Laurie Anne Fleming, and her husband, Richard. Laurie Anne, this is Floyd Cabiniss. You might have seen him out at the flea market, selling seconds. He inspects socks."

For a second, I wondered if this meant he was a new kind of foot fetishist, but figured out that she meant he inspected socks at the mill, and bought the discards to sell to people who didn't mind a missed stitch or two in their tube socks. Floyd was a florid man, with a potbelly and thinning gray hair. Despite his job, or maybe because of it, he wore thick glasses. He looked vaguely familiar, but most people in Byerly do. Either I'd seen him in passing, or knew enough of his relatives to detect a family resemblance. "Pleased to meet you," I said.

He nodded briefly, then went back to his tirade. "You're a union woman, Miz Burnette. I know I can trust you to vote the right way."

"We'll just have to see what happens," Aunt Maggie said mildly.

Floyd must have known that that was the best he was going to get out of her, because he murmured something polite and went into the crowd, no doubt to find a new audience.

"I thought you'd already made up your mind about the buyout," I said.

"I have, but I don't see why what I think is any of Floyd's business. Besides which, all he's worried about is his pension. He's due for retirement this fall, and doesn't want anything to come between him and taking off in that Winnebago he just bought. He's afraid that with the Saunders in charge, he might lose his pension, and that's the only reason he's against them. He doesn't really care about the mill or the union."

"What made up your mind?" Richard asked.

"My gut instinct and Bobbin's nose," she said. "When word of the buyout got out, I went to the mill and told Big Bill I wanted to meet the Saunders right then and there. Bobbin was with me, and you should have seen how that dog acted with them. She let Marshall pet her, but not Grace, even though the woman cooed at her like an idiot. Floyd's right about them being union busters—I can smell it on them just as good as Bobbin does. Maybe I don't work there anymore, but I fought long and hard to get that union into the mill, and I'm not about to let anybody push it out."

There wasn't much I could say to that. Once Aunt Maggie forms an opinion, there's nothing anybody can do to change it, and though Aunt Maggie hadn't had Bobbin a year yet, she'd already started depending on the dog's reactions.

From the other side of the field, I heard a loud call of, "Laurie Anne! Richard!" My cousin Vasti was waving at us wildly as she yelled.

"I suppose y'all are going over there," Aunt Maggie said.

"Yes, ma'am. If that's all right."

"It don't make no nevermind to me. I just didn't realize y'all were in favor of the buyout."

"We're not," I said, but before she could get the wrong idea, I added, "We don't know what to think yet."

"Well," she said with a sniff, "I'll be on this side." She left us to cross no-man's-land by ourselves.

Richard said, "I suggest we walk quickly to get out of the line of fire before the shooting begins."

"I don't think it's going to come to that." Then I looked at some of the angry faces on both sides, and I wasn't so sure.

From the amount of stuff arranged around her, I'd have thought Vasti had come for the weekend rather than just the afternoon. I didn't blame her for bringing a picnic umbrella since there wasn't much shade on the field, but the folding lounger and battery-operated fan were a bit much. She was laid out on the lounger, with the fan aimed at her feet, and the plastic table beside her held a large bottle of ice water.

"Did you even recognize me?" she asked.

"Why wouldn't we?" Her shoulder-length brown hair was still thoroughly permed, and her bright red sundress matched her earrings, necklace, and headband, the same as always. I leaned down to give her a quick hug, and Richard did the same. "You look very nice."

"You're just saying that," she said coyly. "I know I look as big as a whale."

At first, I thought she was fishing for compliments. Then I remembered something Aunt Nora had told me in her last letter. Vasti had worked so hard to get pregnant that she couldn't wait to get into maternity clothes, even though she didn't need them yet. "You are starting to show," I said, even though I couldn't see any difference in her figure. Of course, her dress was big enough for the two of us put together, so it would have been hard to tell even if she had been showing.

"Starting to show?" she said plaintively. "I'm huge! Laurie Anne, you have no idea how hard pregnancy is on a woman's body. Especially as little as I've always been—Mama says it's easier when a woman starts out a little plump, so you don't have to worry."

Maybe Vasti's weight had changed, but her personality hadn't.

"And my poor feet," she wailed. "They've been swelling up like basketballs every day since it started to get so hot. I can't even wear decent shoes."

I looked at her feet and did a double take. Vasti was wearing flats! Ever since she turned sixteen, she'd worn high heels everywhere—even her bedroom shoes had heels.

"At least it's not too hot today," I said. Despite the bright sun, it was cool and breezy, perfect weather for a cookout.

"That's easy for you to say, but I'm carrying my own little heater." She patted her distinctly flat tummy. "I just don't know how I'm going to make it through the summer."

"Are you sure you should be out here in this heat?" Richard said. I was sure my cousin heard only concern, not the sarcasm.

"Oh, I had to be here to show my support for the new mill owners."

"They haven't signed on the dotted line yet," I reminded her.

"It's only a matter of time," she said, waving away my comment.

Of course, I already knew she was in favor from the side of the field she was sitting on, but I didn't know why. "I'm surprised you feel so strongly," I said. Neither she nor her husband Arthur had ever worked for the mill.

"But Laurie Anne," she said, "this goes beyond the mill. It's a chance to bring a new level of sophistication and elegance to Byerly."

"Really?" I said. I'd never known Byerly to display any level of sophistication or elegance.

"Absolutely!" Vasti said, her curls bobbing as she nodded. "And I'm not just thinking about our generation—I've got the future to consider." She patted her tummy again. "I spoke to Grace Saunders earlier this week, and when I told her about my idea of founding a debutante society, she said that she thinks it's just what Byerly needs."

"Is that right?" I said. Trust Vasti to be more concerned about debutante balls than jobs. As for Grace's support, I bet Grace had only offered it after she found out Arthur was on the city council.

"I don't know why people are putting up such a fuss."

She glared at the other side of the picnic grounds. "At least you two understand that."

"Actually, Laura and I haven't made up our minds," Richard said. "It's a pretty complicated issue."

"I don't see what's so complicated about it—" she started, but before she could go any further, Arthur stumbled up, carrying an ice chest. Behind him, a tall man with salt-and-pepper hair was toting two well-filled paper grocery bags.

"It's about time you got back," Vasti said.

"I got here as fast as I could," Arthur said, as he put down the chest, pulled a handkerchief out of his pocket, and mopped sweat from his forehead. "I was lucky Tavis came by to give me a hand."

Now that Arthur said his name, I recognized the man with him as Tavis Montgomery, the local union president, and I wondered if he knew something about the Saunders more useful than Aunt Maggie's gut instinct or Vasti's tunnel vision. "Let me help you with that," I said to him, taking the bags and plopping them down next to Vasti's lounger. If Grace Saunders could suck up to people she wanted something from, so could I.

"Glad to help," Tavis said. "Besides, I was curious to see which side of the field Arthur would end up on."

"Of course we're on this side," Vasti said sharply. "Why wouldn't we be? I think—"

Interrupting her, I said, "We were just talking about the buyout. Is the union as divided over it as everybody else in town?"

"I'm afraid so," Tavis said, "but we're meeting with the Walters and the Saunders Tuesday morning to see what we can work out."

"Do you think you can trust the Saunders?" I asked.

"I'm sure we'll be able to come to some sort of decision that will make everybody happy," he answered, sidestepping the question.

"Of course we can trust them," Vasti said. "You can see what kind of people they are just by looking at the way they act and dress. Arthur thinks so, too, and after selling cars all these years, he knows how to size up people in a hurry. Isn't that right, Arthur?"

I expected Arthur to agree with Vasti because he always agreed with her, but at least he had reasons of his own this time.

He said, "I haven't seen that much of the Saunders, but I do think we need a change at the mill. The place has been going downhill for years, and I don't want to see it shut down. Apart from the immediate ramifications, the impact on local businesses could be disastrous. The buyout is best for Byerly."

From the way he was speaking, I knew he'd been listening to Big Bill at the city council meetings. I also know which local business he was most concerned with. He'd recently broken ground for a new location for his Cadillac and Toyota dealerships, and if people lost their jobs, they sure as heck weren't going to be buying new cars.

"Of course it's for the best," Vasti snapped. "You can go tell the union that I said so, Tavis."

"I'll do that," Tavis said with a chuckle. "Now if y'all will excuse me, I've got some folks to catch up with."

Arthur thanked him again, and Tavis slipped into the crowd.

"I knew he'd see it my way," Vasti said. She pulled a

handful of cookies out of one of the grocery bags and started munching.

I said, "I thought Big Bill was supplying the food."

"He is, but there's no telling how long it will take to serve lunch, and in my condition, I can't afford to let my blood sugar get low. So I brought along a few things to tide me over."

A few things? The grocery bags were filled with chips, dip, cheese, cookies, and other goodies, and the cooler was big enough to carry food for half the Burnettes.

While Richard and I finally got around to shaking Arthur's hand and hugging his neck, respectively, Vasti reached into the cooler and came out with an ice-cream bar. "For the calcium," she explained as she peeled off the wrapper.

My doctor recommended Tums as a calcium supplement, but Vasti's idea was probably tastier. She didn't offer us anything, and I was trying to decide if it would be safe to help myself when Aunt Daphine appeared and hugged onto Richard and me.

"I was wondering if y'all had gotten here yet," she said.

"Just starting to make the rounds," I said.

"What do you think of our little mama?" she said, leaning over to give Vasti a hug. "I never knew how much I wanted a grandbaby until now. We're all so excited!"

Vasti finished up her ice cream and reached for a bag of potato chips, making me wonder just which part of pregnancy excited her the most.

"It won't be too long before you're doing this yourself," Aunt Daphine said, smiling indulgently.

"I'd save my maternity clothes for you," Vasti put in, "but I don't think they'd fit." Before I could assure her that

I had no interest in her hand-me-downs, she added, "You know, Laurie Anne, you're not getting younger. I hope you two are planning on getting started soon."

"Not yet," I said, the way I always do when asked, but was surprised to hear Richard say, "We're thinking about it."

"We are?" I asked.

"Aren't we?"

Aunt Daphine, realizing that she'd put her foot in it, hastily started describing the baby furniture Vasti had picked out and how she was planning to decorate the nursery. Hearing their plans reminded me of why I wasn't ready for a baby. A child was more responsibility than I was ready for.

Aunt Daphine sighed happily. "My baby with her own baby. And me a grandmama!"

"The times they are a' changin'," Richard said.

I looked at him and mouthed, "Bob Dylan?"

He shrugged and went on. "Speaking of changes, Vasti and Arthur were just catching us up on the news about the mill. What's your take on it, Aunt Daphine?"

"I'm all for it. The more money the mill makes, the more money the mill workers make, and the more money they make, the more likely the ladies are to come get their hair done. Anything that helps the mill is good news to me."

"You're sure the buyout will help?" I asked. Aunt Daphine was a pretty good businesswoman. "What about union busting?"

"Oh pooh," Aunt Daphine said. "You've been talking to Aunt Maggie, haven't you? You've got to remember that she's got a blind spot where the union is concerned. I don't know if this is going to hurt the union or not, but to tell you the truth, I don't care. I know the union has helped a lot of people in the past, but the mill is having problems right now, and if Burt Walters can't do anything about it, we may as well get us somebody who can."

Her perspective made sense, but so did Aunt Maggie's. I was starting to wish that Richard and I had been out to dinner when Burt came by our apartment.

Richard must have picked up on how I was feeling, because he said, "We're going to try to catch up with the rest of the family, but we'll see you guys later."

"Be sure to come back over on this side to eat," Vasti said. "You don't want people getting the wrong idea about where you stand."

Chapter 6

▼●▼●▼●▼●▼

"Where do we stand?" I asked Richard as we made our way through the thickening crowd, looking for more Burnettes. "This is awful!"

"How did you expect people to react? They depend on the mill for their livelihoods—threatening it threatens them."

"I know, but I expected the Burnettes to all be on the same side."

"Your whole family? Laura, that many people can't even agree on what to have for dinner."

"True," I admitted. Then I spotted a familiar face in the crowd. Or to be precise, three familiar faces. To be even more precise, three copies of the same familiar face. "Here come the triplets. At least they're all on the same side." I'd only known them to disagree seriously once, and that was over a man. For lesser issues, they'd always been of one mind.

The three of them were talking to a man I didn't know, but when they saw us, Idelle said, "Laurie Anne!", Odelle echoed, "Richard!", and Carlelle skipped all that and rushed over to hug us, her sisters right behind her. I think I was hugged four times instead of three, but darned if I could tell which one got me twice. As usual, they were dressed in matching outfits. This time it was dark blue, red, and green shorts with coordinating striped shirts and Keds. Their hair, usually teased and hair sprayed to imposing heights, was pulled back in simple ponytails, but they'd put on the usual amount of makeup, and even as we spoke, I could see one or the other of them scanning the crowd for eligible men.

I was just wondering if the man with them was a recent conquest, when he said, "I don't believe we've met. I'm Max Wilder."

"Laura Fleming," I said. "This is my husband, Richard." We exchanged handshakes.

"Fleming?" he said thoughtfully. "Y'all must be related to the triplets, but I can't place any Flemings."

"We're cousins, but we don't live in town," I explained. "Ellis Burnette was my grandfather, too, but I don't imagine you've been in town long enough to have known him."

"Only by reputation. Thaddeous and Willis Crawford must be your cousins, too."

"That's right," I said, impressed that he'd been able to make the connections so quickly when he wasn't from Byerly. I'd never heard of any Wilders in town, and was sure that I'd have remembered Max if I'd met him. He had red hair, a curly beard, and a smile as friendly-looking as a teddy bear's grin.

"Isn't this a nice party?" Idelle said.

"It's a wonderful way for us to get to know the new owners," Odelle added.

I said, "Are y'all that sure it's going to go through?"

"Of course it will," Carlelle said.

Odelle said, "The Walters want to sell and the Saunders want to buy."

"It probably would have been a done deal already if

somebody hadn't leaked the news to the *Gazette* and gotten the union all stirred up," Idelle said with disgust. "I bet the Walters would love to know who put Hank Parker up to running that story."

Actually, I had a hunch one of the Walters already knew Hank's source. Hadn't Burt said something about stalling? I only wondered if he'd approached Hank directly or made an anonymous phone call.

"Obviously, you three are in favor," Richard said.

"Of course," they said in unison.

Carlelle said, "It's so bad now that we're taking our lives in our hands every time we walk in the gate. One of the dye vats sprung a leak last week, and boiling dye spilled all over the floor. It's just lucky nobody was standing next to it— that stuff will take the skin right off of you."

"What about when the tension bar on Boyd Wallace's knitting machine broke off?" Odelle said. "Boyd could have lost a finger or worse if he hadn't jumped back in time. It's getting scary."

"What's been done about it?" Richard asked.

"Not a darned thing," Idelle said indignantly. "Is it any wonder that we want somebody new in charge?"

"Burt isn't doing anything?" I asked.

Carlelle made a face. "All he's done is blame us for everything that's gone wrong."

"I don't think Mr. Walters means it that way," Max said, "but he is concerned that maintenance schedules aren't being followed as closely as they should be."

That sounded uncomfortably like what Burt had said to Richard and me when talking about equipment failures. I said to Max, "I take it that you're also in favor of the buyout."

"I've only been at the mill for a few months, so I'm not

sure that I'm entitled to an opinion," he said, "but the more I speak to people whose opinions I trust, including your cousins here, the more it sounds as if it might be a good thing."

After hearing about the recent accidents, I didn't blame him. "What do you think about the Saunders?"

He said, "I just met them this afternoon, so I haven't seen enough to judge them by, yet."

"They've only been in town since Thursday," Idelle explained. "Big Bill's been showing them around the mill, but we hadn't had a chance to actually speak to them until today."

I didn't like hearing that. Questioning friends and family is usually the best way to find out anything in Byerly, but I was afraid it wasn't going to work this time, not with Grace and Marshall being from so far away.

Max said, "I better get going—I promised to help run the grills."

"I swear, Max, is there any dirty job you don't get stuck with?" Carlelle asked.

"I don't mind," he said with a smile. "It gives me a chance to meet people like you lovely ladies and your cousin. I can see that good looks run in your family, if you don't mind my saying so, Richard."

"Not at all," Richard said with a proprietary air. "I always enjoy meeting another man with an eye for beauty."

The triplets giggled as Max ambled away. "So which one of you is dating him?" I asked.

"None of us," Carlelle said. "In fact, we may be the only single women at the mill who aren't dating Max."

"After the old Woolworth's burned down," Idelle said

with a giggle, "folks were saying that Max's house was going to go up next, because of all the hot action going on there."

"Plays the field, does he?" Richard asked.

"And how!" Carlelle rolled her eyes. "He's got a girl in every department, on both shifts. He substitutes for other men a lot, and I think he was telling the truth when he says he does it to meet people. Female people, anyway."

"But not y'all?" I said.

"He tried," Idelle said, "but right after he asked me out, Carlelle heard him asking somebody else out for later the same night."

"Did you let him have it?"

They shook their heads, and Idelle said, "That would have been too easy. What happened is all three of us showed up for the date, and he had to buy three times as much beer. That learned him—I bet he didn't have a dime left when he went to pick up his other date for the evening."

We all laughed, and Richard said, "He doesn't seem to hold a grudge."

"No, Max isn't that way," Odelle agreed. "Everybody likes him—you just can't trust him where women are concerned."

I looked in the direction he'd gone, trying to catch another glimpse. "He didn't strike me as a lady-killer."

"That's the worst kind," Idelle said.

With mill gossip out of the way, we moved on to family gossip. After catching up with most of the aunts, uncles, and cousins, I asked, "What are your parents up to? Are they going to be joining us?"

The triplets hesitated for a minute before Odelle answered. "They're over on the other side of the field. I'm afraid we don't exactly see eye to eye on the buyout, so it's kind of awkward."

"I didn't realize that," I said, wishing I'd kept my mouth shut. I'd just assumed that Aunt Nellie and Uncle Ruben would agree with their daughters.

By then, we could smell hamburgers and hot dogs cooking, and Idelle said, "They're going to start serving lunch soon, so we're going to go stake us out a table while there's still some empty. Y'all want to come?"

"I think we'll go hunt down some more folks," I said, looking at Richard to make sure he agreed. The way things were going, I was afraid it would be our only chance to see everybody in one place.

Chapter 7

▼○▼○▼○▼

"Where to next?" Richard asked, once the triplets had gone.

"Heck if I know. We're supposed to be investigating the Saunders, but nobody in Byerly knows them. How are we going to find out anything about them in only a week?"

He thought for a minute. "The way I understand it, Burt only cares about information that could stop the buyout. In other words, negative information."

"Right."

"Well, it stands to reason that the people in favor of the buyout don't know anything negative, or they wouldn't be in favor. Therefore, we might have better luck if we talk to the Burnettes who are against the buyout."

"Good thought," I said. "Aunt Maggie didn't have anything definite, so we can scratch her off, and Aunt Nora and Thaddeous are for it. Did Aunt Nora tell you about anybody else?"

"Uncle Buddy and Willis are pro, mainly because of the way Burt has been blaming them for not keeping the equipment working. They insist they've been following proper procedures, and it's not their fault that the machines are practically antiques."

"What about Augustus?"

"He's decided not to voice an opinion."

"Good for him," I said, glad that we weren't the only ones avoiding taking sides. Augustus worked with Aunt Maggie at the flea market, so it would probably cause hard feelings if he disagreed with her, but it would also cause hard feelings if he publicly disagreed with his father and brothers. "There's still Aunt Nellie and Uncle Ruben—the triplets said they're against it. Shall we cross the great divide and see if we can find them?"

" 'Once more unto the breach, dear friends, once more,' " Richard said. "*King Henry V*, Act III, Scene 1."

It did feel as if we were going into a breach. The last thing we wanted was to appear to be switching sides, but clearly, that's what people thought. Though nobody said anything as we left the probuyout side, there were plenty of unfriendly looks, while the antibuyout side looked delighted to have fresh recruits, and several people greeted us by name.

It didn't take us long to find Aunt Nellie and Uncle Ruben, mostly because of Aunt Nellie. She was the tallest woman around, and if that didn't make her stand out enough, she was wearing a royal-purple-and-gold blouse with darker purple slacks, colors that dramatically set off her dark hair and fair skin. When I called her name, the crowd seemed to part before her as she came our way. Uncle Ruben, who tended to fade into the background, came along in her wake, looking as proud as ever of his flamboyant wife.

The four of us traded hugs and handshakes, and Aunt Nellie said, "I'm glad to see you two over *here.*" Her emphasis on *here* made me uncomfortable.

"We were talking to the triplets, and they said we could find you in this direction," I said.

"Still on the other side?" Uncle Ruben said sadly. "I never would have thought those three would be so naive about the Saunders."

"I've always thought they were real good judges of people," I said.

"Usually they are," Aunt Nellie said, "but not this time. The Saunders have got the wool pulled over their eyes."

"Or socks, as the case may be," Richard put in.

"That's a good one," Uncle Ruben said, reaching up to pat my husband on the back. "That's just what they've done, pulled the socks over the girls' eyes and over an awful lot of other people's, too."

"So you don't approve of their plans for making changes to the mill?" I asked.

Aunt Nellie said, "I don't care about their plans—it's the Saunders themselves that are the problem. At least, he is."

"Really?" I said, hoping that we'd found pay dirt.

"I don't trust him as far as I could throw him," she declared.

"What have you heard?" I asked.

Aunt Nellie said, "Nothing definite, but we know darned well that Marshall Saunders doesn't know the first thing about management. Tell them what happened, Ruben."

"We ran into him at the post office Friday," Uncle Ruben said, "and since I'd read the article about them in the *Gazette*, I knew who he was, but I didn't let on. I just started talking to him. At first, he seemed nice enough, but then I asked what his line was, and he said he was a management consultant. I told him a friend of mine is a manager at the Winn Dixie, and that I should introduce them sometime because they'd have a lot to talk about. Well, that Saunders did his best to backpedal. He said he didn't think he'd have much free time, but it was pretty obvious that he wanted to stay as far away from a real manager as he could, so as not to get caught." He nodded sagely. "That man doesn't know any more about managing than the man in the moon."

I tried to keep a straight face, but I was afraid to look at Richard for fear I'd burst out laughing. All I could do was nod, and after promising to catch up with them again later, Richard and I moved on before we lost control.

Richard just barely waited until they were out of earshot before saying, "That settles it. We've got the proof Burt Walters wants. I'm only surprised that Uncle Ruben hasn't gone to Hank Parker with this exposé."

Finally, I let myself laugh. "Can you imagine what Burt would say if we told him that? He'd be calling the boys from Dorothea Dix to come take us away."

"Come to think of it," Richard said with a snicker, "if Aunt Nellie and Uncle Ruben don't trust the Saunders, then they must be trustworthy."

"Given their track record, you're probably right," I agreed. They were the ones who'd invested in bogus water filters, and signed up to sell floor wax that changed the color of the floors being waxed. Another time, they'd lent a complete stranger a thousand dollars, and almost got stuck with his collateral, which might have been worth it if they'd known where to sell an elephant. "Seriously, though, this does show that Marshall might not be the right person to run Walters Mill."

"How do you figure that?"

"Because he's not comfortable with the kind of people we've got in Byerly."

"If you mean Aunt Nellie and Uncle Ruben, there aren't any other people like them, in Byerly or anywhere else."

I poked him in the side, but said, "Okay, I admit that they're unusual, but the fact is, a lot of the people in Byerly don't know what the heck a management consultant does. For that matter, there are plenty of people in Boston who don't. It's Marshall's job to explain himself and what he does. He has to learn their language."

"I don't think he can fake a Southern accent."

I poked him again. "Don't you remember how people reacted when you first came to Byerly?"

"They did seem to be taken aback."

"They didn't know how to take you: aback, frontward, or sideways. You had a funny accent, you quoted Shakespeare all the time, and you didn't know anything about the South."

"I wasn't that bad," he said, sounding injured.

"Yes, you were," I insisted, "but you got away with it because you were with me and I could translate for you. Besides, you were willing to learn. That made all the difference in the world."

"What about my charm?"

"That helped."

"And my devastating good looks?"

"That, too."

"And my rapierlike wit?"

"Don't push it. Anyway, you also had other advantages that the Saunders don't. You had me to guide you, and I'd already been through it myself."

"But you're from Byerly," Richard objected.

"I know, but I'd gone away, and I came back talking computers and M.I.T. and Boston, saying things that didn't mean squat to the people here. I had to learn to put it into terms they'd appreciate." It sounded simple now, but I'd really made a fool of myself when I made that first trip back home. Fortunately, Paw had tactfully let me know I was putting on airs. That was a mistake Richard had never made.

I went on, "More importantly, you were never a threat to anybody, while Marshall is going to be in charge of people's jobs. Southerners don't mind an eccentric—heck, we prefer having a good eccentric around—but when the eccentric is the boss, eccentricities lose their charm real quick. If Marshall wants to work here, he's going to have to make himself understood so folks will see what he's trying to do. Otherwise, he'll never be able to get them to go along, and the whole thing will be a disaster."

"You've got a point." He paused. "Does this mean you agree with Uncle Ruben?"

"That's a scary thought, isn't it? I guess I do, but not for the same reasons." Unfortunately, in terms of giving Burt Walters something he could use, my reasons were no better than Uncle Ruben's.

Chapter 8

By then, the grills were doing land-office business and long tables had been covered with chips, potato salad, coleslaw, and fixings for burgers and hot dogs.

"I don't know about you," I said, "but I'm getting hungry."

"I was hoping you'd say that," Richard said.

We took our place in the nearest line, but as we got closer to the business end, I said, "There's only one problem. Which side of the field should we sit on?"

"Good question. Maybe we should eat in the parking lot."

I was seriously considering it, but by the time we made it to the front of the line and filled our paper plates, a bus had driven onto the field and people were unloading speakers and instruments onto a low stage right smack dab in the middle of no-man's-land. "I think we've got an out," I said. "That's the Ramblers' bus. Surely it can't be politically incorrect to eat with the band."

Roger Bailey had become my uncle by marriage twice. During his first marriage to Aunt Ruby Lee, they'd produced my cousin Ilene and some of the most outrageous fights the Burnettes had ever seen, mostly because of the carousing that Roger felt was a necessary part of his life as a country musician. Aunt Ruby Lee didn't think it was at all necessary, so divorced him to marry again.

When that marriage fell apart, Roger was back on the scene, swearing that he was a changed man. So she'd married him again, and apparently he really had changed, because they'd been getting along famously, much to the family's relief. It didn't hurt that Aunt Ruby Lee had started going along with him on the Ramblers' road trips, making sure that prospective groupies knew what they were up against. Even with three children well on their way to being grown-up, Aunt Ruby Lee's blond hair, dimples, and bosomy figure were enough to discourage most competitors.

Uncle Roger was carrying a guitar case out of the bus as we walked up, but when he saw us, he put it down on the grass so he could give us both hugs. Roger is a big man, so a hug from him is an experience, and I lost half of my potato chips in the process.

"I didn't know y'all were in town," he said.

"We just got in a little while ago," I said.

"Why on earth didn't Ruby Lee tell me y'all were coming?" I was about to explain that it had been a last–minute decision when he boomed, "Ruby Lee—why didn't you tell me Laurie Anne and Richard were coming?"

She came out from behind the bus, hugged us with much less loss of food, and said, "Nora only called me this morning, and I didn't get a chance to tell you, Roger." She saw our plates, and said, "Shoot, your lunch is going to get cold." Though Richard and I volunteered to help unload the bus, she wouldn't hear of it and bustled around until she'd found two folding chairs and pulled them up to one of the larger speakers so we could have a table to eat from.

We chatted as the two of them went back and forth

setting up, and found out that it wasn't the Ramblers playing after all, but the band that Ilene and her half brothers Clifford and Earl had put together. The three cousins arrived just as Richard and I were finishing up, and there were more hugs and then we all went to work getting everything ready for the performance.

As always, it amazed me to see how much equipment it took for a concert—instruments, speakers, amplifiers, and miles of power cord snaking everywhere. We were so busy arranging and rearranging that I didn't have a chance to ask what they thought about the buyout, but as things turned out, I didn't need to.

Uncle Roger and Aunt Ruby Lee were making one last adjustment when my cousin Linwood came up to Clifford and said, "I guess you're not planning on working up at the mill again."

Linwood, a stocky, thick-faced man with hair that kinked despite his best efforts, had never been my favorite cousin, and the way he'd just spoken to Clifford was part of the reason why. To start in on a conversation without saying "hello" and "how's your folks" is considered rude anywhere in the South, and to forgo the niceties when talking to somebody in your own family is unheard of. Only certified eccentrics like Aunt Maggie can get away with it, and Linwood was too young and too mean to be an eccentric.

"What's that supposed to mean?" Clifford said.

"It means that you'd better not try to get your job back after taking Big Bill Walters's and Marshall Saunders's money to play for them. You'd wouldn't last a day anywhere in the mill, especially not in my department. There's too many ways to get hurt."

Clifford's face got red, but before he could say anything, Earl spoke up.

"Come on Linwood, it's just a job. We've never even met Saunders. This is just what we do—we play music for people."

"The hell you say! This isn't just playing music. You making things all nice for Saunders is the same as saying you think him throwing us out onto the street is okay." Linwood shook his head. "I'm surprised at you, Earl. I expected better."

Though Linwood and Earl were several years apart in age, they'd always been close, and I could see that Earl was hurt by what his childhood role model was saying.

"Well, this is just exactly what I expected of you," Ilene snapped. "You leave Earl alone, Linwood."

Linwood turned on her. "Aren't we all high-and-mighty for somebody who prances around on stage with her—"

"Linwood!" Aunt Ruby Lee said. "What on earth has gotten into you?"

Uncle Roger was right behind her, looking thunderous. He loved his stepsons Earl and Clifford as if they were his own, and Ilene *was* his own. "If you've got something to say, boy, you can say it to me."

Aunt Ruby Lee added, "The kids are only playing here because Roger and I asked them to so the Ramblers can get some rest before we go on the road. We agreed to do it before we even knew what the cookout was for."

Linwood sneered. "So you'll take anybody's money? Y'all know how it looks to work for the Walters right now."

"I haven't heard anything about you turning down your paycheck," Uncle Roger said.

"That's different," Linwood spat. "I'm loyal to the mill, no matter how they've treated me, but if Walters and Saunders think we're going to bend over and let them—"

"Linwood!" Aunt Ruby Lee gasped.

Linwood had the good sense to rephrase. "If they think the union is going to lie down and let them walk all over us, they've got another think coming. And if y'all think nobody is going to hold it against you that you played for Walters today, y'all better think again, too."

He turned to stomp away, then saw me and Richard. "I should have known you two would be on *this* side of the field."

"We're in the middle," I pointed out.

"Does that mean you're for the buyout or against it?"

"Neither," I said. "We just got to town, and we don't have all the facts yet. Even if we did, it's not our place to say what's what."

"That figures—too mealy-mouthed to take a stand, even when your own family is in trouble."

"Linwood—" I started to say, but then stopped. It wasn't worth the effort. "If you want to tell us why you're so against the buyout, we'd be happy to listen, but I'm not going to stand here and let you insult us."

"Neither am I," Uncle Roger said. "You just go on and get out of here."

"It's a public place," Linwood said defiantly.

Uncle Roger didn't bother to say anything. He just stepped forward, one hand clenched into a fist. Behind him, Clifford followed suit. Linwood glared at them, but he went.

"I wish you hadn't done that, Roger," Aunt Ruby Lee said.

"Honey, if that boy wasn't your flesh and blood, I'd have done a whole lot more than that. He's got no call to be talking to Laurie Anne that way, let alone what he said to Ilene and the boys."

"I know," Aunt Ruby Lee said sadly. "I just hate to fan the flames any worse than they already are."

"How could they get any worse?" I asked. "Linwood has never been my favorite cousin, but I've never known him to be this nasty. Not in public, anyway."

Aunt Ruby Lee said, "This buyout has got him as grumpy as a bear. He hasn't even been back at the mill long enough to get his old rating back, and now he's scared to death that he's going to lose his job altogether."

"It's not just the buyout," Clifford said. "It's Caleb Wilkins dating Aunt Edna that's got Linwood's shorts in a bunch."

"It's hard for him," Aunt Ruby Lee said. "Especially after the way his daddy died."

Though nobody else in the family had mourned Linwood's father Loman, Linwood had never really gotten over his loss.

"Besides," Aunt Ruby Lee added, "having your mama get married again can be rough on anybody." She looked pointedly at Clifford. He hadn't been thrilled when she remarried the first time, or even the second or third, though he seemed happy to have Roger as his stepfather now.

Clifford, remembering some of the tricks he'd played on the men his mother had loved, looked sheepish. "I guess you're right."

"Anyway," Roger said, "I'm glad we're going to be out of this after tonight."

"Did I hear you say you're going on the road?" Richard asked.

"Bright and early tomorrow morning. The kids are coming, too, so I'm glad we got a chance to see y'all. We'll be gone the better part of a month, so I don't guess you'll still be here when we get back."

"Rats," I said. "I was kind of hoping that there'd be somebody else around who's staying neutral on this buyout business."

"If I were you two, I'd stay just as far away from all of this mess as I could," Aunt Ruby Lee said. "It'll blow over soon, one way or the other."

It sounded like good advice to me, and I only wished Richard and I were going to be able to follow it.

Chapter 9

▼◉▼◉▼◉▼

They still had a performance to get ready for, so Richard and I left them to it and went in search of more Burnettes. At least, that's what we meant to do, but we got sidetracked by the dessert table. Then we had to get some lemonade to go with the cookies, which made navigating through the thickening crowd tough. Not wanting to make a political statement, we walked to the far end of the field and had a seat on the bleachers instead of settling on either side.

"I don't suppose the Ramblers could use a couple of extra roadies," I said to Richard as I wiped crumbs from my hands.

"If you want to, we can get a plane home tomorrow."

"No, we can't. What would Burt think if we backed out now?"

"I don't care what he thinks. I care about you."

I reached for his hand. "I know, and I appreciate it. But we've made a commitment, and I wouldn't feel right giving up so easily. I just wish I'd realized how much the family would disagree about the buyout."

"Disagree? The Montagues and the Capulets disagreed. This is all-out war. Their heads are 'as full of quarrels as an egg is full of meat.' *Romeo and Juliet*, Act III, Scene 1."

"I have a feeling it's going to get worse before it gets better," I said sadly. "Would you rather we go home?"

"Of course not, Laura, not if you don't want to. I agreed to make the attempt, too."

"Okay, then. What next?"

"More cookies?"

I grinned. "I'll buy that."

We made our way back to the dessert table without getting caught up in any more arguments, and were picking through the dwindling platters of cookies when Big Bill Walters came onto the stage in the center of the field and announced Carolina Dreaming, the current name the kids were performing under. I was relieved to hear applause from both sides of the field, and Richard and I moved closer to watch them play.

At first I was so happy listening and tapping my foot in time to the music that I didn't notice something was missing. Then I turned to Richard, and yelling over the music, said, "Nobody's dancing."

Ilene must have noticed, too, because she started looking around, and her voice faltered as she started the second number. Then Uncle Roger dragged Aunt Ruby Lee into the cleared area in front of the stage, and started an enthusiastic two-step. Suddenly Richard pulled me out to dance, too.

I'm a lousy dancer, and I wasn't happy about dancing so visibly. Usually I wait until enough other people are on a dance floor that I can safely hide myself in the middle, but the thumbs-up from Uncle Roger and Aunt Ruby Lee mouthing, "Thank you," helped make up for my embarrassment.

The strategy worked, too. Slowly other couples joined in, and though there wasn't any mingling between the pro and con factions, at least people were having a good time instead of glaring at one another. Exhaustion and knowing that we'd helped get things going convinced Richard and me to drop out after the fourth song, and we gladly headed for the lemonade table, which was safely in neutral territory.

I chugged down one cup, refilled it, and was turning away from the table when somebody barreled into me. Half of the lemonade slopped down my leg, and before I could recover, somebody else ran into me, knocking the cup clean out of my hand.

"Crystal, Jason," a resigned voice called. "Why don't y'all watch where you're going?"

Now I recognized the missiles that had hit me as two of my second cousins, and the woman behind them as a cousin-in-law. "Hey, Sue," I said hesitantly. After our encounter with Linwood, I wasn't sure what kind of reception we'd get from his wife and children.

I needn't have worried. Sue had spent much of her married life ignoring Linwood's faults, enough so that they'd produced four alarmingly healthy children. Jason and Crystal were the middle two. Tiffany, the oldest, was behind Sue, pushing the baby, Amber, in a battered umbrella stroller. If that stroller had made it through all four of those kids, I didn't blame it for being battered.

"Hey, there," Sue said, and gave Richard and me quick hugs. "Laurie Anne, did they make you spill your drink?"

"No big deal," I said, reaching for napkins.

Sue frowned at Jason and Crystal, who were shoving each other to determine who'd get to the lemonade first. "Y'all apologize to Laurie Anne."

"Sorry," they muttered in unison, but didn't stop shoving.

"You two are going to have to do better than that, or neither of y'all are getting any lemonade."

Crystal quickly said, "I'm sorry I made you spill your drink, Laurie Anne," but Jason whined, "But Mama, you said I could."

"You heard me," Sue said, not relenting.

"I'm sorry, Laurie Anne," Jason said grudgingly.

"That's all right," I said, giving up the battle with the thin paper napkins. My leg was just going to have to stay sticky for a while. I only hoped that there weren't any bees around.

"Are y'all enjoying the cookout?" I asked. I'd seen which side of the field they'd come from, so I didn't need to ask what Sue thought about the Saunders and their plans.

"It's not bad," she said. "It got me out of the kitchen for a change. You haven't seen Linwood, have you?"

"We talked to him a while ago," I said, "but haven't seen him lately."

Sue frowned, and looked around at the crowd.

"Do you need help with the kids?" Richard asked.

"Nothing a good set of leashes wouldn't take care of," Sue said, looking at the lemonade table, which was getting sloppy with spills as Jason and Crystal tried to see which of them could fill a cup higher. Then Tiffany pushed both of them aside, while Amber wailed and kicked her feet.

The baby reminded me of the other baby on the way. "Have you seen Vasti?" I asked with a grin.

Sue rolled her eyes. "Is she still moaning and groaning about what a trial being pregnant is?"

" 'Great with child, and longing for stewed prunes,' " Richard said. *Measure for Measure*, Act II, Scene 1."

"I don't know about prunes," Sue said, "but she's eating

everything else in sight. I sure hope she doesn't want a second child. She'd never survive."

"The rest of us certainly wouldn't," I joked.

Sue's kids, still spilling as much lemonade as they were drinking, suddenly yelled, "Grandmama!"

Aunt Edna arrived and was immediately surrounded by sticky-faced children. Even little Amber giggled happily and said, "Gran-ma!" Behind her, Aunt Edna's beau, Caleb Wilkins, beamed at them indulgently, but when Jason saw him, he turned away, and Aunt Edna winced. Obviously Jason had picked up on his father's feelings about her dating.

"Hey, Aunt Edna," I said, hoping to distract her. "Good to see you, too, Caleb."

There was a round of hugs and handshakes. It was funny how Aunt Edna seemed to get younger instead of older. The way she was dressing and fixing her hair helped, of course. She'd let her hair out of its bun and let Aunt Daphine cut it becomingly, and replaced the shapeless housedresses with outfits like the slacks and blazer she was wearing. But the biggest change came from Caleb, the handsome man with salt-and-pepper hair who was holding her hand. Everybody in the family agreed that he deserved the credit. Everybody, that is, except for Linwood.

Since Caleb and Aunt Edna had also come from the anti-buyout side, I didn't bother to ask what their feelings were, either. Instead I caught up on what they'd been doing and shared a few more jokes at Vasti's expense. I probably should have felt guilty about it, but I think we needed an excuse to laugh.

We were speculating about how Vasti would act in labor when Aunt Edna said, "Do I smell smoke?"

I inhaled and caught a whiff of something. "Just a cigarette, I think."

She kept sniffing, and looked at the horizon as if she expected to see something more threatening. "I guess you're right," she finally said.

Caleb patted her shoulder, and said, "I don't know if you and Richard have heard, but we've had a couple of fires around town the past few months."

"I know about the Woolworth's fire," I said. Aunt Nora had written me that the old storefront had burned down, but she'd said that nobody was hurt and that the fire brigade caught it before anything else was damaged. Since Aunt Daphine's beauty shop was in the same strip mall, that was all I'd cared about.

"Well, it looks as if it was arson," Caleb said.

"For insurance?" I guessed.

"Nope, the owner's policy just barely took care of boarding it all up. I guess he lowered his coverage after the store closed down."

"Have there been other fires?" Richard asked.

Caleb nodded. "A couple of storage buildings have gone up, too. It may be the owners were storing gasoline or something else inflammable in them, but they said they hadn't been. Anyway, it's gotten everybody in town a little on edge." Certainly Aunt Edna looked nervous, and Sue looked tense, too.

The music stopped then, and Big Bill, Burt, and the Saunders came onstage. There were boos and hisses from the side of the field we were on, and at first I thought even little Crystal was joining in, but all she wanted was the music to start up again. Sue shushed Crystal, and we all moved closer so we could hear what he had to say—after all, that's why we were there.

When I paid attention to Big Bill's actual words, I realized that his speech contained almost no real information. It was nothing but platitudes about a new day dawning, and passing the torch, and good things for Byerly; but somehow, it was still a darned good speech, not because of what he said but because of the way he said it. I'd never realized how forceful a speaker the man was. If he hadn't gone into business and politics, he'd have made a fine hellfire-and-damnation preacher. By the time he was done, I was nigh about ready to tell Burt to let his father do whatever he wanted to do with the mill.

To Big Bill's increasingly obvious annoyance, I was in the minority, at least on the side of the field where we were standing. Every time he paused to take a breath, there were catcalls and comments yelled from the crowd, all of them rude and some bordering on vulgar. I could see Big Bill looking around, trying to see who the hecklers were; but they were smart enough to duck. Still, I was pretty sure I recognized Linwood's voice at least once, his words a little slurred as if he'd been drinking more than lemonade. I wasn't at all surprised that when Big Bill came to the end of his speech, there was applause from half the field, but mostly boos from the other.

Next Marshall Saunders took the microphone. I'd expected Grace to do the talking, but maybe they assumed a Southern audience would be more receptive to a man. Whatever the reason, it was a mistake. Marshall was a terrible speaker. He mumbled, and I couldn't hear enough of what he was saying over the catcalls to figure out what he was getting at. People on the probuyout side started yelling for the other side to hush up, which only made things worse. Marshall rushed through his speech to get to the end; but by then, people were so distracted by fussing at one another that there wasn't even a pretense of applause from anybody other than the folks onstage. Big Bill was furious, but when he reached for the microphone, Burt pulled him away. As the arguing continued, the Walters and the Saunders left the stage.

I was starting to worry that it was going to turn violent, and was trying to figure out the best way to get out of there, when somebody managed to make himself heard over the crowd. "Fire! FIRE!"

I turned and saw black smoke rising from the direction of the parking lot, but I was too short to see the actual flames or what it was that was burning. There was mass confusion, with shrieks and yells, but even that was drowned out by a woman screaming, "Crystal! Where's Crystal!"

It was Sue.

Chapter 10

An authoritative voice came over the loudspeaker and said, "Fire brigade—grab what buckets and water you can and head on over there. Everybody else, stay out of the way and don't panic. I repeat, do not panic!" I recognized Tavis Montgomery, who ran Byerly's fire brigade as well as the union chapter, and thanked the Lord that somebody was in charge.

I was trying hard to follow Tavis's instructions about not panicking, but all I could think of was Crystal getting trapped in that fire. Sue was staring toward the smoke, her knuckles white from gripping the handle of Amber's stroller. "I leaned over to change Amber's diaper," she said, "and when I looked up, Crystal was gone."

"Sweet Jesus!" Aunt Edna breathed.

Caleb took her hand and paused just long enough to say, "Stay here. We'll find her," before pulling Aunt Edna into the throng of people.

Richard tried to put one arm around Jason, but he twisted away to grab on to Sue's shirt. I don't think she knew he was there, any more than she saw Tiffany and Amber crying. The baby seemed to be crying as much from unhappiness at being held so tightly by her sister as from anything else.

I took a deep breath. Though I didn't have a clue as to what Sue was feeling, I was going to have to act as if I did. First things first, and that meant Amber. I gently pried the baby away from Tiffany, and started jiggling her the way I'd seen mothers do to fussy children my whole life. Wonder of wonders, it worked, and Amber calmed down. That was one of them, anyway.

"Where the hell is Linwood!" Sue said.

"He's probably helping with the fire," I said, trying to make it sound as if putting out a fire were an everyday event. I knew my cousin was with the fire brigade, so it was a reasonable answer. Wherever he was, Linwood probably didn't even know that his daughter was missing. "Richard, see if you can find him."

Richard knew that I also meant for him to tell the rest of the fire brigade that a child might be in danger, but there was no reason to say that. He wove through the crowd, which was starting to get frenzied despite the warning we'd been given.

Still holding Amber, I leaned toward Tiffany. "Honey, you've got to calm down. Your mama needs you."

It took a minute, but Tiffany did manage to staunch her tears and went to put her arm around Sue's waist. From the other side, Jason did the same. Sue finally looked away from the smoke, saw her two oldest looking up at her with fear in their eyes, and pulled them toward her in a fierce embrace.

While they huddled, I looked around the crowd, trying to spot anybody who looked as if he knew what was going on. I saw the tall, thin figure of Uncle Buddy pushing his way through, followed by his sons Augustus, Thaddeous, and Willis.

"Uncle Buddy! Crystal is missing!" I yelled.

Uncle Buddy doesn't say much, but he's not a stupid man, and he could tell what Sue and I were thinking. "We'll find her," was all he said, but as I watched, he took one direction and sent his boys in others designed to make sure they covered the entire field. I knew they'd enlist any other Burnettes they found along the way. The feud over the buyout was forgotten.

From the rumors spreading via the people going past us, I learned that the fire was in a ramshackle wooden building that used to be the field's snack bar. It had been abandoned years ago when the cooking equipment wore out, and a new snack bar had been built closer to the bleachers. As far as anyone knew, there was nothing stored in it, and the fire brigade had got to it before it could spread to anything more valuable. Still, since the brigade had to wait for the volunteers on call to get the truck and bring their equipment, it was taking a long time to put out. And nobody knew anything about a lost little girl.

A few minutes later, Aunt Nora found us, having been alerted by Uncle Buddy. She took Amber from me, and cuddled her as much to comfort herself as the child. I couldn't bear to stand there waiting for news, so I told Sue I was going to search, and dived into the crowd.

The problem wasn't finding towheaded little girls—it was finding the right one. I squeezed my way through clusters of people five times in pursuit of tiny blondes, only to find that I was chasing the wrong one. I'd never realized how much children look the same from the back. Then I tried to remember what Crystal had been wearing. Something pink? No, purple. Purple shorts, and a white T-shirt with the latest Disney heroine, that was it! Only after nearly grabbing two little Mulans did I decide that I needed something else to go on.

The key, I told myself, was to think like a four-year-old. Or was she five? I was embarrassed that I wasn't sure. However old she was, the last time I'd seen Crystal, she'd been spinning in time to the music. No, she'd stopped spinning while Big Bill gave his speech, and started whining that she wanted to dance. Sue had shushed her so we could listen, but Crystal had kept pouting that she wanted to hear Ilene sing some more. Now if I were four or five, and wanted to hear my cousin sing, wouldn't I go find her? So wouldn't the stage be the logical place for me to hunt for Crystal?

I decided that anything was better than searching randomly, and I headed that way. Nobody was onstage, and I didn't see Crystal, but the abandoned microphone gave me an idea. After making sure it was still on, I spoke into it as clearly as I could.

"Attention! A little girl is missing. Crystal Randolph is five years old, has curly blond hair, and is wearing a Mulan T-shirt and purple shorts. If anybody sees her, please bring her to the stage." I wasn't sure if anybody heard me over all the uproar, so I waited a couple of minutes and repeated the message, this time calling Crystal a four-year-old, just to cover my bets.

The only immediate reaction was for Aunt Maggie to appear and gesture for me to pull her up onto the stage. "God bless a milk cow, Laurie Anne, why didn't you speak up? I think I'm the only one who heard you." She took the mike herself and yelled, "Listen up, people! We've lost a little girl, so y'all calm down before somebody runs her right over." Nobody reacted. Aunt Maggie took a deep breath, and roared, "I SAID, PAY ATTENTION! WE'VE LOST A LITTLE GIRL!"

Folks started looking our way, and when Aunt Maggie described Crystal again, I could see them searching for my little cousin. Aunt Maggie and I peered over the heads as best we could, using the extra foot of height the stage provided. A few minutes later, I heard somebody calling, "I've found her! I've found her." Out from the crowd came Earl, carrying Crystal on his shoulder. A cheer went up, and as I helped Earl and Crystal onto the stage, Aunt Maggie yelled into the microphone, "Linwood! Sue! Get yourselves over to the stage and pick up your young'un."

Crystal seemed to enjoy all the attention at first, but as the crowd made way for Sue, the little girl burst into tears and started calling for her mama. As fast as Sue was already going, she started running faster when she saw that, and she almost flew onto the stage to grab up her daughter.

"She'd gotten onto the bus," Earl explained. "Said she wanted Ilene to sing some more, but then she found one of our guitars and was playing to beat the band. That's how I found her—I heard the noise."

Sue was too caught up to say anything, but Aunt Maggie patted his shoulder, and said, "Good work, Earl." From Aunt Maggie, that was as good as a twenty-one-gun salute, and Earl beamed.

Linwood broke out of the crowd just then. "What the hell is going on?"

"Where were you?" Sue snapped. "Here Crystal gets lost, and you're nowhere to be found."

"Are you telling me you can't keep up with your own children? I'd have left y'all at home if I'd known that."

The two of them glared at one another, then seemed to

remember that they were standing on a stage in front of almost everybody in Byerly.

In a calmer voice, Linwood said, "Is she all right?"

"She's fine," Sue said. "Just scared. She wandered off when I was changing Amber's diaper, and when I heard there was a fire, I was afraid—" She couldn't say what she'd been afraid of.

"I found her on the Ramblers' bus," Earl said, obviously proud of himself. "She'd picked up one of our guitars and was playing it as if she knew what she was doing. We might have to let her into the band one of these days."

"Over my dead body," Linwood snapped.

Earl's smile melted.

"The fire's out," Linwood said to Sue. "Let's get the kids out of here."

The family feud hadn't ended after all—it had only been a temporary truce, and the truce was over.

Chapter 11

▼♥▼♥▼♥▼

Linwood was right about the fire being out. The fire truck had arrived while we were looking for Crystal. People started drifting toward their cars, but Aunt Maggie suggested that she and I stay where we were so Richard could find us.

When he did show up, I hugged him nearly as hard as Sue had hugged Crystal. "You knew we found her, didn't you?" I asked.

"I think I could have heard Aunt Maggie if we'd still been in Boston."

I explained what had happened, and said, "Linwood was just awful to Earl, but I guess we have to cut him some slack under the circumstances. He must have been pretty upset when you told him Crystal was missing."

"Actually, I didn't tell him."

"Why not?"

"I never found him. I got to the fire, but he wasn't there, and I was drafted for the bucket line until the fire engine arrived. I don't know where Linwood was, but he wasn't helping put out the fire."

I don't know how much longer Big Bill had expected the cookout to last, but by that point, most people had already gone, and I saw Clifford and Earl loading equipment onto the bus. I turned to Aunt Maggie. "Are you about ready to go?"

"Not yet. Tavis Montgomery is going to be meeting with Big Bill and the Saunders later this week, and I want to put a bug in his ear." Reaching into her voluminous beige vinyl pocketbook, she pulled out her key ring. "Y'all go on out to the van and wait for me." Then she hopped off the stage.

While Richard and I were heading for Aunt Maggie's van, I saw blue lights flashing over by where the fire was still smoking. "Junior must be here. Let's go say hello."

"Are you sure this is a good time?" Richard said.

"Junior won't mind," I said confidently, but as it turned out, I couldn't have been more wrong.

Junior Norton, Byerly's chief of police, is either burdened or gifted with an unusual first name, depending on who you ask. A lot of folks think it was a dirty trick for our old police chief Andy Norton to play on his fifth daughter, just because he'd given up hope on getting a son to follow in his footsteps. Others say that since Junior made it plain right from the start that she was going to be the child Andy wanted her to be, her name made it easier for her to deal with police officers from elsewhere. As for Junior, I don't think she worried about it one way or the other.

Junior was a short woman, even in the black cowboy boots she always wore, but her sturdy build and callused hands kept her from looking petite. She was standing next to the smoldering building, holding a blackened piece of something and looking disgusted.

"Hey, Junior," I said.

"Hey," she said, not sounding at all surprised that Richard and I were in town. I think that I could walk into town at midnight, without warning anybody I was coming, and Junior would still know about it by the time I got up the next morning.

"What a mess!" I must have seen the old building when we drove into the parking lot, but it had been there so long that I hadn't really noticed it. They'd boarded it up when they quit using it, but it quickly became a prime target for vandalism and graffiti. After each generation of kids broke in, a new generation of boards was used to repair the damage, making it a patchwork quilt of different colored paint and wood. Now it was all one color: black.

"There wasn't anybody hurt, was there?" I asked Junior, who still hadn't turned to look at us.

"Not this time."

"We heard there'd been some other fires lately."

"Quite a few."

"Is there really an arsonist in town?"

"Oh, yeah. Our firebug has been keeping himself real busy."

I made a face, hating the idea of something so nasty in Byerly. "Was this one arson, too?"

"Apparently. The man who spotted the fire smelled gasoline."

"Any idea of who might be doing it?"

"Laurie Anne, if I knew who it was, do you think that person would still be loose to set fires?" she asked, sounding tired.

"I guess not," I said sheepishly.

"Are y'all planning on investigating this?" she asked.

"No, thanks," I said. "We don't know anything about arson."

"Is that right? I would have thought that you'd know

quite a bit." Before I could respond to that odd comment, she said, "So you two just came to town to visit?"

"We do have family here," I reminded her, which kept me from having to lie outright. Lying to family was bad enough—lying to the chief of police didn't appeal to me.

"Quite a coincidence, y'all showing up right in the middle of these fires." Now she turned, and I knew she was watching my face as I spoke.

"Junior, I swear that we don't know anything about the fires," I said, taken aback by her suspicion. "Heck, until a little while ago, the only one I'd even heard about was the one at the Woolworth's, and I thought that one was an accident."

"I suppose your visit doesn't have anything to do with the mill buyout either?"

I tried not to react visibly, but I sure wished that she'd stuck to questions about arson. "What do you think about it?" I said, knowing that she'd pick up on my evasion.

"I don't care one way or the other. All I care about is making sure that none of these hotheads decides to beat up on the other side."

A red pickup truck labelled *"Fire Investigation"* pulled up, and Junior said, "If y'all will excuse me, I want to see what the experts think about this fire. Unless there's something about it you want to tell me."

I just stared at her, not knowing what she was getting at. "Junior, I don't know anything—"

"That's right—you're not interested in arson. Well, then, y'all enjoy your visit."

While she went toward the investigator's truck, Richard and I headed for Aunt Maggie's van, one of the few vehicles left in the parking lot.

"I wonder what that was that all about," Richard said.

"I don't have any idea," I said, "but Junior sure has a bee in her bonnet about something."

"You don't think the arson has anything to do with the buyout, do you?"

"I don't see how. The Woolworth's burned down a couple of months ago, long before the Saunders came into the picture." I believed what I was saying, but what Junior had said about coincidences bothered me. An arsonist came to town right before the first time anybody tried to buy the mill. Could it just have been a coincidence?

Chapter 12

Aunt Maggie got back to her van just as Richard and I did.

"Did you find Tavis?" I asked her.

"I sure did, and I told him that he ought to take into account the fact that the Saunders didn't so much as lend a hand when that building caught fire."

"Tavis asked everybody but the fire brigade to stay out of the way," I pointed out.

"That's what Tavis said, too," she said, "but I just wanted him to have that in mind when he goes into that meeting. In fact, I told him I want to be there, too. Tavis is a right smart fellow, but when it comes down to it, he's a politician. Nobody would spend half his free time running the fire brigade and the other half running the union if he didn't have something bigger in mind. He only started working nights at the mill so he could have his days free for glad-handing. I want to make sure that he remembers the people he's supposed to be working for."

It was just starting to get dark as we pulled out of the parking lot, and Aunt Maggie said, "Do y'all have any plans for the evening?"

"Not a one," I said.

"Y'all can have my car, if you want. Augustus is picking

me and Bobbin up in his truck so we can go to an auction. Unless y'all want to go with us, that is."

I looked at Richard, and though he said, "Whatever you want," he looked tired. Or maybe I felt tired myself at the thought of staying at an auction as long as Aunt Maggie always did. "I think I'd just as soon get to bed early tonight. I don't know what it is about traveling that's so tiring, but I'm beat."

"Suit yourself," she said.

We got back to the house, and found Augustus already waiting, and they took off while Richard and I went inside to grab cold bottles of Coke and head down to the den in the basement. The living room is much nicer, and the television set in there is larger, but somehow we always end up in the den. The carpet has worn through to the bare concrete in places, the couch is upholstered in a hideous floral pattern that unfortunately never fades, and the recliner has been battered by countless children and grandchildren, but it's an incredibly comfortable place to hang out.

Richard and I planted ourselves in front of the television, and were debating whether or not to order a pizza when we heard the front door open. Somebody called out, "Hello? Anybody home?"

"We're down in the den," I said, and a minute later, Aunt Edna came in.

"Hey there," she said. "I was driving by and saw the light on, and thought I'd see if y'all were here."

"Well, we're glad you did," I said. "Come on in and have a seat." I'd been looking forward to loafing, not visiting, but at least Aunt Edna didn't work for the mill, so maybe she wouldn't start debating the buyout. "Can I get you a Coke-Cola?"

"Not right now," she said, sitting down in the armchair opposite us. "What are y'all watching?"

"*Xena: Warrior Princess.*"

"Oh, I like that. You ought to see Tiffany and Crystal pretending to be Xena and that little gal Gabrielle who runs around with her."

"I bet they're cute," I said, wondering if Aunt Edna knew about the show's enthusiastic following among the lesbian community, who were convinced that Xena and Gabrielle were more than just friends. From the gleam in Richard's eye, I had a hunch he was thinking about the same thing, and I gently poked him with my elbow as a hint not to say anything.

The show started, and the three of us watched without speaking for a while, but by the first commercial, I decided that Aunt Edna hadn't just been passing by. There wasn't anyplace I could think of that she could have been going that would lead her past Aunt Maggie's house, and she wasn't even watching the show. Her eyes were aimed in that direction, but as far as I could tell, she was staring above the television, at a rack of demitasse cups that made up Aunt Maggie's latest collection.

"Aunt Edna," I finally said, "is there something on your mind?"

"Why do you ask?" she said, not very convincingly.

I just looked at her.

"You're right, Laurie Anne. There's something I want y'all to do for me."

"I'll turn off the TV," Richard said, reaching for the remote.

"Lord, I don't know where to start," Aunt Edna said, and the sadness in her voice made my heart ache. "I'm not much of a letter writer, but I imagine Nora has kept y'all up to date on what's been going on with me and Caleb."

I said, "We hear y'all are getting along real well."

She smiled for a second, but then it was gone. "I guess that's part of the problem. Linwood doesn't approve."

"I'd heard that," I said carefully.

"I don't think it's Caleb," she said thoughtfully. "He's been just as nice as he can be to Linwood, Sue, and the kids, and Linwood seemed to like him at first. They even talked about Linwood going to work for him. But somewhere along the line, somebody made a joke about Caleb and me getting married someday. That's when Linwood started making trouble.

"First, Linwood started showing up when Caleb and I wanted to be alone. He always acted like it was a coincidence, but he didn't fool me for a minute. I swear, it reminded me of when Ruby Lee used to go sit on the front porch right around the time my dates would bring me home, so she could keep us from kissing good night. Of course, Ruby Lee was a child then; Linwood's supposed to be a grown man.

"I've tried to be patient with him, because I know it must be hard for him, and I've tried to explain the way I feel. He won't listen—every time I bring it up, he has something he has to do or someplace he has to go.

"When Linwood realized that Caleb wasn't going to go away, he really started acting up. He says terrible things to Caleb for no reason other than to pick a fight. Of course, Caleb understands what's going on, so he lets it roll off of him like water off a duck's back. I'm just lucky he's put up with it as long as he has."

"Obviously he realizes how lucky he is to have you," Richard said gallantly.

"Aren't you sweet?" Aunt Edna said with a fleeting smile, but the smile disappeared as she went on. "These days, Linwood is so aggravating that nobody in the family wants to be around him. Even Earl has stopped coming to visit."

"Linwood said some pretty awful things to him today," I put in.

"I know he did," Aunt Edna said with a sigh. "The last time anybody other than me or Caleb would have anything to do with Linwood was Tiffany's birthday party, back in February. I'd asked Sue what Tiffany wanted, and she told me that she wanted a boom box. Caleb went shopping with me, and wouldn't let me get the one I was going to get— he wanted us to get a better one together. I let him talk me into it, and naturally I put both our names on the card.

"Come the day of the party, Tiffany opened it and was just thrilled, but when Linwood saw Caleb's name on the card, he accused Caleb of trying to show him up by buying his daughter a big gift. I tried to tell him it was half from me, but Linwood wouldn't listen. He said Tiffany had to give it back. He even tried to take it from her, but she got upset and wouldn't let go. With the two of them tugging on it, it hit the ground and broke, and Tiffany was just heartbroken. Linwood started kicking it, calling it a piece of junk, and by the time he was done, there wasn't enough left to try to fix. Tiffany ran to her room crying—she didn't even want a piece of her own birthday cake."

"The poor thing," I said sympathetically. Tiffany was right on the edge of puberty, a tricky time for anybody. To have had her birthday spoiled that way must have been devastating.

"That got Sue all worked up, and you know Sue has never been one to sit quietly when Linwood does something she doesn't like. She lit into him something good, and told him he was going to have to replace that boom box and he'd better do it right quick. He tried to argue with her, but she wasn't having any, and wouldn't let up until he got in his truck and took off. Nobody was in the mood for a party after that, so after helping Sue straighten things up, the rest of us left, too."

"Did Linwood get the boom box?" I asked.

"I don't know, Laurie Anne. I've been afraid to ask. You see, that was the night the Woolworth's caught fire."

I stared at her. "You don't think . . . ?"

"Laurie Anne, I don't know what to think. All I know is what I found out from Daphine the next day. She said that Tavis Montgomery called her that night to let her know because of the fire being so close to her shop. Daphine went running down there, but it was all over by the time she showed up, and her shop wasn't hurt. She asked Tavis what had happened, and he said they were just lucky that Linwood had been driving by when the fire started so he could call for help. Of course, Daphine and Tavis made a big deal of him being a hero and saving all the other businesses, and so did the rest of us when we heard. Hank Parker even put a picture of him in the *Gazette*."

"But you don't believe that's what happened?" Richard said.

"At first, I did. It never occurred to me to think otherwise until the next fire, a couple of weeks later. That night was like Tiffany's birthday all over again. Caleb and I had stopped over at Linwood's house, and sat down to watch the basketball game on TV. Then Linwood started arguing with Caleb about which coach is better or some such non-sense. Even though Caleb doesn't usually let Linwood get to him, there are some things he won't back down on, and basketball is one of those things."

Richard looked mystified, but I nodded. College basketball in North Carolina is darned close to a religion to its rabid fans, and though I didn't follow that particular faith myself, I was familiar with some of its tenets.

Aunt Edna said, "Sue finally told Linwood to hush up, and he stormed out the door again, and Caleb and I left not long after that. The next morning, I heard that Drew Wiley's old chicken coop had burned down, and that Linwood had been the one to find it."

I was feeling sick to my stomach by that point, but I could tell from Aunt Edna's face that there was more to come.

"Linwood was a hero again," she said, "but people didn't make so much of him that time. The chicken coop was nearly falling down already, and there was nothing nearby that could have caught fire. Besides, by that time, everybody in town knew that the Woolworth's fire had been arson, and it looked as if the chicken-coop fire was, too."

She rubbed her eyes wearily. "There have been four or five more fires since then, Laurie Anne: an abandoned barn, somebody's outhouse, some empty storage buildings. And every one of them was arson."

"Was Linwood the first one on the scene for all of them?" I said.

"No, only the first two. The others were reported anonymously."

"Was he away from home every time?"

Aunt Edna bit her lip. "I'm not sure. I've tried to ask Sue, but she won't even talk to me about it, which is why I think she suspects Linwood, too. I called their house one night and asked for him, and she said he was busy, but when I went by there a few minutes later on my way to the drugstore, his truck wasn't in the driveway."

"Was there a fire that night?" I had to ask.

"No, not that time," she said, not sounding much comforted by it. "But it proves that they've both been lying to me. Anyway, I imagine y'all can guess why I'm telling y'all all of this. I know it's not fair for all of us Burnettes to expect you two to solve our problems for us, but when you came to town this week, I thought maybe it was a sign from God that I should ask for help. Laurie Anne, Richard, I want y'all to find out whether or not Linwood is setting these fires."

"What do we do if he is?" I asked.

"We stop him before anybody gets hurt. When Drew's chicken coop went up, the whole roof collapsed. What if one of the firemen had been in there when it happened? What if Crystal had been in that building that burned today? I've read in the paper about old buildings going up and them finding out that homeless people had been living inside without anybody knowing it. Somebody could get killed, Laurie Anne, and that would be on Linwood's head for the rest of his life.

"You don't know how hard it is for me to think this about my own son, but I have to know the truth. If he hasn't been setting the fires, I'll beg his forgiveness, but if he has been, we have to stop him."

"How?" I had to ask.

"I don't know. We'll get the rest of the family to help if we have to." She hesitated. "Until then, I'd just as soon you didn't tell anybody else what I'm thinking. It's bad enough to suspect my boy of something like this—I couldn't stand my sisters knowing about it."

"What about the police?" I asked softly.

She looked more troubled than ever. "I'm praying it won't come to that, Laurie Anne. Would you have to go to Junior?"

I hesitated. Junior was my friend before she was police chief—I'd edged around the truth with her once already that day, and didn't like the idea of doing it again. But Linwood was family, even if I didn't get along with him. Besides, there was Aunt Edna to think of, not to mention Sue and the kids. Weren't they worth bending the law for? "I don't know that I can lie outright to Junior," I said slowly, "but I'll try to keep her out of it."

"Does that mean you'll help?"

I glanced at Richard to confirm what I already knew. "We'll do what we can, Aunt Edna."

Tears came to her eyes, and she kneeled between the two of us to pull us both to her. "Y'all just don't know how much this means to me."

Richard and I hugged her back, but when I looked over at him, I could see he was worried. So was I.

Chapter 13

Aunt Edna left after that, clearly relieved to know that we were on the job. Though I appreciated her confidence in us, I still felt a little overwhelmed. I'd been worried about only having a week to investigate the Saunders. Now we had to find out about Linwood, too. I slid down on the couch so that my head rested in Richard's lap.

"You must love me to put up with this," I said to him.

"Yup."

"Just yup?"

"Is there something wrong with 'yup'?"

"It's not exactly Shakespearean."

"How about this? 'Doubt thou the stars are fire, doubt that the sun doth move, doubt truth to be a liar, but never doubt that I love.' *Hamlet*, Act II, Scene 2."

"Much better." I let him stroke my hair, trying to relax. "First Burt's Yankees, and now my cousin the arsonist. Maybe it's time I started learning to say 'no.'"

"Just as long as you don't start with my next suggestion," Richard said with a leer.

"Tell me, is it Xena or Gabrielle that gets you into this mood?"

"Only you, my programmer princess. So . . . What do you say?"

I considered the matter. "Pepperoni," I finally said. "With extra cheese."

"Your wish is my command."

He left the couch long enough to call Domino's, then returned to his role as my pillow. We probably should have started planning our strategy, but instead we channel-surfed while waiting for the pizza to arrive. Only when we'd both munched our way through a piece did I reluctantly turn the conversation back to the business at hand. "I wish I found it harder to believe that Linwood could be an arsonist."

"If his own mother can believe it, then why shouldn't you?"

"It just feels so ugly to think such a thing about my own cousin."

"Laura, most criminals have families. I remember reading about the Yorkshire Ripper's brother and father coming to visit him in prison."

"Weren't they ashamed to admit it?"

"Maybe," he said, "but they must have known that they weren't to blame for what he did."

As usual, Richard had put his finger right on what was bothering me. Even considering the possibility of Linwood as an arsonist made me feel guilty, as if I'd been setting fires myself. Earlier in the day I'd taken pride in the musical abilities of Clifford, Earl, and Ilene. Was I going to have to accept the flip side of having a criminal in the family? I didn't want to think about it. "Now we know why Junior was so hostile," I said.

"You think she suspects Linwood?"

"She must. Don't you remember how she nigh about

accused us of knowing something about the fires? Once she finds out that we're sniffing around, she's going to think we were lying."

"But we weren't. At the time, we had no intention of chasing an arsonist, and we certainly didn't suspect anybody."

"I know that, and you know that, but it's not going to look that way to Junior." I sighed. "Goodness knows we were telling the truth when we said we don't know anything about arson."

"That's something we should remedy, don't you think?"

"That sounds like a job for Research Man." After years of writing scholarly papers, there's nothing Richard can't find in a library.

"Does this mean I get to wear a spandex costume?"

Though the picture that appeared in my mind was highly diverting, I forced myself to say, "My family has been very patient about your Northern birth and accent, and has even learned to appreciate your penchant for quoting the Bard, but I think they would have problems accepting you in spandex."

"Perhaps you're right," he said. "I'll have to retain my mild-mannered disguise."

"You can wear really tight jeans," I offered.

"That's very generous of you," he said dryly. "I think I'll hit the library in Hickory to see what I can find out."

"Sounds perfect."

"What about you?"

"Two things. First off, I thought I'd try to move forward with Marshall and Grace Saunders. Burt said his father had done some background research on them—there must be a report that we can read and get some ideas of where to go next. I'll call and see about getting a copy."

"Good idea. And the second thing?"

I wasn't crazy about the next job, but it had to be done. "I know Aunt Edna said Sue wouldn't talk to her, but I think I should give it a try."

"Do you think she believes Linwood is an arsonist, or will admit it if she does?"

"Who knows?" With the mill-buyout feud raging, the last thing I wanted was to get involved in another family argument, but I'd promised Aunt Edna I'd do what I could.

Richard said, "You know transportation is going to be a problem."

"I'll tell Burt he has to pay for a rental car. He'll love that."

"He agreed to pay our expenses," Richard said. "If he balks, we'll have an excuse to back out."

Between family animosity over the buyout, and Aunt Edna's request, the idea of backing out of mill business definitely appealed to me, though I didn't dare hope that it would actually happen.

With the next day's plans made, we felt justified in concentrating on the rest of the pizza, and once that was done, we headed for bed. Despite the day's ups and downs, or maybe because of them, I fell asleep immediately.

Chapter 14

Despite having been out late the night before, Aunt Maggie was gone by the time we got up the next morning. She had left us a bag of sausage biscuits from Hardee's and, more importantly, her car keys, along with a note telling us that Augustus could drive her. At least, I thought the car keys were more important, but when I bit into the first sausage biscuit, I wasn't so sure.

Once we were showered and dressed, I found the phone book and called to reserve a rental car at the airport in Hickory. Then I tried Burt at the mill, but only got as far as Hortense Hunsucker, the secretary who'd been guarding his door for as long as I could remember. She said he was out of the office and didn't know when he'd be back, so I left a message for him to call back.

The next step was a trip to the airport, and after filling out a sheaf of paperwork Richard swore was longer than *Hamlet*, we arranged to meet for lunch, then went our separate ways. I let Richard indulge himself by driving the bright red rental car to the library, while I drove Aunt Maggie's van back to Byerly.

It was hotter than it had been the day before, closer to the temperature Vasti had claimed it was, so I wasn't surprised to hear yells and splashing from the backyard when I got to Linwood and Sue's house. I walked around to the chain-link fence, and called, "Hello?" from the gate.

"Around back," Sue yelled, and I went on inside the yard.

The grass was still that bright, spring green, and was long enough to tickle my legs as I walked. There was a kiddie pool in the middle of the yard, next to a tired-looking swing set. The pool was maybe three feet deep, but there was no more than a foot and a half of water left inside. The rest was either turning the dirt around the pool into mud, or flying through the air as Crystal and Jason used plastic buckets to drench each other. Sue and a sleeping Amber were sitting on a plastic chair in the shade, while Tiffany sunned herself on a towel as far away from the noisy kids as possible.

"Hey there," I said.

"Hey yourself," Sue said. "Have a seat."

I took the other plastic chair, which was far enough from the pool to be mostly dry. "Richard had a project to work on, so I thought I'd come bother y'all for a while," I explained. "Looks as if you found a good way to keep those two cool."

"It's a lot easier than giving them baths," Sue said. "Getting them into the tub is like pulling teeth, but they'll stay in there until they turn into prunes."

"I was the same way at their age," I said.

"You want something to drink?" Before I could answer, Sue yelled, "Tiffany! Why don't you get Laurie Anne and me something to drink?"

Tiffany didn't move.

"Tiffany!"

Still no reaction.

"Jason, you want to take that bucket of water over there and help your sister? I think the heat's gotten to her and made her pass out."

Jason was halfway out of the pool before Sue could finish speaking, but he wasn't fast enough to catch Tiffany, who went past us so quickly on her way in the back door that all I saw was her glare.

"It looks like Crystal is okay," I said. From the way she was leaping around, she sure didn't look as if she'd suffered any ill effects.

"She is this time," Sue said ominously, "but she won't be if she goes sneaking away from me again."

Sue had been speaking loudly enough for her daughter to hear, and Crystal did look abashed for two or three seconds.

Tiffany returned with three glasses of Coke, handed one to me and one to her mother, and after we thanked her, started back to her towel.

"Where's mine?" Jason wailed.

"I want some," Crystal whined.

Tiffany glowered, but turned around to go back to the house.

"That's all right," Sue said. "Jason and Crystal can get their own."

"But we're wet," Jason said.

"Then dry off. And don't go tracking mud onto the floor."

"I'm not thirsty," Crystal announced.

After a moment's thought, Jason said, "Me, neither."

They went back to splashing while Tiffany went back to sunning. I asked Sue the usual questions about Amber's teething, walking, and so forth, and Sue asked me the usual questions about Boston. Then we sat and sipped Coke for a while, content to let Crystal and Jason move around enough for all of us.

I'd always liked Sue, though we had almost nothing in common. She'd barely made it through high school, and despite being younger than me, started dating while I still had my nose stuck firmly in books. I always felt as if my family was smothering me, while the best way I could describe Sue's treatment by hers was benign neglect. She'd started dating Linwood while still in high school, and got pregnant with Tiffany a month or two before their wedding. Now she had four children, while I still wasn't sure if I could handle one. Despite all that, we'd always gotten along, which is why I thought I could get away with bringing up the subject that was the reason for my visit.

"I hear that fire at the cookout wasn't the first one lately," I said, trying to sound nonchalant.

"Every town has a fire now and again," Sue said.

"I suppose, but this batch seems to have everybody spooked."

Sue switched Amber to her other shoulder, but didn't answer.

I tried again. "Is it true that somebody's been setting them?"

"That's what the paper says."

"I wonder why somebody would do something like that. Setting fires, I mean."

There was a long pause, and I tried to think of something else I could say without flat out asking Sue if she thought Linwood was doing it.

Before I came up with anything, Sue said, "Is that why you and Richard came down here? To snoop around a bunch of burnt-out buildings that nobody cares about?"

"Of course not," I said. "I was just asking—"

"Because not one of those shacks was worth the money it would have taken to repair them."

"What about the Woolworth's?" I asked. "If they hadn't caught it, it could have spread to the businesses next door. Aunt Daphine's place is only a few doors down, you know."

"I know where Daphine's shop is," she snapped, "but it didn't get hurt, did it?"

"It could have."

"An earthquake *could* hit tomorrow and swallow up the whole town—what difference would a closed-down dime store make then?"

Sue's voice had gotten louder and louder as she spoke, and by the time she stopped, Amber had woken and was squirming fretfully against her shoulder.

"I've got to feed the kids," she announced. "Crystal, Jason, get on out of there and dry off. It's lunchtime."

"You said we could eat out here," Jason objected.

"I can watch them while you're inside," I said.

"Why? So you can 'just ask' them things, too?"

My face reddened. "That's not why I offered—"

She turned away from me. "Crystal! Jason! I said go inside. You, too, Tiffany!"

"I'm not hungry," Tiffany mumbled, turning her face to make sure the left side got well baked.

"Now!" Sue barked.

The kids must have been able to tell that their mother

wasn't kidding, because they obeyed without saying another word.

Nobody said anything to me, either, as they disappeared into the house. I was still holding my empty glass, but since I didn't think Sue would want me to go inside to give it back, I left it on the seat of my chair. I had a hunch that they'd be back outside as soon as I was gone, anyway.

Chapter 15

I got to Pigwick's Barbecue ahead of Richard, and went on inside to get a table, drink iced tea, and brood over my conversation with Sue. Tim Topper, who owns the place, usually stops to visit when I go in, but he was busy with the lunch crowd and settled for a wave. It was just as well—I wouldn't have been good company. I cycled between anger, embarrassment, and guilt, and was feeling all three when Richard came in.

He immediately gave me a hug. "From the look on your face, I assume it didn't go well."

"You are a master of understatement." I told him about it, finishing with, "Needless to say, Sue didn't ask me to stay for lunch."

"I'm sorry, love, but did you really expect anything different?"

"I suppose not, but I was hoping. I mean, if I suspected you were in that kind of trouble, I'd want to talk about it to somebody, just for my own sanity."

"Even if I were involved in something illegal?"

"Maybe not," I admitted. "I hope you had better luck at the library."

"I did, but perhaps it should wait until after we order."

He'd seen the waitress coming, carrying a basket of hush puppies for us to start with, and I quickly asked for my usual: a large plate of pulled-pork barbecue with french fries and coleslaw. Richard took a while to make up his mind, which is unusual, but eventually ordered the same thing.

After the waitress had gone, I asked, "What's the matter? Aren't you hungry?"

"Starved," he said. "I'm just not sure I have a taste for barbecue today."

"Really?" Eating barbecue has always been one of the high points of our visits to Byerly. There are a few places in Boston that serve barbecue, but there's nothing like eastern-North-Carolina-style barbecue, pulled off the pig and marinated in a vinegar sauce. Just thinking about it was putting me in a better mood.

Then I realized what Richard had been doing all morning. "Oh Richard, what was I thinking? Were the books on arson . . . Gruesome?"

He shrugged, which meant that they had been.

"Do you want me to call the waitress back so you can order something else?"

"No, I'll be fine. Let's just get the dirty work over with before the food arrives." He pulled out a small three-ring notebook with the Boston College logo. "I started out with the basics of arson investigation, but decided we don't really need to know the effect of various accelerants on wood, plaster, mattresses, and other materials."

"Mattresses?"

"Don't ask."

No wonder barbecue didn't appeal to him.

He went on. "I also didn't think we needed to know how

arson investigation is conducted, though I was fascinated by stories of arson dogs trained to sniff out hydrocarbons."

"Why hydrocarbons?"

"Most accelerants are hydrocarbons, of course."

"Of course."

"From what I did read, I realize why Junior has had such a hard time with the case. About the only ways to prove arson are by catching the arsonist in the act, or by exclusive opportunity. Since he's hit buildings in public areas, I don't think she could prove exclusive opportunity to any of them, and to catch him in the act, she'd have to stake out every conceivable target in the area."

"No wonder she was as ill as a hornet when we spoke to her," I said.

"Obviously we can't compete with Junior and the experts in formal investigation, so I focused on the reasons for arson. Most arson fires fall into certain categories. A popular one is insurance fraud."

"That's what people originally thought the Woolworth's fire was, but it turns out the place wasn't insured enough to make burning worthwhile."

"Next there are larceny arsonists, who rob a place, then burn it to destroy the evidence."

"I haven't heard of anything worth stealing in any of the buildings."

"Occasionally, arson is used to cover up other crimes, such as murder."

"To get rid of the body?"

He nodded.

"Thank goodness that one doesn't fit."

"Then there are people who want to get relocation priority in public housing. There's arson as part of gang fights.

Arson can be used as a weapon in domestic disputes, as in burning down an ex-wife's house as part of a pattern of abuse or harassment. Obviously none of those apply here."

"Which leaves us what?"

"Pyromaniacs, for one. Or as the literature refers to them, pathological fire-setters."

"Linwood isn't a pyromaniac," I said, hoping it was true.

Thankfully, Richard agreed. "Probably not," he said. "Pyromaniacs usually demonstrate extreme isolation from society, and nobody in your family could get away with extreme isolation for more than a week."

I stuck my tongue out at him, but he was right. I'd moved to Boston and Augustus had gone to Germany with the army, but even we couldn't claim extreme isolation.

Richard said, "Pyromaniacs tend to achieve sexual gratification from fire, and I suppose Linwood could be getting his jollies watching the fires, but the rest of the profile doesn't fit him. Pyromaniacs generally don't enjoy the result of their fires."

"Meaning what?"

"Meaning that they avoid the bedlam that ensues after the fire: the fire trucks with sirens blaring, the adrenaline rush of firefighters rushing to and fro, the excitement of the crowd."

"But Linwood is a volunteer firefighter, and was the first on the scene for the first two fires. Obviously, he can handle bedlam." Considering his kids, he had to. "So what is he?"

"The question isn't so much what, as why. If Linwood is our arsonist, why does he set fires?" Always the dramatic storyteller, Richard picked that moment to take a long swallow of iced tea.

"All right, why?" I prompted.

"As a demonstration of rage, and a way to get attention," Richard said. "The rage could be from a number of things: Aunt Edna getting closer to Caleb, frustration with work, aggravation over the proposed buyout, even leftover emotion from his father's death."

"He does have a lot of anger in him."

"One other thing. Though rage arsonists enjoy watching the fires they set, sometimes they also enjoy helping to put them out. It's not at all uncommon to find them working at a fire department."

"Or in a volunteer fire brigade?" I suggested.

Richard nodded. "They crave attention, and by assisting with the fires, they become heroes."

"The way Linwood did after the Woolworth's fire."

"The problem is that the attention doesn't last forever, so the arsonist strikes again."

"But Linwood didn't get as much attention the second time."

"Which could fuel the rage even more."

"That does sound like Linwood, doesn't it?" I said unhappily.

Richard closed his notebook. "Laura, that sounds like a lot of people."

"I suppose you're right," I said.

Our lunch arrived then, and I did my best to forget what we'd just been talking about so I could focus on the barbecue. Goodness knows it was worth my attention, and I managed to clean my plate and eat my share of hush puppies.

It wasn't until we were drinking down the last of our iced tea that I let myself think about arson again. "You know, Junior must have suspects other than Linwood," I said speculatively.

"Probably," Richard agreed. "Byerly isn't so small that there might not be other people who fit the profile."

"What do you think about going to see her?"

"I thought we promised Aunt Edna not to."

"I'm not going to tell her what Aunt Edna told us," I assured him. "I just want to see what Junior knows. Maybe there's something that would eliminate Linwood as a suspect."

"Maybe," he said.

I thought then that he sounded reluctant, and I should have asked him why. Instead we paid our check, dropped the van off at Aunt Maggie's, and drove to Byerly's police station.

Chapter 16

As we came into the police station, Junior was reading a file at the battered metal desk she'd inherited from her father; but when she saw us, she closed the folder.

"Hey, Junior," I said, as Richard and I sat in the two wooden chairs opposite her.

"What brings y'all down here this afternoon?"

"Just coming to visit." Then, realizing how ridiculous that sounded, I said, "And we want your opinion about something."

"Is that right?"

I nodded vigorously, starting to wish I'd planned what I was going to say so I wouldn't have to make it up as I went along. Or even better, that Richard would take over. "It's about the Saunders. What do you think about them?"

"I don't know that I've seen enough of them to have an opinion."

"What about the buyout? Do you think it's a good idea?"

"I told you yesterday, all I want is for it to be decided. I've already had to break up half a dozen brawls over it, which is a waste of time and paperwork when I've got more important things to worry about." She looked me right in the eye. "Like this arsonist, for instance."

"Actually, Richard and I were just talking about the fires."

"I thought you didn't have any interest in catching arsonists."

"There's been so much talk that we got curious. It sounds as if you've got a serial fire-setter, the kind who gets a kick out of setting fires."

"Y'all know much about arson?"

"We've done a little reading," I said.

"Recently?"

"Fairly," I said vaguely. "Of course, if you've found evidence of arson for gain . . ."

"I don't know that I should be talking about an open case, particularly not to you."

"You have before," I said, stung.

"Not when somebody in your family was my chief suspect."

"Somebody in *my* family?" I said unconvincingly.

"Laurie Anne, you and I have known each other too long for you to start playing dumb. I'm talking about Linwood Randolph, and you know it."

"Why Linwood? Do you have any proof that he's involved?"

"Not yet, but with all your vast knowledge of arsonists, doesn't it seem to you that Linwood just might match the usual profile?"

"Other people in Byerly match that profile."

"Name one," she said, but before I could, she held up a hand to stop me. "Never mind—there's no need for me to encourage you. I know you'd say just about anything to get me to look at somebody else."

"That's not fair!"

"Isn't it? Tell me the truth, Laurie Anne. If you knew that Linwood had set those fires, would you tell me?"

I wanted to say that I would, but I honestly wasn't sure. "I don't know, Junior."

"That's what I figured. I don't blame you—I don't know that I'd turn in a cousin of mine, either."

"I can tell you this much, Junior. I don't *know* that Linwood is setting the fires."

"You mean you don't know for sure. I don't know for sure, either, but I mean to find out. You might want to tell him."

"I don't think I have to. He already knows." I looked longingly at the file on her desk, sure that it had something to do with the fires. "If I knew more about the case, I might could help you."

But she shook her head. "Not this time, Laurie Anne. I know I can't stop you and Richard from nosing around and trying to find somebody else to pin it on, but I don't want you to come running to me anytime you find somebody with a book of matches, saying that he's got to be the one. I've let you get away with playing fast and loose before, but it's not going to happen this time."

Maybe she was right, but it made me mad anyway. "Thanks for the warning," I said stiffly.

"One other thing," Junior said. "You might want to think about what could happen if somebody happens to be in the next building that goes up. Fire does nasty things to the human body, Laurie Anne. Have you ever seen scars from a real bad burn, the kind where the skin doesn't look human anymore? Are you sure you want to take responsibility for that, especially for a cousin you don't even like?"

There wasn't anything I could say to that, so I didn't bother trying. Richard and I just left.

When we got back to the car, I had to take a deep breath to help me let go of some of the anger or I never would have been able to unclench my fists enough to drive. I didn't know if I was angrier because I thought Junior was wrong or because I thought she was right. "Did you expect Junior to react that way?" I asked Richard.

"I had a feeling she might."

"You could have warned me."

"Would that have kept you from going?"

"Probably not." I didn't say anything else for a while, just concentrated on driving.

"Are you brooding?" Richard finally asked.

"Maybe a little, but I was also thinking about what you said at lunch about Junior not being able to stake out every possible target."

"Please don't tell me you want us to watch them all."

"No, there are way too many abandoned buildings around here for that. But we could watch Linwood. Junior may suspect him, but she doesn't have the manpower to put a tail on him. She and her deputies have their hands full already."

"And we don't?"

He was right, so I ignored the remark. "Since Linwood works all day, we'd only have to worry about the evenings. All it would take is one fire to be set during a time when we know where he is, and then we'd know he's innocent. What do you think?"

"'Our doubts are traitors, and make us lose the good we oft might win, by fearing to attempt,'" Richard said. *"Measure for Measure*, Act I, Scene 4."

"Does that mean that you think we should do it?"

"Let me put it another way—"

"Could you just give me a 'yes' or 'no'?"

"If you insist. Yes, I think we should do it."

It turned out we didn't have to start watching Linwood that night. When we got back to Aunt Maggie's house and called Aunt Edna, she said Linwood, Sue, and the kids were coming to her house that night for dinner with her and Caleb, leaving us free to focus on the Saunders.

Unfortunately, we didn't have much luck. I tried to get Burt Walters again in hopes of getting a copy of the investigator's report, but couldn't reach him at the office or at his home. Neither Richard nor I could come up with another place to start our snooping that wouldn't let everybody in Byerly know what we were up to, so we were stuck until we heard from Burt.

Then Aunt Maggie and Augustus showed up with a big load of stuff to sell at their flea market booth, and enlisted us to help unload, price, pack, and reload it all, which took a while.

After that, Aunt Nora called and insisted that Richard and I come home with Augustus for chicken and dumplings, which we were happy to do. Aunt Maggie was tempted, too, but was still holding a grudge over the buyout, and said she'd just eat the leftover pizza from the night before. Nobody talked about the buyout during or after dinner, which was a relief, and nobody talked about fires, either. We had more than enough to talk about just gossiping about the family, so it was fairly late when Richard and I got back to Aunt Maggie's, carrying the leftover chicken and dumplings I was sure she'd been hoping for. After keeping her company while she ate a big helping, we all headed for bed.

That night, I dreamt about fires and smoking mattresses, but most of the memories faded the next morning. I just wish what I found out after waking up had been as easy to forget.

Chapter 17

Richard was still asleep when I woke up. I thought I'd heard the phone ring, and I stumbled downstairs to answer it, but Aunt Maggie had gotten there ahead of me. I looked at the clock. It was a little after nine o'clock, which meant that Aunt Maggie would normally have already been making the rounds of the thrift stores, and I wondered if there was something wrong. Since she was mostly listening, I couldn't tell who she was talking to, so I got a glass and some water from the faucet, rummaged around to see if there was anything in the refrigerator I could eat for breakfast, and waited for her to get off the phone.

Finally she said, "I appreciate your letting me know, Tavis. I'll talk to you later."

"What are you still doing here?" I asked, stifling a yawn as she hung up. "No thrift stores open today?"

"I sent Augustus to make the rounds without me because I was planning to go to the union meeting with Saunders this morning."

"I'd forgotten about that. When's the meeting?"

"There isn't going to be any meeting, at least not with Marshall Saunders."

"They're withdrawing their bid for the mill?" I asked,

selfishly hoping that they had so I wouldn't have to worry about them anymore.

"Marshall is dead, Laurie Anne."

I guess I blinked, but I don't think I did anything else for a few seconds. I know I didn't speak, because so many questions were trying to crowd their way out that I couldn't decide which one to ask first.

Aunt Maggie said, "You know that old warehouse out by the train tracks, the one where they used to store shipments for the mill before they started shipping by truck? They found him in there. What was left of him, anyway. The place burned to the ground last night, and he was inside. Tavis said they put the fire out last night, but it wasn't until this morning that they realized he was in there."

"Marshall wasn't the one setting the fires, was he?" I asked, almost hoping he had been. It was terrible of me, but it was better than thinking Linwood could have done it.

Aunt Maggie snorted. "Not unless he set the fire and then tied himself up."

My stomach rolled. Aunt Edna had only been worried about somebody being hurt by accident. Neither she nor I had even considered murder. I remembered how angry Linwood was about the proposed changes at the mill. Could he be angry enough to kill?

Aunt Maggie leaned over and touched my arm. "Are you all right, Laurie Anne? You look like you just saw a ghost. I thought you only met Marshall the other day."

"I'm fine," I said, knowing that I couldn't explain the truth without mentioning Aunt Edna and Linwood. "It's just hard to imagine Marshall dead."

"People die every day, Laurie Anne," Aunt Maggie said. "One time I was talking to a friend of mine, and she left my house to go to the grocery store and got hit by a car not ten minutes later. It throws you, but it does happen."

I was a little leery of asking the next question, but I tried to make it sound casual. "Do they have any idea who did it?"

"Not that Tavis knew of. I imagine Junior will be keeping busy with this one."

"How is the murder going to affect the buyout? Is Mrs. Saunders going to go through with it?"

"Nobody's sure yet. I think that even Big Bill has enough sense not to ask a brand-new widow a question like that, but I hope she says something soon. Tavis says he's going to see what he can find out and get back to me. I'm going to see if I can catch up with Augustus." She got up and gathered her pocketbook, but stopped at the kitchen door to look at me. "Are you *sure* you're all right?"

"I'm fine." It was a lie, but it satisfied her, and she left.

I sat at the kitchen table while too many thoughts ran through my head. First was the shock of somebody I'd just met dying, especially since I'd liked him. Second was the idea that my cousin might have been involved. And third was what Junior had talked about: coincidences. The day after Richard and I showed up to investigate Marshall and his wife, he was murdered. What with the problems with Linwood and not being able to get in touch with Burt, we hadn't done much yet—certainly nothing that could have pushed somebody to murder Marshall—but it was a big enough coincidence that I couldn't help but feel guilty.

Eventually, Richard came downstairs, rubbing his eyes. "Good morning," he said cheerfully.

I didn't answer.

"No sausage biscuits?" he asked.

The thought of well-done meat made my stomach roll again. "I'm not hungry."

He sat down across from me and studied my face. "What's wrong?"

"Marshall Saunders was murdered last night."

"Good God! What happened?"

"He was burned to death," I said and told him what Aunt Maggie had told me.

"Do you think Linwood did it?" he asked once I was finished.

"I just don't know, Richard." Suspecting Linwood of arson was one thing; suspecting him of murder was something horribly different. Then I remembered something. "He couldn't have!" I said. "He was at Aunt Edna's house last night."

"You're right," he said, sounding as relieved as I was. "Let's call Aunt Edna and give her the good news."

Unfortunately, there was no answer at Aunt Edna's house.

"What about Burt?" Richard said when I hung up the phone.

"I'm sure he knows about Marshall already."

"Don't you think we should find out if he still wants us to investigate?"

"I hadn't thought of that." I tried Burt at the mill and at home again and left messages at both places. "No luck," I said, "but surely he'll call us sometime today."

Realizing that Linwood was off the hook had given me my appetite back, but there still wasn't anything to eat in the house, so Richard and I took turns in the shower and were about ready to head for Hardee's when we heard Aunt Edna at the front door.

"Thank goodness y'all are here!" she said, rushing into the kitchen. "I tried to call, but the line was busy, so I came on over. Have y'all heard about Marshall Saunders?"

I nodded. "Tavis Montgomery called Aunt Maggie and told her about it."

"Then it's true!" She burst into tears.

"Aunt Edna?" I said, mystified by her reaction. "This is good news, isn't it? Not about Saunders being dead, of course, but at least it clears Linwood. He was with you last night, so he couldn't have set the fire."

Aunt Edna started crying even harder, and I got that sick feeling in my stomach again. "Linwood *was* with you last night, wasn't he?"

"No, Laurie Anne, he wasn't." She made a visible effort to pull herself together. "Linwood, Sue, and the kids did come to my house for dinner last night, just like they were supposed to, and things went real well at first. Caleb was really working hard to kind of bring Linwood out of his shell—playing with the kids, and talking to Sue about cars because he knows they've been looking at minivans—and it was going so well. Linwood didn't talk much, but at least he wasn't saying ugly things the way he has before."

"Then what?" I asked.

"We ate dinner, and the kids were cranking homemade ice cream when Caleb said, 'Linwood, I've been seeing your mother for quite a while now—I think it's pretty obvious how I feel about her. I want you to know that I'm going to ask Edna to marry me, but I want your blessing first.'"

Aunt Edna's eyes shone as she remembered Caleb's words, but then they teared up again. "Laurie Anne, I swear that was the first I'd heard of it. Oh, we'd talked about marriage, but I didn't know Caleb was going to say anything to Linwood like that."

"How did Linwood react?" I asked.

"It was awful. He said there was no way in hell that he'd let me marry Caleb. And that Caleb had no right to come sniffing around me the way he had been—that everybody knew he was only after one thing." Aunt Edna snorted. "As if a good-looking man like Caleb couldn't get *that* anyplace he wanted it. Sue was trying to hush him up in front of the children, but then Linwood turned on me. I know he didn't mean it, but—" She paused to wipe her eyes again, and I reached over to take her hand and squeeze it gently. "He said that I should be ashamed of myself for running around with Caleb, that I was being disrespectful of Loman's memory." She shook her head. "Everybody knows what he did to me. He doesn't deserve any respect. But still, I've tried to do the right thing. Loman had been dead over a year before I started seeing Caleb. Don't I have a right to be happy?"

"Of course you do," I said firmly. "There's not one thing wrong with your seeing anybody you want to."

"I told Linwood that, but he said that if I married Caleb, I'd be no better than ... no better than a whore!"

"He said that?" I said, aghast. I'd known Linwood was mighty messed up, but him saying that to his own mama shocked me worse than the idea of him burning down buildings.

Aunt Edna looked down at her hands as if she were ashamed, and I went from being shocked to being furious at Linwood for making her feel that way.

"I had to hold Caleb back, as you might imagine," Aunt Edna said.

I nodded, thinking what Richard would have done in that situation. My husband isn't a violent man, but he can be when it comes to people he loves.

"Then I told Linwood that he had no business talking to Caleb or to me that way, and that maybe he was a grown man, but while he was in my house, he darned well better watch his mouth. He started to say something about it being his daddy's house, but I told him it was *my* house and *my* life and who I decide to spend my time with is *my* business. And moreover, if and when I decide to get married again, that's my business, too."

Now her eyes were flashing, and I remembered stories Aunt Nora had told me about Aunt Edna as a young woman, how she was the spirited one in the family. The spirit was still there, even after her years of being browbeaten by Uncle Loman, and when it came out, it was something to behold. Then she seemed to deflate as she remembered the next part.

"Linwood got real still, the same way Loman used to when he got mad. It wasn't Loman yelling that you had to worry about—it was when he was quiet that you knew it was bad. Then he stood up and walked out the front door. A minute later, we heard the station wagon start up. He just drove off, with Sue and the kids sitting right there."

"What time was it?" I asked.

"Early enough for him to have set the fire, if that's what you're asking. Caleb kept apologizing for springing it on me and Linwood that way, and Sue didn't say much of anything other than to tell us that she and the kids needed a ride home. The poor kids didn't know what to think—I felt so bad for them having to see and hear that. Of course, being kids, they still wanted their ice cream, so it was probably an hour or more before we finally got ready to go, but I figured it was just as well because Linwood needed some time alone. Caleb wanted to come with us, but I told him to go on home because I thought I should talk to Linwood by myself. I had Sue in the front seat with me with me, so I saw her face when we got to their house and the station wagon wasn't there. She looked scared, Laurie Anne, and she wouldn't say a word. She just took the kids inside.

"After that, I couldn't seem to make myself go home. I kept hearing what Linwood had said about it being Loman's house. So I went to the church and got Reverend Glass to let me in so I could sit and think things through. It was close to midnight before I finally left there, and when I drove back by Linwood's house, he still wasn't home. This morning Nora called to tell me about Marshall Saunders being dead. I tried to call Sue and Linwood, but they didn't answer, and when I went to their house, I saw Junior Norton's squad car in the driveway."

"Did she arrest him?" I asked.

"No, but she wanted to know where he'd been last night. Sue swore that he'd been with her and the kids the whole time."

"Even though he hadn't been," Richard said.

"I was so glad the kids weren't in the room to hear their mother lie that way, but the thing is, if Junior had asked me, I'd have lied, too. I've never lied to the police before, but maybe not telling her the truth is the same thing."

I patted her hand. "I'd probably have done the same thing. What else did Junior say?"

"She asked Linwood about gasoline. I guess she'd checked around town and found out that Sid Honeywell has sold Linwood gasoline in a can several times these past few months. Linwood said he needed it for the lawn mower."

"Oh Lord," I said, remembering how high the grass had been at Linwood and Sue's house. "What did Junior say to that?"

"There wasn't much she could say, but after she left Sue and Linwood's house, I saw her going up the drive to the neighbor's place. I know she's going to try to find out if anybody saw him coming or going last night. Maybe he was lucky and nobody was looking out the window. I don't know because I wasn't there long enough to see if she came back."

"Why not? What did Linwood do?"

She sighed so deeply it hurt to hear it. "As soon as Junior was gone, he looked at me so hateful and said, 'This is *my* house.' I tried to talk to him, but he wouldn't listen, and Sue said that she thought I should go."

"Oh, Aunt Edna, you know he's just mad—he'll get over it."

"I hope so, Laurie Anne. But no matter what, there are two things I decided while I was at the church last night. First off, I can't marry Caleb if it's going to ruin things between me and Linwood. I love Caleb, Laurie Anne, and I don't think I'll ever stop loving him, but I can't stand the idea of losing Linwood. I'd be miserable if I went ahead and married Caleb, and it would just sour our relationship." I started to object, but she said, "I know what you're thinking: that I ought not let Linwood keep me from what I want. But I don't want to lose my boy. He's the only child I could ever have—I had to have a hysterectomy when he was just a little thing—and he and his children are the world to me. You'll know what I mean someday."

She was right. Until I had a child of my own, there was

no way I could understand how the possible loss of one would affect me. I already knew I'd lie to the police for Linwood— I didn't know what lengths I'd go to to protect a child.

"I decided something else, too," Aunt Edna said. "You two and I have never talked about religion, but there are some things I believe. One of those is that a person has to redeem himself when he sins. Murder puts a blot on a man's soul, one that stays there until he repents. If Linwood killed that man, he's got to admit it and ask for forgiveness. If he doesn't, he'll be damned for all eternity." She took a ragged breath. "I won't have that, Laurie Anne. I asked y'all before to find out if he was setting those fires so we could stop him ourselves, but it's too late for that. If Linwood didn't do it, I don't want him taking the blame for it, but if he did, he's got to go to jail and redeem himself, even if that means my losing him forever. I'd rather lose him than have him lose his soul.

"Laurie Anne, I know y'all don't want to be responsible for sending your own cousin to jail. It should be my responsibility, and I'd do it if I could, but I don't know how. So I'm asking you two to help me save my boy's soul."

It should have sounded melodramatic—people just don't talk about redemption and saving souls that way—but I knew Aunt Edna meant every word of it. She was willing to forgo her own happiness with Caleb, but she wouldn't risk her son's eternal soul for anything. Could I live with myself if I didn't take a risk to help her?

I repeated what I'd told her before. "We'll do what we can, Aunt Edna. That's a promise."

Chapter 18

▼○▼○▼○▼○▼

Aunt Edna gave us both long hugs after that, and then went back home. She didn't say so, but I think she hoped Linwood would come by to apologize. I didn't have any idea that that would happen, so I called Aunt Nora and, without giving her any details, suggested that Aunt Edna needed company. A hint was all it took, and Aunt Nora rushed off to be with her sister.

"Damn it!" Richard said when I got off the phone. "I should have watched him last night."

"Come on, Richard, we thought he'd be at Aunt Edna's. How could we have guessed that he'd go off like that?"

"After the way he's been acting, I should have known better than to try to predict what he'd do. He's not rational, Laura. This latest fire only proves that."

"*If* he set it. We still don't know that for sure."

Richard didn't say anything.

"Richard, you don't honestly believe Linwood killed Marshall Saunders, do you?"

He still didn't say anything.

"*Do* you think he did it?"

"I don't know, Laura. What do *you* think?"

I wanted to tell him that there was no way Linwood

could have committed a murder, but I just couldn't. It was funny, there was a time when I'd suspected Thaddeous of murder, even though I'd always liked Thaddeous better than I had Linwood. The difference was that I hadn't much felt like a Burnette then. Now that I'd found my place in the family, I couldn't stand the thought of turning against one of my own. Could I put my own cousin in jail if it came to that?

"I need a quote," I said sadly. "Something about honor before family, or the truth coming out no matter what."

Richard put his arms around me and kissed me on the forehead. "You don't need a quote to tell you what to do. You'll do the right thing. You always do."

"I don't know about that," I said, "but I know I did the right thing when I married you." I leaned up against him, just breathing in his scent and feeling glad that he was there. I could have stayed that way all day, but the phone picked that moment to ring, and I had to get up to answer it.

"Burnette residence."

"May I speak to Laurie Anne, please?" a voice whispered.

"Mr. Walters? This is Laura."

"Have you heard the news about Saunders?"

"Yes, sir, we did. That's one of the reasons we've been trying to get in touch with you."

"Miss Hunsucker gave me the messages, but I haven't had a chance to call back until now. It took a while for me to come up with a good excuse."

I knew it wasn't really any of my business, but I couldn't help asking, "You needed an excuse for your secretary?"

"Miss Hunsucker is a distant cousin of my wife's," he said, which explained a lot. I'd always known that Dorcas Walters kept Burt on a tight leash, which didn't keep him from slipping out of it now and again, but did make it a lot harder. "Please don't call here again unless it's absolutely necessary. Even if you don't leave a message, Miss Hunsucker has caller ID, so she'll know where you're calling from."

"I'll keep that in mind. That is, assuming that we're still on the job."

"Y'all aren't backing out, are you?"

"To tell you the truth, we didn't know if you wanted us to go on with Mr. Saunders dead. Is the buyout still going to happen?"

"Grace says she wants to go through with it, and I think Daddy wants to move quickly before she changes her mind. I don't know what else I can do to stall."

More time pressure was the last thing I wanted, but I said, "Then we're still on the job."

"Good," he said, sounding relieved.

"We do need some help from you. You said your father had the Saunders investigated—we want a copy of the report."

"But I told you there was nothing useful in there."

"I know, but we've got to start somewhere. We can't go to a lot of our usual sources without word getting around. After all, we've got no legitimate reason to be nosing around the Saunders."

"With Saunders dead, can't you pretend to be trying to solve his murder?"

I blinked. His solution was perfect, not just for his purposes but for ours, too. What better way to prove Linwood innocent than to find the actual murderer? Admittedly, I was assuming that Linwood was innocent despite the circumstantial evidence to the contrary, but I just couldn't think about it any other way right then. "That's a great idea," I told him. "It might not fool everybody, but it should be enough to cloud the issue."

"Good."

"But we still want that report," I said.

"All right, but I have to figure out how to get it to you."

"Don't you have a copy?"

"Yes, but it's in Miss Hunsucker's files."

The dread Miss Hunsucker again. "Can't you get it while she's at lunch?"

"She eats at her desk."

"How about after she leaves for the day?"

"She never leaves before I do."

"Could you get in early tomorrow morning?"

"Sometimes I'd swear that woman comes in at bedtime and sleeps at her desk." I was starting to think that we'd have to have to stage a terrorist attack to distract her when Burt said, "Why don't you two come with me to the mill this evening? I can make a copy of the file and put back the original, so Miss Hunsucker will never know."

"All right," I said. We arranged to meet at the Methodist church parking lot, not far from the mill. That way, we could all go in Burt's car and maybe nobody would notice Richard and me.

I did consider asking Burt to copy the file without us, but from the way he was talking, I was afraid he wouldn't be able to find it. Besides, I wanted a chance to find out what he knew about Marshall's murder. Big Bill was almost certainly breathing down Junior's neck to get the details of the investigation, and he was sure to pass them on to Burt.

As soon as I hung up the phone, I explained the plan to Richard. He reminded me that we wouldn't be able to keep watch over Linwood if we both went to the mill, and after what had happened the night before, we weren't about to risk that. Fortunately, a quick call to Aunt Edna took care of the problem. The fire brigade was having its monthly meeting that night, and Aunt Edna was sure Linwood wouldn't miss that. I was glad he was out of the picture for the night, but I hated knowing that Linwood's enthusiasm was all too typical of arsonists.

Chapter 19

▼●▼●▼●▼

Once that was settled, we had the rest of the day free, and with the week slipping away, I should have been ready to get to work, but what I wanted was to crawl into bed and hide. Richard knew me well enough to know that what I really needed was something to eat.

Hardee's had quit serving breakfast by the time we got there, so we had to settle for hamburgers and fries, but at least we had something to read. Somebody had left a copy of Sunday morning's *Byerly Gazette* on the table next to ours, and I flipped through it as we ate.

The *Gazette* only came out on Sundays and Wednesdays, which was usually more than enough to cover any news in Byerly, but the past two weeks had been exceptional. From the looks of this issue, Hank Parker had been having a field day writing about it all. The front-page story was about the buyout, and most of the second page was devoted to a background piece about Marshall and Grace.

I read through it twice, hoping to find something useful, but it was pretty bland stuff. They'd been married just over five years, and had met through mutual business acquaintances. Grace's field was marketing, which didn't surprise me, and as I'd suspected from things Marshall had told me, his family was old money. The family owned a home in Boston's Louisburg Square, a piece of Beacon Hill so exclusive that you had to wait for somebody to die before you could hope to buy your way in. If Marshall had owned the place himself, I could almost consider it as a motive for murder, but since his parents lived there, it wasn't likely.

Still, looking at the paper gave me an idea. I said, "For now, I'd like to assume that Linwood had nothing to do with Marshall's death. That means that somebody else killed him."

"Logical."

"Now, since Marshall and Grace only came to town last week, and probably spent most of their time on mill business, I don't imagine they had time to make any personal enemies around here. That gives us two kinds of motive. One, something to do with the buyout."

"Such as a disgruntled mill worker trying to stop it?"

That came too close to describing Linwood for comfort, but I said, "Right. Or two, it was something Marshall brought to Byerly with him. Does that make sense?"

"Absolutely."

I pointed to the article in the *Gazette*. "Hank Parker has been digging into the Saunders's background. What do you say we go visit him and see what he knows?"

"Don't you think he'd have put it all in the paper?"

"Not necessarily. He could have heard hints of something more, or rumors he couldn't print. He loves to twit Big Bill, but he knows better than to go too far."

"Then I say it's an excellent idea."

The office of the *Byerly Gazette* looks more like an old dress store than a newspaper office, but since it used to be a dress store, that's no surprise. I vaguely remembered the old office, which was appropriately fitted with mahogany railings and such, but the *Gazette* had moved years ago, lured by closer proximity to the highway, a parking lot, and probably the most important, central air conditioning. The current location was smaller than the old, but since the huge printing presses had been left behind for the wonders of desktop publishing, they had more room than they needed.

The only staff who actually worked in the office were the editor/publisher, a man from Statesville who owned several small papers around the state so was rarely around; a secretary, who took subscription orders, dealt with the paper carriers, and sold advertising; and star reporter Hank Parker. Other than his articles, the paper's pages were filled with wire stories and the work of half a dozen stringers scattered around town, most of whom covered society events like weddings and church socials.

With the paper scheduled to be printed that night, I halfway expected Hank to be out chasing the murder story, but we found him typing away at his keyboard. When the bell over the door jingled as we walked into the office, he looked up and smiled.

"Mr. and Mrs. Fleming," he said. "I'd heard y'all were in town." Hank's reddish brown hair was thinning, but he usually wore a hat that covered his bald spot. From Labor Day to Memorial Day, it was a brown fedora, and from Memorial Day to Labor Day, a straw boater. Either way, he always had a press pass stuck in his hat band—maybe that was the reason for the hats.

Most people in Byerly are on a first-name basis, unless from different generations, and Hank wasn't that much older than us, but he preferred to keep things more formal. He said it helped him keep his journalistic distance. How anybody could keep any kind of distance from anybody in Byerly, I'll never know, but I was willing to go along if it made him happy.

He went on. "Of course, after Marshall Saunders's murder, I'd have expected you to show up even if you hadn't already been visiting."

I winced. "Are we that ghoulish?"

"Not at all," he said with apparent sincerity. "I look forward to your visits—when else do I get the opportunity to write about such intriguing events?"

I still thought it made us sound like assistants to the Grim Reaper, but I could see his point. "Speaking of the murder, have you found out much about it? At this point, all we've heard is gossip."

"Does that mean that y'all are involving yourself in the case?"

"We can't confirm that at this time," Richard said solemnly. It was the perfect thing to say, because Hank would assume that the murder was our only interest.

"Let's just say we're curious," I added.

"Then let me assuage your curiosity now, rather than make you wait for tomorrow's edition." He reached for a long, narrow spiral-bound pad labeled *Professional Reporter's Notebook*, and flipped it open with the flair of Captain Kirk with a communicator. "At eleven o'clock last night, the fire department received a call that there was a fire at the old Walters Mill warehouse. The fire brigade was notified, and assembled at the site of the fire. Junior Norton was there, also. In light of the recent spate of fires, she had asked to be informed of any additional reports. As the firefighters began their efforts, they quickly realized that an accelerant had been used, just as in the previous suspicious fires. The fire had been going on for some time before the brigade arrived, and though the blaze was eventually contained, the warehouse was completely destroyed.

"The firefighters then soaked down the site, both to ensure that there would be no flare-ups and to render the area cool enough to be inspected. They were in no particular hurry, because they'd been informed that nothing of value was stored in the building, and they were waiting for daylight to make their inspection easier. As the sun rose, they entered what was left of the building, checking for any traces of the arsonist and tracking the blaze's progress. Then, in the area where the fire started, they found the remains of a human being.

"Though I did not see the body in situ, I did view it as it was removed, and it was quite gruesome." He grimaced, and I could tell he'd been hard-pressed to maintain his professional objectivity. "We could tell it hadn't been an accident because the victim's wrists and ankles were still bound. Had the killer used hemp or cotton rope, it might have burned away, but he used nylon cord, which melted in place."

I must have made some sort of noise, because he quickly added, "Dr. Connelly, who was called immediately, informed me that the victim almost certainly perished of smoke inhalation before the flames claimed him. The rope would have melted after his death."

Though I wasn't sure if dying from smoke inhalation was any better, I appreciated the thought. I wondered how much of this Grace had heard, and if she was hoping Marshall had been unaware of what was happening to him.

"How did they identify him so quickly?" Richard asked. "It sounds as if he wasn't recognizable."

"The first clue was the rental car he left nearby. Since so many firefighters had driven themselves, it wasn't immediately noticeable that it wasn't one of theirs, but eventually they broke inside and found papers identifying him as the lessor. I understand his laptop computer was also inside, tucked under the front seat."

Marshall had been a Bostonian, all right. Somebody from Byerly would probably have left it in plain sight.

Hank went on. "Next, Mrs. Saunders was called, and she verified that Marshall was missing."

"Was she at a hotel?" I asked.

"No, they were staying at the Walters home. Though they had both been at the mill most of the day, she says that after dinner, Marshall returned to the mill to finish something he'd been working on. I understand that he often preferred working at night, when there were fewer distractions. He frequently didn't return from such expeditions until quite late, so she thought nothing of it when he hadn't returned by the time she retired. The phone call from Chief Norton was the first time she realized that he had never returned at all."

"She didn't have to identify him, did she?" The idea of having to see anybody in that condition, let alone a husband, horrified me.

"Dr. Connelly and Chief Norton agreed that seeing the remains would not be necessary because any identification made that way would be suspect, at best. Mrs. Saunders contacted her husband's physician and dentist, who faxed the necessary records to identify him."

"This quickly?"

Hank shrugged. "Marshall Saunders was a wealthy man, and even the medical profession moves swiftly when large sums of money are involved."

"How did Mrs. Saunders react to the news?" Richard asked.

"I don't know. Chief Norton was alone with her at the time, and when I asked her, her response was, 'How do you think she acted?' Oh well, it's nothing I could have used in a story, anyway." Not that that would have stopped Hank from trying to find out. The prevailing opinion in Byerly was that he'd become a reporter just so he'd have an excuse to be nosy.

"Does she have an alibi?" I asked.

"Not a good one. She said she was at the Walters home all night, but nobody saw her after dinner—she told them she wanted to work in her room. The house is quite large and has a number of exits, so she could easily have snuck out. Since she and her husband had both rented cars, she had her own means of transportation."

"Does Junior suspect her? Or anybody else, for that matter?"

"Not that she's told me, and she had no comment on the possible connection with the previous fires." He closed his notebook and looked at us expectantly. "Do y'all have somebody in mind?"

"Not a soul," I lied, hoping that I sounded convincing.

I guess I did, because Hank didn't look suspicious, just disappointed. "I was hoping for something I could add to the story."

"Sorry about that," Richard said.

"I hope you'll keep me in mind if you do learn something.

As I said before, your visits usually provide intriguing events to write about."

"Thanks," I said, still not happy with that particular compliment. "Of course, you've had plenty of intriguing events to write about lately, even without the murder."

He smiled like a cat who'd had his fill of milk. "It has been a gratifying time to be a member of the Fourth Estate."

"Breaking the story about the buyout was mighty impressive," I said. "How did you manage that?" I was pretty sure Burt had been the one to tell him, but I was curious to see what Hank would say.

He didn't answer, just kept on smiling. Though he worked for the *Byerly Gazette*, Hank's journalistic standards were as rigorous in their way as those of any reporter for the *New York Times* or *Washington Post*. He wasn't about to give up a source. "Is there something else I can help you with?"

"Actually, yes," I said. "I know the Saunders only got to town last week, but what can you tell us about them?"

"I had a rather long article in Sunday's issue," Hank said, reaching for a copy of the paper.

I said, "We read that, but I wanted to find out if there was anything you weren't able to use in your article. Anything unusual."

"Any dirt?" Hank said flatly.

"Any dirt," I agreed.

"Regrettably, no. I performed the usual on-line searches and spoke to my contact in Massachusetts, but found nothing that even hinted at irregularity. Most of what I found was in the society columns, with the occasional business piece. The Saunders have the bluest of blood, and are leaders in finance, society, charity, and academia."

"No dirt at all?" I said, disappointed.

Hank shook his head, looking regretful. "The closest to scandal was the fact that Marshall had been married before, but the marriage to Grace occurred a comfortable time after the first marriage ended. There was a hint that Grace was marrying above herself, but apparently she makes up for her lack of breeding with an indomitable will to fit in among the rich."

"Rats!" I said.

"Exactly," Hank agreed. "Hardly the kind of information needed to affect the mill buyout. The only thing I could take advantage of was the fact that neither of them had been involved in this kind of venture before."

"Does this mean you're against the buyout?" Richard asked.

"I have no opinion. I merely want to place all available information before those who will be making the decision," he said piously.

"But dirt does make better stories," I said.

"Definitely. So if you two should manage to happen across anything, I would be most interested."

"We don't have anything so far," I said, which was true enough. "Did you speak to the ex-wife? If there was any dirt, I bet she'd know it."

"I did, but she had nothing negative to say. Apparently it was an amicable parting, and they still saw each other frequently because of the children."

"Marshall had kids?"

"Two boys. Since they live with their mother, I didn't include it in the article. Does it make a difference?"

"I guess not," I said. "I just feel sorry for them, that's

all." Having lost both my parents as a teenager, I knew all too well how they must feel. "Thanks for your help."

"Anytime," he said, politely walking us to the door. "And please, keep in touch."

Chapter 20

▼◉▼◉▼◉▼◉▼

"Where to next?" Richard asked as we left the *Gazette* office.

"I'd love to go talk to Grace," I said, "but even if I could bring myself to interrogate a bereaved widow, I don't think I could come up with a decent excuse to get her to talk to us. Besides, chances are that I wouldn't get anything out of her that Junior didn't get."

"So much for *cherchez la femme*."

"That's hardly Shakespeare."

"Then how about, 'We'll do anything for gold.' *Timon of Athens*, Act IV, Scene 3."

"Meaning what?"

"Meaning that where large sums of money are involved, so are large piles of paper to document that money. I sat in when my parents closed on their house, and was staggered by the amount and variety of documentation. Buying a business like the mill must cause ten times that amount."

"You're right, but I don't think Burt would let us see any of it." Maybe we knew some of his family's secrets, but financial information was perhaps even more intimate. "There is somebody else who might could help us. Earl's daddy, Alton." Alton Brown had been Aunt Ruby Lee's second husband, and they were still on pretty good terms, and because of Earl, he'd stayed friendly with the rest of the Burnettes, too.

"Who works at the bank," Richard said, nodding.

"He got a promotion not long ago, so I'll lay odds he's involved in the financial wranglings."

"Very funny."

"What?"

" 'Lay odds,' indeed."

I realized what he was talking about, and said, "Purely accidental." Or perhaps it was a Freudian slip. In addition to working at the bank, Alton Brown was a frequent and enthusiastic gambler.

No doubt as a result of his promotion, Alton now had a private office at the First Bank of Byerly, instead of a desk in the main area. I was glad for him because of the increased status, and even more glad for us, because it gave us a private place to talk.

I saw Alton at his desk through the glass in the door, and tapped on it. He looked up and smiled widely before coming to let us in and close the door behind us. First the warm welcome from Hank, and then this one from Alton. I'd have been more gratified if I hadn't known that both men had ulterior motives.

Alton always had been a snappy dresser, never coming to work in anything less than a neatly pressed suit and a freshly laundered shirt, but I guess he'd decided he had to live up to his promotion. He was wearing a charcoal gray pin-striped suit, complete with a silk handkerchief to match his tie and a tasteful tie tack. I didn't get a chance to peek at his shoes before he got back behind his desk, but I was sure that I could have seen my reflection if I had.

"Laurie Anne and Richard," Alton said with satisfaction. "This is a pleasant surprise."

"I'm glad you think so, Alton," I said. At least he didn't see us as harbingers of death.

"What brings you to Byerly? Surely you weren't able to get here so quickly after the murder?"

Then again, maybe he did see us as harbingers. "We just happened to be in town visiting," I said.

"But . . . ?"

"But since we are here, we are curious about Marshall Saunders's death."

"Of course," he said, and pulled off his wire-rimmed glasses to hold them up to the light and check for dust. There never was any, but he carefully wiped them with a tissue anyway. "I have a passing interest in the case myself."

"A monetary interest?" Richard asked.

Alton nodded. "On a hunch, I took out a wager that the mill buyout wouldn't happen."

"Then there's something fishy about the financial arrangements with the Saunders?" I asked hopefully.

"Actually, I made the bet before I'd even seen any financial statements. I was counting on union intervention, or perhaps Big Bill's capriciousness. It wouldn't have been sporting to make such a bet once I had insider knowledge."

"Plus it would have been difficult to get someone to take the bet," Richard pointed out.

Alton acknowledged that fact with a nod. "Unfortunately for me, once I did examine the documentation, I saw nothing to cause any roadblocks in the process. The Saunders's offer, though not as large as the amount Big Bill was hoping for, is backed by substantial assets."

"How substantial?"

"Do you need a dollar figure?"

"No, I'm just wondering about the widow. She's going to be awfully well-off now, isn't she?" Could it be that simple, that Grace had killed Marshall for the money? I hadn't seen them enough to get a feel for how firm their marriage was—maybe she wanted to be rid of him, but didn't want the fuss of a divorce. Maybe she'd signed a prenuptial agreement. Even more convoluted, maybe the whole mill buyout scheme was just a way to get Marshall away from home, to a place where she could cover her tracks. Maybe she thought she'd be able to fool a small-town police force in a way she'd never be able to do with the Wellesley cops. It was a wonderful structure of maybes, but if Alton's next words didn't bring it tumbling down, they certainly made it wobble.

"She'll be well-off, but probably not as well-off as she was with Marshall alive. Half the money goes to Marshall's sons by his first wife."

"Rats!"

"Of course," he added, "there are always insurance policies."

"Still, it's not likely that she'd go to so much trouble to end up poorer than she is now," I said.

"Perhaps not," Alton conceded, "but people have killed for far less."

He was right, but from what I'd seen of her, it was hard for me to imagine Grace doing anything that would lose her money.

"How have the odds for and against the buyout been affected by Marshall's death?" I asked.

"Initially, the thought was that the deal would be canceled immediately. Then word came down that Big Bill and Mrs. Saunders intend to continue negotiations, and the pendulum swung the other way. They've rescheduled the meeting with the union, but there's no way of telling how that will affect the odds until afterward."

"What about the odds in Marshall's murder?" Richard asked Alton.

"You don't bet on murders, do you?" I said.

"There are those that do," Alton said. "Mrs. Saunders is a leading contender, along with various mill workers and union leaders, and I heard that Saunders has an ex-wife to consider."

"You *are* betting on it!" I said.

"Not personally, but I have been following the contest because of the effect it could have on the mill buyout. If Mrs. Saunders is the killer, for instance, that would certainly put a crimp in Big Bill's plans."

"And if Big Bill is the killer, that could cause problems, too," Richard joked.

Alton and he laughed, though it seemed to me that betting on a murderer was awfully tacky. Of course, the same thing could be said about all my questions, so maybe I was in no position to judge.

Alton said, "Even though I don't intend to bet on the investigation, if you don't object, I'd like to tell those who are that you two have shown interest."

I looked at Richard, who shrugged, so I said, "I don't see why not."

"Thank you. Exchanging tips is part of the game—this information could help me acquire information I need later on. Along those lines, if you have any early thoughts as to whether the mill buyout is going to happen, I would very much appreciate hearing about it." That was why he'd been so glad to see us in the first place, of course.

After the information Alton had given us, we did owe him something; but while I wondered how the odds would be affected if it became known that Burt opposed the plan, I had to say, "We can't tell you anything now, but we'll call if we do learn anything we can share. Fair enough?"

"Eminently fair." As he escorted us to the door, I finally saw his shoes. They were mirror-bright, as expected. It was just a shame I hadn't been able to lay a bet that they would be.

Chapter 21

As we headed back to the car, Richard said, "I wonder what the odds are for Burt having murdered Marshall?"

"Richard!"

"We know that he's against the buyout—why not kill Saunders to stop it? The fact that nobody knows what he's really hoping for would provide one heck of a cover."

"But Marshall's death didn't stop anything," I reminded him.

"Burt probably assumed that Grace would be too distraught to go ahead with the deal."

"Then why go to the trouble and expense of bringing us down here? You know doggoned well Burt wouldn't spend money on plane tickets and rental cars unless he thought he had no other choice."

"All part of his insidious plan. Since we're the only ones who know about his nephew, we're the only ones who'd know why he wants to stop the buyout. He got us here so he can take care of us, too."

"You are kidding, aren't you?"

"Don't you think it's suspicious that he's invited the two of us to meet him at the mill? Alone? At night? And he doesn't want us to tell anybody where we're going."

For a minute or two, it almost made sense. Then I tried to imagine Burt as the master manipulator that he'd have to be to have come up with such a plan. It didn't work. "Cut it out!" I said, poking him. "You're just trying to scare me."

Richard grinned. "I had you going for a minute there, didn't I?"

"You did not."

"I did."

"Not for a whole minute. Ten seconds, tops."

"At least fifty."

We ended the auction at thirty seconds as we got into the car. Checking my watch showed that we had several hours before time to go meet Burt, but I had no brilliant ideas of how to fill them productively. Then Richard got a different kind of idea that might not have been productive, but it sounded good to me. So we headed back to Aunt Maggie's, and after making sure we had the house to ourselves, took advantage of the time alone the best way we knew how.

Richard was taking a quick shower when I heard the front door open. I quickly finished getting dressed and went downstairs, expecting to find Aunt Maggie. What I didn't expect was to find Linwood at the bottom of the stairs, glaring at me.

"If you're looking for Aunt Maggie, she's not here," I said.

"I wasn't looking for her. I was looking for you."

"Well, you found me," I said. "I was just about to get something to drink. Can I get you something, too?"

"I don't want nothing from you."

"Okay," I said, and stepped past him to get to the kitchen. Linwood stomped in behind me.

Linwood continued to glare as I got a cold bottle of Coke out of the refrigerator and leaned against the kitchen counter to drink it. I knew Linwood wanted me to speak first, and at first I thought I'd wait him out, but looking at Aunt Maggie's clock reminded me that Richard and I had an appointment, so I broke the silence first. "You said you were looking for me?"

"Sue told me what you're up to," he said.

"Meaning what?"

"Meaning that I want you to keep your nose out of my business! Going to my house behind my back and asking her a bunch of fool questions, and trying to pretend you were just curious. Did you really think my own wife would bad-mouth me?"

I took a breath before answering, partially to calm down and partially to make sure that I worded the next sentences carefully. "All I did was bring up some of the fires that have been set around here lately. I never mentioned your name, so why would you assume I was asking about you?"

"Don't try to fast-talk me! I know damned well you're trying to pin those fires on me. I bet it was you who set Junior Norton on me."

"I did no such thing!"

"Who gave you the right to go stirring up trouble, any-way? Who the hell do you think you are?"

"I thought I was your cousin," I said. "I thought I owed it to you to find out if you were in trouble, so I could help you if you are."

"Since when do you want to help me? You've never had any use for me before."

The awful thing was, he was right. "I know we've never gotten along, Linwood. At this point, I don't know whose fault it is, and I don't think it even matters anymore. What matters is that we're family, and if you need help, I'll do what I can for you."

"I don't need your help!"

"Fine!" I snapped. "You go ahead and keep setting fires until you burn the whole town down, if that's what you want."

"Who said I set those fires?"

I was tempted to tell him his own mother suspected him, but I couldn't hurt Aunt Edna that way. So I sidestepped the question. "If you didn't set them, then where have you been all those nights you weren't at home? Where were you when the fire broke out at the cookout?"

"Where I go is none of your business."

"You weren't with the rest of the fire brigade, and you weren't with your family. Don't you realize that your own daughter could have been hurt?"

"You leave Crystal out of this! She wasn't anywhere near that fire, and you know it!"

"I know it now, but did you know it then? Where were you, Linwood? Prove to me that you weren't anywhere around the fire, and I'll quit asking questions about you."

"I don't have to prove a damned thing to you!" He stepped closer, and even though I stood as straight as I could, he still loomed over me. "I'm only going to tell you this once: you stay the hell out of my business or I'll—"

"What you'll do is get away from my wife," Richard said. Though he didn't raise his voice, somehow the implied threat was more effective than all of Linwood's blustering.

Linwood must have thought so, too, because he backed off. "I was telling her, and now I'm telling you: stay out of my business or I'll—"

"Let me tell you something," Richard said in that same tone. "If you ever do anything to hurt Laura, you *will* regret it." Linwood started to say something, but Richard held up one finger and Linwood stopped. "Don't make idle threats. I don't."

Linwood tried his best to stare my husband down, but got nowhere. I didn't even see Richard blink. Finally, Linwood turned on his heel, muttering something profane under his breath, and, a few seconds later, we heard the front door slam as he went out.

Richard put his arms around me. "Are you all right?"

"No," I said, burying my face in his chest.

"He didn't—"

"He didn't hit me, but I could tell he wanted to. Now I know how Aunt Edna must have felt. Lord, Richard, has he always been so awful? I mean, I've known since he was little that Linwood had a mean streak, but this . . ."

"He's out of control. Promise me that you won't be alone with him, not until he's acting normal again. Or as normal as he ever acts."

"I promise." I hadn't really had time to be afraid of Linwood, but now that he was gone, I was very relieved that Richard had come down when he had. Peeking around him to look at the clock on the stove, I said, "We'd better get going if we're going to meet Burt on time."

"Are you sure you're up to it?"

"I'm fine." I wasn't, but I wanted to get the meeting over with. The sooner we answered our questions about Marshall and Grace Saunders, the sooner we'd be able to get out of Byerly, and the way things were going, the sooner we got out of Byerly, the better I'd like it.

Chapter 22

▼◉▼◉▼◉▼◉▼

I must have been estimating by Boston's traffic, rather than by Byerly's, because we got to the Methodist church more than half an hour before time to meet Burt. Rather than sit in the parking lot where somebody might notice us, I decided just to drive for a while. And that's when we ended up in that line of cars going by the burnt-out warehouse where Marshall Saunders had died.

Seeing how awful the building looked made me wonder what Marshall's body must have looked like. All I could think of was the time I forgot to set the timer for a meat loaf and how the pan had looked and smelled by the time I remembered to take it out of the oven.

The worst part about driving by that husk of a building was knowing that the road ended just a little way past it, meaning that I had to turn around and go past it again.

As we made the turn, I said, "Richard, when do you suppose Sue told Linwood about my talk with her?"

"Last night before dinner with Aunt Edna, I suppose. Why?"

"I'm just wondering how mad it made him." By then, we were passing the burnt warehouse again, and though I wanted to ignore it that second time, I couldn't help but stare at it.

"Laura, listen to me," Richard said emphatically. "We don't know that Linwood killed Marshall. That's why we decided this morning to assume that he didn't."

"I know, but that was before he came after me," I said. "The way he was today, I'm not sure I'd put anything past him."

"Okay, maybe he did do it. But *if* he did, he did it for his own sick, twisted reasons. It was not your fault."

"Wasn't it? I got him all riled up, didn't I?"

"No, it was Aunt Edna's fault."

"Aunt Edna didn't do anything, and you know it. All she's done is fall in love with Caleb. She didn't know he was going to propose last night."

"Then it was Caleb's fault."

"It was not. He's been trying to do the right thing by Aunt Edna, and by Linwood, too. It's not his fault if Linwood reacted the way he did. There's no way he could have guessed what Linwood would do, and even if he had, it was Linwood who set the fire, not him. How can you say it was his fault?"

Richard didn't answer, and though I may be slow sometimes, I'm not stupid. "Okay," I said, "I get it. Even if Linwood murdered Marshall, it's not my fault any more than it's Aunt Edna's or Caleb's."

"That's right," he said.

"What if Linwood didn't do it?" I asked.

"Then it couldn't possibly be your fault."

"Are you sure? Maybe our being in town scared somebody enough to want to kill Marshall."

"How? We haven't done anything yet to scare anybody."

I nodded. I still felt uneasy at the possibility that we'd even inadvertently contributed to Marshall's death, but I pushed the feeling away.

Burt showed up in the church parking lot right on schedule, and Richard and I climbed into the backseat of his white Cadillac. "The windows are tinted," he said, "so if y'all scrunch down, the guard at the gate probably won't see y'all."

That seemed reasonable, and the car was more than big enough. Heck, it was so big that in Boston, he'd have been able to sublet the backseat as a studio apartment.

Burt didn't bother to sign in at the gate, just waved and drove on through as befitted the boss. Unfortunately, after going to the trouble of making sure Richard and I got inside the gate unseen, Burt parked in his reserved spot, right in front. I didn't realize it until Richard and I got out, and I saw people looking out the windows of the break room, and by then it was too late to do anything but follow Burt inside.

Though we didn't actually see anybody as we went in through the front door and rode the elevator up to Burt's office, I could hear people's voices and plenty of footsteps. So much for a discreet entrance—we might as well have come in and asked Miss Hunsucker for the file.

When we got to Burt's office, he waved at a bank of file cabinets, and said, "The file's somewhere in there."

"What's it filed under?" I asked, but wasn't surprised when he looked blank.

"I've never gone into the files myself—I just ask Miss Hunsucker and she brings me what I want."

I should have known. "I'll see what I can find," I said, and nudged Richard. While I was going through files, he could find out what Burt knew about Junior's investigation into Marshall's death.

"Has Chief Norton learned anything new about the murder?" Richard began.

"Nothing important," Burt said. "Why?"

"It is our cover story," Richard reminded him, "and if anybody asks, we should have some details."

In the meantime, I found the *S* drawer and looked for a file marked *Saunders*. No such luck.

"I see what you mean," Burt said. "I heard that Junior got Dr. Connelly to perform the autopsy right away. Apparently Saunders was knocked unconscious before he died from smoke inhalation, so it was definitely murder."

As if we hadn't known that already. Next I looked under *buyout*. Nothing there.

"Are there any witnesses or suspects?" Richard asked.

"Not that I've heard. Junior has been questioning people about Marshall, including me and Daddy, but I can't tell that she's come to any conclusions. Of course, the arsonist has hidden his tracks pretty well up to now, so it only stands to reason that he'd do an especially good job when there was so much more on the line."

I racked my brains, trying to come up with another place to look. "Mr. Walters, what was the name of the detective agency your father used to check out the Saunders?"

"It's in the file," he said.

"I haven't found the file yet. Are you sure you don't know what she filed it under?"

He shrugged his shoulders helplessly.

"I'll keep looking." Maybe *D* for *detective?* Nope.

"So Junior thinks that Marshall's killer and the arsonist are one and the same?" Richard said.

"Naturally," Burt said, sounding surprised that he'd asked. "What else could it be?"

"The buyout has roused a lot of strong feelings," Richard pointed out. "You aren't the only one in town who wished the Saunders had never heard of Byerly or Walters Mill."

"Surely that had nothing to do with it," Burt said, sounding troubled.

At first I thought Burt was just being naive, but then I wondered if maybe he was feeling guilty. If he hadn't leaked the news about the buyout to the *Gazette*, nobody would have found out about it until it was too late. There would still have been hard feelings, but people would have settled down pretty quickly once they realized it was a done deal. Instead they'd had a week to stew about it. Not that I blamed Burt, of course. With Richard's lesson still fresh in my mind, the only one I blamed was the killer.

Burt went on, "I'm thinking that Marshall saw something he wasn't meant to see, and the arsonist did away with him to protect himself."

"Does Junior think that, too?" Richard asked.

"She didn't say so in so many words, but it is the most reasonable explanation, don't you think?"

Though Richard nodded, I couldn't imagine that Junior wasn't considering all the same possibilities that he and I had come up with, and probably others as well. I've always thought she was born to do her job, and I'd have been more than happy to leave the whole mess in her capable hands had I not made that promise to Aunt Edna.

I glared at the file cabinets and tried to think like Hortense Hunsucker. If the buyout were to go through, she'd have a new boss, so I looked under *boss*. Nothing there. Okay, maybe she didn't think of Burt as her boss, but as the owner of the mill, and ownership of the mill was what was in transition. Not getting my hopes up, I looked under *owner*, and there it was: a fat folder labeled, *Owner, new.*

"Here it is," I announced. Inside were several pages of typewritten notes about the Saunders, apparently gleaned from phone conversations with them, and several letters from them and their lawyers. At the back was a sheaf stapled together with a piece of letterhead from the Lyman Gibson Detective Agency. "Here's the detective's report."

"Be sure to put it right back where you found it," Burt said worriedly, "and don't get anything out of order."

"I'll be careful," I said. The last thing I wanted was to alert Miss Hunsucker that anything was awry, because she'd tell Mrs. Walters, who'd tell Big Bill. So far, Burt was managing to hide his feelings from his father, but I wasn't sure that he'd be able to keep hiding them if Big Bill confronted him directly.

Burt didn't even know how to turn on the copier, so it took a few minutes for me to figure it out and copy everything in the file. In the meantime, Richard kept trying to get something useful out of him.

"How is Mrs. Saunders holding up?" he asked.

"Remarkably well," Burt said. "She's a mighty strong woman."

"She must be to continue on with the deal under the circumstances," Richard said.

"You've said a mouthful there—I'd have thought she'd give it up and go home."

For a minute, I remembered Richard's theory about Burt being the murderer, but would a man who couldn't run his own copier be able to set a fire?

Burt went on. "You know, if she'd been a widow beforehand, I don't know that Daddy would even have considered the offer."

"Why not?" I asked sharply. "Doesn't your father think a woman could handle the job?"

"Lord, no," Burt said. Then he saw the expression on my face, and quickly added, "Daddy is old-fashioned that way. I'd never make that mistake myself."

"Glad to hear it," I said, though I didn't believe him for one hot minute. I would have bet dollars to doughnuts that he wouldn't have asked my help if he hadn't known Richard would come along with the deal.

"Has Junior spent much time talking with her?" Richard asked.

Burt looked flabbergasted. "You're not implying . . . You don't think she's involved, do you? Her own husband?"

So much for his being gender blind. "It's been known to happen," I said.

"I guess it has," Burt said, and rubbed his chin speculatively. "You know, if she did kill Marshall, that would certainly give me the excuse I need to stop the buyout. Daddy wouldn't deal with a murderer."

"That's good to know," I said. "Have you gotten any hints that Junior is thinking that way?"

"Not a one," he said almost regretfully. "Junior has been holding her cards pretty close to her chest with this case."

I didn't blame her, considering how politically ticklish it was; but since I knew she wouldn't talk to us while Linwood was a suspect, I sure wished she had let something slip in front of Burt.

By then, I had the file copied, and after making sure everything was back where I'd found it, we headed back downstairs.

I thought about suggesting a more circumspect exit, but decided it wouldn't be worth the trouble. Anybody who hadn't seen us arrive would have heard about it by then anyway—the mill may not make socks as well as it used to, but it's still good at manufacturing gossip.

Chapter 23

▼◉▼◉▼◉▼◉▼

After Burt left us back at our car, I said, "Richard, tell me that wasn't as big a waste of time as I think it was."

"Of course it was, at least as far as getting anything out of Burt goes. But now we've got the information on the Saunders."

"Go ahead and look at it, and please find something we can use."

"I'll try." Richard flipped through the file as best he could in the dark on the way home, but said he didn't see anything that jumped out at him. I was hoping that we'd have better luck at Aunt Maggie's, where we could examine it more thoroughly, but it turned out that we didn't get a chance to look until much later. As we came in the front door, we found Aunt Maggie waiting for us, sitting on the living room couch with her arms folded tightly over her chest.

"Hey, Aunt Maggie," I said hesitantly, wondering what she was so mad about.

"Have y'all got a minute? I want to talk to you."

"Sure," I said.

Richard casually folded the copies into a thick packet and slipped it into his back pocket as we sat down on the couch.

"I just got a call from Floyd Cabiniss," Aunt Maggie said.

I remembered that Cabiniss was the one who'd spoken so emotionally against the buyout, and nodded.

She went on. "Floyd's on the night shift, and he said he saw you two up there just now with Burt Walters."

Damn! Why couldn't Burt have been more careful?

Aunt Maggie said, "Y'all want to tell me what that's all about?"

I looked at Richard, but he shrugged, putting the ball back in my court. "It's kind of confidential."

"I see," she said, kicking her foot back and forth. "Then can you tell me again why it is y'all decided to come visit all of a sudden?"

"Since when do we need an excuse to come visit?" I said, trying to make it sound light, but knowing I was failing miserably.

"Y'all are welcome to *visit* anytime y'all want, but this isn't just a visit, is it?"

I couldn't lie to her. "Not exactly," I said.

"That's what I thought. You two have been running all over town ever since you got here." She held up one hand. "Don't bother telling me you were just *visiting* people. You don't generally visit Hank Parker or Alton Brown, do you?"

"No, ma'am." I wondered who had seen us at the *Gazette* and the bank, but it didn't really matter. The only reason Byerly's grapevine is slower than the mill's is because there's more distance involved.

"Then let me see if I've got this straight. Y'all come into town unexpectedly, right when this whole mill buyout comes up. And you've been going to see all kinds of other people, asking questions. Then you go off for a secret meeting with

Burt Walters. Now I know you two have spent right much time solving problems before, but that was for the family. You're not doing this for the family, are you?"

We were, at least partially, but I couldn't tell her that without betraying Aunt Edna's confidence. "Marshall Saunders was murdered, Aunt Maggie," I said, not answering her directly.

"Were you talking to Burt Walters about that man's murder?"

"Yes, ma'am, we were," I said, grateful for the chance to tell the truth without hesitation.

She kicked her foot once or twice. "That's all you were talking about? Nothing about the buyout?"

"It might be connected," I said lamely.

"And you still say you don't have an opinion about the buyout?"

"No, ma'am. I don't have an opinion." That was the truth, too, but I didn't think she believed it.

She didn't say anything for a few minutes, just kicked some more. "Laurie Anne, do you have any idea of what life for people at the mill was like before the union came? It used to be, if you took sick or had some other reason you couldn't come to work for more than a day or two, Big Bill Walters would fire you, no matter what the reason was. When things got tight at the mill, he'd send people home early and dock their pay without a second thought—what did he care if you had bills to pay and children to feed? If you complained, he'd fire you for that. You know why? Because he could. Because nobody made him do the right thing.

"Then the union men came to town. At first, almost nobody took them seriously. Big Bill pure out laughed at them—he didn't even bother to fire the first folks who joined up. Well, your grandfather and I were among those first members, Laurie Anne. We knew the union could help if we gave it a chance.

"The union leaders tried to get Big Bill to treat us workers like decent human beings, but he wouldn't listen, so they called the first strike to show him that they meant business. It was just for one day, but even so, it was hard to get people to go along with it. When we finally got enough people to stay out that Big Bill couldn't afford to fire us all, he realized that he was going to have to deal with the union, one way or another. That's when it got nasty.

"The first thing Big Bill did was to hire men from out of town to break up the union meetings. We were at the Baptist church when a dozen thugs broke in carrying ax handles and wearing brass knuckles. We were in a house of God, but that didn't bother them a bit. They told us that if we didn't clear out right that minute, we'd be sorry.

"Some of the folks started to go, but your grandfather stood up and told those men that we had rights, that nobody was going to stop us.

"They hadn't expected that, and they didn't like it. Their leader walked right up to Ellis. He was a big man, and you know Ellis wasn't real tall. That man raised an ax handle over his head, and I thought sure I was going to see blood in the church that night, but Ellis reached up and took it right out of his hand. Then he used it to poke the man in the stomach so hard he fell right on the floor. I don't know where Ellis learned how to do that, but it knocked the stuffing out of that man and rattled the whole crew. They got out of there as fast as they could, dragging the leader with them, because he couldn't even walk."

I smiled, thinking of Paw and how he must have looked.

"Don't look too proud yet," Aunt Maggie warned. "The next night, Big Bill told Ellis he had to stay late at the mill. By the time he got out, his car wouldn't start, and there wasn't anybody around to give him a lift, but it was a nice night, so he didn't bother to call somebody to come get him. He just started walking home.

"Ellis should have been back in plenty of time for dinner, but he didn't make it, so your grandmother called around and found out that he'd stayed late at the mill, and got us to go look for him. I'm the one who found him—I'd never seen so much blood in my life."

I flinched, and Richard took my hand and gripped it tightly.

"Later on, he told me that when he was on his way home, a truck drove up and six or seven men jumped out. They were wearing masks, but he knew it was Walters's thugs. They beat him like a dog, Laurie Anne, and left him on the side of the road as if he were so much garbage. When I first saw him, I thought sure he was dead, but we got him to the doctor, and he fixed him up and told us to keep him in bed for a week.

"That was Friday night, and on Monday morning, Ellis was so bad off he could barely move, but he made me drive him to the mill. He knew word had gotten around about his beating, and he wanted people to see him and to know that he still supported the union. He wasn't going to give Walters a chance to say he was laying out of work so he could fire him."

"Big Bill Walters really had Paw beaten?" I asked, not wanting to believe it.

"I don't know if Big Bill meant it to happen or not. The

tale he told was that he just wanted those men to scare Ellis. He said he had no idea that they'd go so far, and he got rid of them right away. He paid Ellis's doctor bill, too. Then he started talking to the union and realized it would cost more to hire scabs than it would to treat us right, so things settled down. And it all happened because your grandfather risked his life to get the union into the mill. Now his own granddaughter is working with people who want to break it. Do you know what your grandfather would say about that if he were here today?"

She wanted me to feel guilty, but what I felt was anger at the way she was trying to manipulate me. "I think I do, but I'm not sure you do."

"Are you saying that you knew Ellis better than his own sister?" she said indignantly.

"Maybe I did, because I know darned well that Paw would never have tried to guilt me into doing what he wanted. He might not have agreed with every choice I ever made—heck, I know he didn't. But he never tried to bully me, and that's exactly what you're trying to do."

"I've got a right to—"

"You've got the right to do whatever you want," I said, interrupting her, "but so do I. Maybe I haven't told you the whole truth about what Richard and I have been doing, but I would think you'd trust me enough to know I'm not going to do anything to hurt this family. I've got reasons for keeping what I'm doing a secret. I'm pretty good at keeping other people's secrets, too." I gave her a long look, and without my saying anything more, she knew what I was talking about. The previous summer, Richard and I had solved a murder because Aunt Maggie had wanted us to, and in the process, had learned things she didn't want anybody else to know. Just to make sure she got the message, I added, "You didn't seem to have any problems trusting me when I was working for you."

We glared at one another for a long time, and I was starting to wonder if we were going to have to stay that way, because it didn't look as if she was going to back down, and I knew I wasn't going to. But finally she admitted, "You might have a point there."

"Does that mean you trust me to do what I have to do?"

She hesitated. "If you could tell me—"

I shook my head. "You either trust me, or you don't. I know we didn't see much of each other when I was young, but you know how I was raised, and you've had a chance to get to know me better these past few years. If you don't trust me now, there's nothing I can tell you that would change that."

She looked me in the eye, but I didn't flinch. "You're right. I do trust you, Laurie Anne."

I took a deep breath, suddenly unsure of how long it had been since the last one. "Thank you."

"But people will talk. Floyd wasn't the only one to see you at the mill, and other folks have seen the places you've been going and the people you've been seeing."

"People in Byerly always talk," I said. "I may as well give them something worth talking about."

She shook her head. "You sound just like Ellis some-times."

"Thank you," I said again, because I considered it a compliment. "Now if it's going to be a problem for you, Richard and I can go stay someplace else." Of course, if we stayed with any of the other Burnettes, they'd be in the same boat, so I added, "We could get a hotel room in Hickory."

"Laurie Anne, have you ever known me to care about people talking? Would I dress the way I do if I gave a hoot about what people think?"

"There's nothing wrong with the way you dress," I objected, though I avoided looking at the bright red sneakers with purple stripes she was wearing.

"Not a thing, but some people think there is, the same way some people might think there's something wrong with you staying here. But this is your home, and nobody can say anything to change that." She flashed a big grin. "Not even me."

That's when I was sure that things were going to be all right between us.

Chapter 24

Richard and I never got around to taking a closer look at the Saunders file that night—all the confrontations had worn us out. I would cheerfully have slept until noon the next day, but the phone rang considerably before that and woke me. I waited through six rings, hoping Aunt Maggie would answer it, but finally decided she'd gone out and dragged myself downstairs to get it.

"Burnette residence," I said as politely as I could.

"This is Burt Walters. Could I speak to Laurie Anne Fleming, please?"

"This is Laura Fleming."

"Miz Fleming! I'm glad I caught you. I realize you and your husband are on vacation, but I need your help."

Finally I caught on to the fact that somebody must be close enough to hear him. Just in case whoever it was could hear me, too, I avoided saying anything compromising. "What can I help you with?"

"I understand that you're quite the computer expert, and we have a problem over here that none of our people can solve."

I didn't laugh, but I was tempted. There were a few folks at the mill who could use computers, but only if told exactly what buttons to push. I once asked one of the finance people what kind of computer she had, and her answer was, "Beige." I've never known if she was kidding or not. "What kind of problem?"

His voice grew solemn. "I imagine you know about Marshall Saunders's death."

"Yes, sir."

"Well, Mr. Saunders had some important files on his computer, and we're just not sure how to get to them. His wife is here with me, and we were wondering if you could come by and see if you could get into those those files for us, and perhaps print them out."

"I could certainly try. Do you know what the problem is? Is it a crashed hard disk or a bad sector?"

There was dead silence on the other end of the line.

"Maybe it would be better for me to see for myself," I said diplomatically.

"Do you suppose you could take a look this morning? Miz Saunders is very anxious for the information."

"That'll be fine. Just give me an hour or two to take care of a couple of things, and Richard and I will be over there."

"I'll leave word at the front desk that you're expected."

An hour and half later, I'd taken a shower, gotten Richard up and moving, made a quick stop at the Kmart, gone by Hardee's to get biscuits for breakfast, and driven to the mill. As I told Richard, I was so delighted to get a chance at Marshall's computer that I would almost have been willing to skip the biscuits.

The receptionist at the front door sent us on up toward Burt's office, where Miss Hunsucker herself was waiting.

In all the years she's been at the mill, neither I nor anybody in my family has ever seen Miss Hunsucker smile, so I wasn't surprised that she looked disapproving today. Her mouse brown hair was tucked into a bun so tight that I was surprised she could move her face enough to frown, but she managed as she looked at her watch. In a tone that implied the enormity of our transgression, she said, "Mr. Walters has been waiting for you."

"Good," I said cheerfully. "Then we can get right to work."

I'd say that her features froze in disapproval, but her features had apparently frozen in that configuration long before, and she radiated indignation as she led us to an ostentatious conference room next to Burt's office. The cherrywood conference table was nearly big enough for all the Burnettes to eat Sunday dinner off of, and the chairs were plush enough to settle in for a long football game afterward. A window filled one wall, and though the curtains were drawn to keep the sun from fading the carpet, I knew it looked out onto the parking lot. Burt had been known to peek out to check and see if anybody was leaving work early.

Burt and Grace Saunders were sitting next to each other at one end of the table, Grace looking impatient while Burt looked uncomfortable.

For the first time since Burt had called me, it occurred to me that it was odd for Grace to be working so soon after her husband's murder. She'd only found out about it the morning before, after all. True, she was wearing black, a new suit what was probably the nicest one that could be found around Byerly, but I wouldn't have expected a woman in mourning to be worried about accessing computer files.

As soon as he saw us, Burt smiled widely and not terribly sincerely. "Here's our computer expert. Didn't I tell you she'd be right along?"

Grace looked at her watch, and had I not wanted to look at Marshall's computer for my own reasons, I'd have been tempted to turn around and walk out. Still, I wasn't about to apologize for taking less time to get there than I'd promised.

"Grace, you remember Laurie Anne Fleming and her husband Richard from the cookout the other day."

"Of course," Grace said, but I wasn't sure she was telling the truth.

Burt said, "I'm useless here, so why don't I leave y'all to take care of this?"

"Good enough," Grace said. "I'll let you know if I need anything else."

Burt kept smiling as he left the room, but something about the way his jaw tightened told me he wasn't thrilled at being at somebody else's beck and call. I felt sorry for him, but only a little. He'd had an awful lot of my family members at his beck and call for years—maybe it was time he got a taste of it for himself.

"Here's the problem," Grace said, turning to the top-of-the-line laptop on the conference table. It was already turned on and booted, with a program window showing, but the screen was mostly filled with a message box asking for a password.

"You don't know your husband's password?" I said.

"It never occurred to me to ask him."

My first thought was that Marshall had been hiding something from Grace, and that's why he hadn't given her his password, but I realized that I hadn't given my most recent passwords to Richard, either, and I didn't have anything to hide from him.

"Missing passwords can be a real bear to work around,"

I said, and put my own laptop down on the table next to Marshall's. "What program is this?"

"Something called STAT."

"Have you called tech support to see if the STAT people can help?"

"I don't have their number. Marshall didn't bring the manual with him."

I sighed. "I *might* be able to help you, but it's going to take some time, and I may have to get in touch with a specialist back in Boston. How much of a hurry are you in?"

"I need it yesterday," she said bluntly. Then, as if remembering what had happened yesterday, she explained, "Marshall had just completed some analyses of performance data for us to use when talking with the union. He intended to print out the latest graphs before he . . ." Her voice broke. "At any rate, he never got the chance, and I'm meeting with the union tonight."

"I'll see what I can do," I said as I booted my laptop.

Grace leaned back in her chair, apparently intending to watch, so I gave Richard a significant look. I'm not fond of having people watching over my shoulder, and besides, I wanted time alone with Marshall's computer.

Richard, bless his heart, knew just what to do. "It will be better if you and I find someplace else to wait," he said. "You know how these computer artists are—they want their privacy." Just in case that didn't convince her, he added, "While we've got the chance, I've been meaning to ask some questions about your plans for the mill."

"I didn't realize you were interested," she said.

"On the contrary. I'm very interested. What I've heard so far sounds quite promising, and I wondered if you were planning to invite other investors to join in. I have friends from my undergraduate days at Harvard who are looking to spend some money—we're all at the age when our trust funds are coming into our hands, and we hate to miss out on lucrative opportunities."

I don't know if it was the glamour of Harvard or the lure of trust funds that did it, but from the look in her eye, Grace would have followed Richard nigh about anywhere after that.

I kept a frown on my face until I was sure they were gone, then grinned. I couldn't have planned a better setup if I'd tried. Passwords aren't nearly as hard to crack as most people think. All it takes it the right piece of software and time. I had the right software on my own hard disk, and with Richard on duty, I should have plenty of time, too.

Even if the software wouldn't do the trick, I was sure I could find out what I needed from the company that made STAT. It just so happened that I'd worked at that company briefly, and if worse came to worst, I'd just call a friend there. I knew they'd left a back door that would get me into the program—I'd seen the source code myself.

The first thing I did was to shut down STAT. Then I quickly looked through the directories on Marshall's hard disk, grateful that he'd arranged his files in a reasonable way. I had no way of knowing what might be useful, so I pulled out the boxes of diskettes I'd picked up at Kmart and copied every file. Byerly must have entered the computer age if even the Kmart carried diskettes.

Once that was done, I tucked the diskettes in my pocketbook and got down to business. Cracking a password is a crapshoot—it's a matter of the system guessing the right configuration of characters. The more characters the program has, the longer it can take, anywhere from two minutes for three characters to two days for eight. Fortunately for me, STAT only allows five-character passwords, and it only took me an hour to find the right one. Actually, Marshall's laptop did the work while I played solitaire on my own computer. I did keep an eye on the door in case I had to cover up what I was doing quickly, but I found the password before anybody came to check on me.

A freelance programmer once told me that it's better for the client to think you've been working hard, especially if you haven't been. So once I was done, I mussed my hair as if I'd been running my fingers through it in frustration, jotted some meaningless notes on a pad of yellow stickies and cluttered up the table with them, and rubbed my eyes to make them look red. Then I walked stiffly to the door to look for Richard and Grace. I didn't have to fake the stiffness—I always forget to stretch when I'm playing computer games.

I stuck my head out the door, and in a voice intended to convey triumph mixed with weariness, said, "I think I've got it." Miss Hunsucker jumped up and went into Burt's office, and came back out a few seconds later, followed by Grace, Burt, and Richard, all three of whom looked mighty relieved.

"Can I access the files now?" Grace asked.

"They're all yours."

"Finally," she said, and brushed by me on her way to the computer.

I suppose I could have been offended, but I decided to take it as a comment on how badly she needed them rather than a criticism of my ability. Though just for a second, I did consider changing the password and not telling her what the new one was.

By the time Burt, Richard, and I joined her in the conference room, she was already at the computer, scrolling through a file. "It looks as if it's all here."

"Of course," I said. "There wasn't any data lost—only the password was missing." I handed her the yellow sticky on which I'd written it. "Here it is, but you might want to change it to something you'll remember."

"Can you do that for me? And print the reports?" she asked eagerly.

It only took a few minutes more to help Grace choose a new password, move the computer to Miss Hunsucker's desk so I could hook it up to a printer, and show Grace how to print the reports she wanted.

Then Mr. Walters said, "You see, Miz Saunders, I told you that if it could be done, Laurie Anne would know how to do it."

"All in a day's work," I said modestly.

"Well, we sure do appreciate it, don't we, Miz Saunders?"

"Hmm?" she said, her nose buried in the first page of a report. "Oh yes, thank you."

"Don't mention it," I said dryly. Then Richard helped me pack up my own computer.

Once that was done, Burt said, "We sure don't want to take up any more of your vacation, so let me walk you out. If you'll excuse me for a minute, Miz Saunders."

She grunted something that might have been appropriate had I been able to understand it.

The elevator door had just barely closed when Mr. Walters's smile dropped off. "That woman is going to drive me to distraction. You'd think she already owned the place! Using my conference room and my office as if I wasn't even there. She's even got Miss Hunsucker getting her coffee.

Laurie Anne, please tell me there's something incriminating in those files."

"I haven't had a chance to look at them," I said, "but I will as soon as we get back to Aunt Maggie's."

"I suppose you couldn't look at them with Grace next door," he admitted, "but please call me if you find anything."

"I will," I promised.

Richard said, "It was very clever of you to arrange this chance for Laura to get at Marshall's computer."

"I had to do something," Burt said. "I've got to get that woman out of my mill!"

"We're doing our best," I said defensively, all too aware that Burt wouldn't appreciate the time we'd been spending on family business. "We've only been here a few days."

"I don't mean to complain, but the pressure is getting to me. The union meeting is tonight, and if Grace sells them on the project, I may be out of time."

"We'll do what we can," Richard said, and Burt had to settle for that.

Once Richard and I got to the car, he asked, "Was it really that hard to fix the computer?"

"Are you implying that cracking a password protection system didn't require every iota of my skill and experience as a programming professional?"

" 'The lady doth protest too much, methinks,' " he said, "*Hamlet*, Act III, Scene 2."

"You're right. I could have done it in my sleep."

"Whereas I was trapped in a room with the yuppie from hell, who was trying her best to convince me to give her my money. I'm only glad that I have no money to give, or I might have done it just to get away from her."

"I take it that Grace gives a hard sell."

"Compared to her, time-share salesmen are laid back."

"You poor thing," I said sympathetically. "How would you like a chance to sit and read once we get back to Aunt Maggie's?"

"There are other activities that would tempt me more," he said with a leer.

I was tempted myself, but the time pressure was getting to me as much as it was to Burt. "Wouldn't you rather curl up with a nice report while I snoop through Marshall's files?"

"Are you suggesting that I take a closer look at the detective's report we got last night?"

"I am."

"It probably won't have much of a plot, but I suppose I could take a look."

As we drove, I said, "Other than trying to get her hands on your checkbook, how did Grace act?"

"You mean, did she act like a woman whose husband had recently been murdered? Or was she acting like a woman who'd recently murdered her husband?"

"Exactly."

"I couldn't say, Laura. On one hand, I admired her strength—work could be her way of keeping the pain away. But on the other hand, I had to wonder if she weren't being callous. She never mentioned Marshall other than that once in the conference room. Is that a normal reaction?"

I thought about it. "One time Aunt Maggie told me that there's no way to predict the way somebody is going to react to losing somebody. Some people go numb, some break down, and some try to pretend it never happened. People don't even react to different deaths the same way. Aunt Nora cried for a week when my parents died, but she was much stronger when Paw died. I don't think it means that she loved Mama more—it just hit her differently."

"So despite the TV shows, police can't really gauge people's reactions when they tell them about a death."

"Actually, Junior says that she does watch people pretty carefully, but only to see if it's an honest reaction."

"You lost me."

"Both innocent and guilty people cry all over the place when somebody dies. It can be honest grief, or it can be guilt. And sometimes both innocent and guilty people act as if they don't care—not everybody who dies is loved. What Junior looks for are phony reactions: a husband acting upset when he's not, or a wife trying to hide her feelings when she really is upset. If somebody takes the effort to fake it at a time like that, there's usually a reason."

"Then our question should be, was Grace faking it?"

"Right."

"I don't think she was, but from what you're saying, that doesn't tell us anything."

"Probably not," I agreed. Then I tapped the lump of diskettes in my pocketbook. "Maybe the files on here *will* tell us something."

Chapter 25

▼◊▼◊▼◊▼

I'm not sure what I expected to find in Marshall's computer files. I didn't look for a file named "evilplan.doc" which detailed the way in which the Saunders were going to transform Walters Mill into a sweatshop, or a file called "dirt.doc" containing scandalous information about their unsavory history. But Marshall had struck me as the kind of man who did everything using his computer, from setting budgets to writing letters to filling out tax forms. Most of the other computer geeks I knew did, including me. And all that information can tell somebody an awful lot about a person. Unfortunately, either Marshall stored such work on another hard drive, did it by hand, or had somebody else do it for him. There were no personal files at all, not even any games. Had his disk not been nearly full, I'd have wondered if somebody had deleted the files I was hoping for.

What I did find were files about Marshall's work: reports and case studies from previous clients, journal articles about reengineering where every other word was a buzzword, and tables of statistics I couldn't begin to decipher. I perked up when I located a directory of Walters Mill data, but that was no help, either. There were tables that tracked and predicted production, and bullet lists of ideas for improving the situation, but nowhere did I find anything that gave any insight into the man or an idea of who might have wanted to kill him.

I hated giving up, so I kept on looking through files for most of the afternoon, stopping only when Richard threatened to pull the plug on my laptop.

"I must be missing something," I insisted, rubbing my eyes. "I just can't believe we had this handed to us, and then can't use it."

"You win some, you lose some," Richard said.

"That's real profound," I groused.

"If you want something Shakespearean—"

"No, thanks," I said quickly. Not that I don't love the Bard's words of wisdom, but I wasn't in the mood. "It's just discouraging. Cracking Marshall's password wasn't all that hard, but I hate that I did the work for nothing. Please tell me you had better luck with the file on the Saunders."

But he said, "Sorry, love. There was plenty of information, but nothing helpful. Grace was born in Lowell, by the way, and attended UMass-Lowell."

"Not exactly Ivy League, is it? Hank Parker was right about her marrying up." Then, not wanting to sound like a snob, I added, "At least, that's how some people would see it."

"Of course, we are above such speculations," Richard said sarcastically. "At any rate, I learned about Marshall's and Grace's college careers, and I know what jobs they've held since graduation, and I found out all the articles on management that Marshall has published. None of which provides a motive for murder. The only vaguely pertinent thing I found out is that the Saunders have an impressive amount of money, but we knew that already."

"Rats! Two dead ends in one day."

"There's still the meeting with the union tonight," he reminded me.

"That would be great if I had an excuse to attend it."

"You could go with me."

"I beg your pardon?"

He looked superior. "I mentioned to Grace that I'd be interested in her presentation, and she said I was welcome to come. I'm sure she wouldn't mind if you accompanied me."

"That's perfect! Why didn't you tell me that before?"

"I was saving it to cheer you up in case you didn't find anything in the computer files."

"You know you're brilliant, don't you?"

He just smiled, but then said, "There's only one problem. Linwood."

"That's right—one of us should keep an eye on him tonight. Why don't you go to the meeting, and I'll follow Linwood?"

"No way! After the way he acted yesterday, I'm not about to risk your being alone with him."

"I'll be in the car," I said. "And if I'm careful, he won't see me anyway."

"He won't see you because you're not going to be there. You go to the meeting—I'll watch Linwood."

I might have been able to talk him out of it, but I was uneasy enough about Linwood that I didn't try. Instead I looked at my watch and decided it was time to get ready for the meeting.

When my mother was still living, she'd told me never to take a trip without at least one nice outfit, "because you never know if you'll need it." I'd taken that advice ever since, so I had a navy blue dress, high heels, and panty hose with me. As I dressed the way I thought a prospective investor should dress, I looked enviously at Richard, who'd pulled on a comfortable black T-shirt over his jeans and sneakers.

Suddenly suspicious, I said, "Are you sure you're not skipping the meeting to keep from having to get dressed up?"

"I'm crushed that you'd even consider such a thing."

I wasn't convinced.

Aunt Maggie arrived while we were getting ready, and when I found out that she was also planning to go to the meeting, I asked if I could ride with her to save Richard from having to drop me off.

Even though we'd made up with Aunt Maggie after last night's argument, I wasn't real sure how carefully I should tread, but on the way to the meeting, I asked her how the union was reacting to the idea of Grace Saunders taking over Walters Mill without her husband.

"Still up in the air," she said. "Some who were in favor are now against because they don't want a woman running things—you can guess how well that set with me."

I wondered what she'd said to whoever it was who'd dared to make that comment. At the very least, she would have given him the look, a piercing gaze that Southern women learn early on as a way to let their opinions be known. I've always thought that the less a woman cusses, the more powerful a look she develops. Aunt Maggie never cusses.

"Then there are those who went the other way, saying that they'd rather have a woman, especially since it looks like she had the smarts in that family."

"What about you?" I asked.

"I don't see that it makes much difference. If Grace Saunders wants to try and break the union, she's going to try it with or without her husband around."

The meeting was being held at the Walters's house, a grandiose structure with enough columns and honeysuckle vines to make Scarlett O'Hara feel right at home. Grace met us at the door with a smile and her firm handshake, but the smile faded when she saw there were only two of us.

"Isn't Richard with you?" she asked me.

"I'm afraid not," I said. "He had a conference call with his broker scheduled, so he sent me in his place." I hadn't warned Aunt Maggie, but she managed to keep a straight face anyway.

"You're interested in investments?" Grace asked doubtfully.

"Not really. I'm just here to take notes for him."

She ushered us into the Walters's living room and quickly moved on to greener pastures.

Though we were right on time, the room was already filled, and with the buffet table of hors d'oeuvres and trays of drinks being passed around by the Walters's maid, it could almost have been a cocktail party. The only thing missing was party conversation. People were talking, but it clearly wasn't about the weather or sports, and nobody was mingling. The way people were arranged reminded me of the cookout. Big Bill, Grace, Burt, and Miss Hunsucker were clustered together on one side of the room, and on the opposite side, there was a group of union folks, including Tavis Montgomery, Max Wilder, and Floyd Cabiniss. Everybody was keeping their voices low, and the only communication between the two groups was the occasional dark look.

Aunt Maggie headed for the union group, and I thought

about joining her, but when Floyd Cabiniss glared at me, I remembered it was he who'd told Aunt Maggie that Richard and I had been with Burt at the mill. So I decided staying in a central location would be more diplomatic.

Just when I was starting to feel like the stranger at the wedding, Carlelle, Odelle, and Idelle arrived, and I gratefully waved them over. "What are y'all doing here?"

Carlelle made a face. "Our department's rep has a cold, and I'm the alternate, so I got stuck."

"Odelle and I just came along to get a look at the inside of the Walters's house," Idelle explained. "Vasti keeps raving about how nice it looks since Mrs. Walters redecorated, and we wanted to see for ourselves. What about you? And where's Richard?"

Before I could come up with an answer, Odelle said, "Idelle, you know you're not supposed to ask Laurie Anne any questions." To me, she added, "Aunt Maggie laid down the law that nobody in the family is supposed to bother y'all."

"Really?" I said, touched. I couldn't imagine a more sincere display of trust than for Aunt Maggie to order the family around on my behalf.

A few more people came in, and Big Bill announced that it was time to get started.

He led the way into the dining room, where an overhead projector and screen had been set up at the head of the long, elegant table. Aunt Maggie claimed the chair at the foot of the table, and I saw irritation on Tavis Montgomery's face. He recovered quickly, though, and sat on her right. The other union folks took seats around them, while Miss Hunsucker and Burt sat by the head of the table, making it plain that this wasn't exactly a friendly meeting. I picked a spot close to the middle.

Once everybody was settled, Big Bill greeted us, delicately referred to the tragedy of Marshall's death and how he was sure he'd have wanted the project to continue, and passed the floor to Grace.

Grace had enough sense to know she had strong opposition to deal with, so wasted no time in social amenities before launching into a presentation of what she saw as the problems at the mill, managing to lay it all out without directly criticizing Burt. Then she explained her plans for solving those problems and making the mill a growing concern.

Having spent the afternoon looking at Marshall's files, I recognized most of the overheads she displayed, but I did notice a few changes, especially in her bulleted list of proposed changes. I'd have felt uneasy about it if Aunt Maggie hadn't been in the room, and when Grace asked if there were any questions, my faith in my great-aunt was confirmed. She had her hand up almost before Grace finished speaking.

"Now you're saying you can provide more benefits and flextime and all kinds of new things. That sounds real nice." She smiled, and I could see Grace relax, which was a mistake. "Just *when* do you expect all this to happen?"

I hid a smile of my own. Aunt Maggie had put her finger on exactly what I'd noticed. The original file had a tentative time line—Grace had deleted those dates.

"Well, Mrs.—"

"Miss," Aunt Maggie corrected her.

"Miss Burnette, obviously I can't commit to any firm dates at this time. Everything is contingent on performance."

"Is that right?" Aunt Maggie said, her tone telling everybody in the room what she thought about contingencies.

"Other questions?" Grace asked, looking at anybody other than Aunt Maggie.

Aunt Maggie spoke up again, and I saw another flash of irritation on Tavis's face. "You don't have anything in your graphs and lists about hiring and firing. Are you planning to keep everybody, or are you going to be laying people off?"

Grace's smile started to look strained, and I wasn't surprised. That was the other thing I'd noticed that was missing in her presentation. The file I'd looked at had included plans for downsizing.

"I assure you that your job is safe," Grace said.

Aunt Maggie snorted. "I haven't worked at the mill in a coon's age."

"Then why—?"

Big Bill whispered something to her. Grace looked confused, but went on. "At this point I can't guarantee that staffing levels will stay the same, but I'm hoping that any necessary changes will be achieved with normal attrition."

Aunt Maggie snorted again.

Grace stiffened, but went on. "Current attrition is eight percent annually, but from looking at personnel records, I see that we have a number of workers about to reach retirement, which would bring this year's attrition rate to nearly ten percent. I think it unlikely that we'll need to trim the workforce any more than that."

Before Aunt Maggie could ask any more questions, Tavis jumped in with a few of his own, and Grace gratefully focused on him. His big concern was new equipment, and I could see most of the union reps nodding approvingly when Grace outlined her plans for replacing some of the older machinery. They smiled outright when she put up a chart that demonstrated how they could recover the money spent in less than a year because of reduced repair costs.

Then Tavis went into technical equipment-maintenance issues that went right over my head, so I quit listening and instead concentrated on people's faces, trying to figure out what they were thinking. Big Bill made a show of nodding enthusiastically at everything Grace said, and Miss Hunsucker watched him so she could mirror his reactions. Burt kept his expression blank, while I was pretty sure the triplets were more interested in figuring out which men were available than they were in maintenance schedules.

Despite her hard questions, Aunt Maggie didn't seem as hostile as she had been earlier, but I could tell she wasn't completely convinced. Most of the other union reps did seem won over, and Tavis seemed to be leaning that way, too, but Floyd Cabiniss's face got angrier and angrier as time went on.

Finally he interrupted Tavis in mid-question, and said, "I don't give a rat's ass about maintenance schedules—I want to know if you're going to keep the promises made to me!"

Grace looked startled, and Tavis smoothly said, "Calm down, Floyd. No offense, but we all know your main concern is holding on to your pension."

"Are you saying Floyd doesn't deserve his pension?" Aunt Maggie asked.

"Of course I'm not saying that, Miz Burnette, and I'd appreciate it if you didn't go putting words into my mouth."

"Then put something in your own mouth other than your foot," she shot back.

There was a titter of laughter, and even Tavis had to smile. "All I'm saying is that Floyd's perspective might not be the same as the rest of ours."

There were agreeing murmurs from around the table, and Grace said, "As owner, I would naturally assume all legal obligations, including pension plans."

Floyd looked relieved, but I was still suspicious, wondering if that pension plan was written down in black and white. Then I saw Aunt Maggie scribble a note to herself, and decided to let it go.

There were a few more questions after that, but most people seemed a lot happier than they had been before. I was impressed that Grace had done as well as she had. It hadn't been easy for her to overcome the union folks' distrust of an outsider, especially a Yankee. The union would still have to vote privately on whether or not it would support the buyout, but it was my guess that it would. How the hardliners like Linwood would react was another question.

Seeing that things were winding down, Big Bill thanked us for coming and reminded everybody that there was plenty of food laid out. Tavis and Aunt Maggie headed straight for Grace, clearly planning to ask more questions, but everybody else wandered back into the living room and lined up for tiny ham biscuits, deviled eggs, cheese, melon balls, grapes, and other finger foods. I'd missed dinner, so I filled a plate and eavesdropped shamelessly while waiting for Aunt Maggie.

Most of what I heard confirmed what I'd guessed, but

nothing helped me with what I really cared about. Not that I really expected any whispered confessions to Marshall's murder, but I was hoping for something interesting. In fact, the subject rarely came up, and when it did, it was hushed quickly as the speakers remembered that Marshall's widow was present.

I was starting to feel sorry for myself. Here I'd put on high heels and panty hose, and I hadn't even had a chance to speak with Grace alone and get a feel for what kind of woman she was. As if in answer to that thought, I saw Grace make it out of the dining room and head down the hall. I assumed she was going to the bathroom, and quickly left my plate on the serving table so I could follow her. I'd had plenty of conversations while waiting in line for an available bathroom—maybe I could get something out of Grace.

I turned the corner and saw the bathroom door open, but it was Miss Hunsucker coming out, and Grace wasn't in sight. I went farther down the hall, thinking that maybe there was another bathroom nearby. Then I heard her voice coming from a partially open door. Thinking that Aunt Maggie or Floyd Cabiniss had cornered her, I tiptoed over there to find out what questions she was dodging. Only when I peeked inside, it wasn't Aunt Maggie or Floyd in the small sitting room with Grace. It was Max Wilder.

My first thought was that Max was expressing sympathy for Grace's loss, but that didn't seem to match the body language. I couldn't actually hear what they were saying, but they were talking much too earnestly for condolences. Then I remembered what the triplets had told me about Max's eye for the ladies, and though I thought flirting with a brand-new widow more than a little tasteless, I knew there were men who wouldn't hesitate. But Max didn't seem flirtatious, either. The fact that they were talking in whispers intrigued me, standing closer to one another than you would expect from acquaintances.

So how did Grace Saunders know a lowly mill worker like Max Wilder?

Chapter 26

Whatever Max and Grace were saying, they finished and I got away from the door and dived into the bathroom just as they were coming out. After staying in there long enough to be convincing, I went looking for gossip.

Aunt Nora is the best source for general Byerly gossip, and because of her beauty parlor, Aunt Daphine is the best for news about couples, married and otherwise. But for mill gossip, the triplets are the ones to talk to.

I found the three of them avidly critiquing the Walters's furniture, window treatments, and decorative accents.

Lowering my voice, I said, "If y'all don't mind, I need to pick your brains about somebody at the mill."

"Who do you want to know about?" Odelle asked.

"Max Wilder."

"Laurie Anne Fleming, I'm shocked!" Carlelle said. "What would your husband say?"

"It's not like that—" I started to say.

Idelle interrupted me. "I bet Richard wouldn't let you out alone if he knew you were going to go asking about other men."

I let them tease me for a few more minutes, knowing

that they weren't serious, but finally broke in to say, "I really do need to know about Max."

Idelle whispered, "You don't think Max had anything to do with Marshall Saunders's murder, do you?"

"I'm not sure yet," I said honestly. "What can you tell me about him?"

They'd mentioned Max's many romantic triumphs at the cookout, but now they gave me the names and marital status of as many of the women as they could remember. There were so many that I had to write them down, and even then, they said they suspected there were others he'd kept under wraps. I sure hoped he and those women were using protection, or there were going to be a lot of redheaded children born over the next year.

Max lived alone in a rented house, and spent most of his off hours at Dusty's, the bar that got the mill workers' business by virtue of being just outside the front gate. As for Max's performance on the job, other than his tendency to flirt with every woman in sight, he had a good reputation. He was a floater, meaning that instead of working a permanent position, he filled in wherever needed. Many new workers started out that way, waiting until there was an opening in the department they wanted, but Max had already turned down two or three assignments, saying that he preferred floating. He was a hard worker, always got to work on time, and didn't mind extra hours. Occasionally he disappeared for fifteen or twenty minutes, presumably to meet one of his lady friends, but he always got his work done.

The union had a policy of approaching new workers, and Max had signed on right away. He went to meetings regularly, including the boring policy meetings that were usually only attended by those who had to go, and was the first to volunteer for the union's car washes and doughnut sales.

Between his friendliness and his willingness to help out whenever asked, Max had quickly become as popular as many men who'd been born and raised in Byerly. There'd been a couple of spats when women learned they weren't his one and only, but he'd always managed to smooth things over. If there was anybody who didn't like him, neither one of the triplets had heard tell of it.

Unfortunately, that's where their knowledge of the man ended. His accent, though Southern, wasn't from North Carolina, and they had a vague idea that he was from Georgia. Since Max never spoke about his family, other than to look sad when people mentioned theirs, people assumed he was an orphan. He'd never mentioned an ex-wife or girlfriend, and never talked about any previous jobs. He didn't seem to have any hobbies, which Odelle attributed to lack of time, considering how many women he kept up with.

When I asked about Max knowing the Saunders, the sisters said they'd seen him go through the receiving line at the cookout, and he'd shown no sign of having met either of them before.

Though I came up with a few more questions, the triplets had no more answers, so I thanked them for their help and left them to try to guess how much the Walters had paid for the love seat they were sitting on.

I knew I might be making a mountain out of a molehill—there was no reason Grace couldn't talk to anybody she wanted to. But it was odd that my inquisitive cousins didn't know more about Max than they did. It's not impossible to keep secrets in Byerly, but it's not easy. That Max had kept so much of his history to himself was mighty unusual.

There was one person in Byerly who should know more about Max: Burt, the man who'd hired him. Unfortunately, he was talking with Tavis, and I had to wait a while to get a chance at him alone. When I saw him heading toward the bathroom, I followed him, and as soon as he came out, I nodded toward the room where I'd seen Max and Grace. Looking around nervously, Burt followed me inside.

"What is it?" he asked.

"I need to ask you some questions about Max Wilder."

"Wilder? How is he involved?"

"I'm not sure that he is," I had to admit, "but I saw something that's got me wondering. Did you hire him yourself?"

"Of course. I never let anybody come into the mill without my personal approval."

"How did he end up in Byerly?"

"He said he was passing through and liked the look of the town. When he saw our ad in the *Gazette*, he came in to fill out an application. He didn't have mill experience, but he had worked in manufacturing, so I was sure he'd do well."

"Where did he come from? Where had he worked before?"

"I don't remember all the details," Burt said, sounding irritated, maybe because he thought I was questioning his judgment. "I can assure you that Miss Hunsucker thoroughly checked out his references, or we wouldn't have hired him."

"Do you still have his application?"

"Of course. We keep all that information on file."

"Perfect. I need to see his file: the job application, tax forms, insurance forms—whatever you've got about him."

"But Miss Hunsucker—"

"I'm sorry, but Miss Hunsucker is your problem. Richard and I don't have time to go sneaking over to the mill in the middle of the night. Besides, I found out that people noticed us when we were over there before. We don't want that happening again, do we?"

"Lord, no," he said reverently.

"That's what I thought. You're going to have to find what we need yourself and get a copy to us as soon as you can."

I know he wanted to argue about it, so I gave him my best look. I'm not Aunt Maggie, but then again, he's not the strongest-willed man in Byerly, either. So he nodded.

"Thank you." I heard somebody in the hall, and said, "You'd better go on back before anybody comes looking for you."

He nodded, checked to make sure the coast was clear, and scurried away. After waiting a few minutes, I went to see if Aunt Maggie was ready to go. I was anxious to hear what Richard thought of what I'd found out.

Chapter 27

On the way home, Aunt Maggie and I agreed that while Grace was smart, she was also a little too slick. Either she was hiding something, or she was desperate. Either way, it would be a mistake to trust her too far. Or, as Aunt Maggie put it, "When somebody wants as badly as Grace wants Walters Mill, you'd better watch yourself."

Other than that, neither of us said much. I think we were both being careful not to ask too many questions. I was still keeping Burt's assignment secret, and I figured that Aunt Maggie didn't want to say too much about the union's position without knowing what I was up to. She seemed as uncomfortable with the invisible barrier between us as I was, so when we got to the house and saw that Richard wasn't back, we settled in front of the television, glad to use it as an excuse not to talk.

Aunt Maggie dozed off after a while, so I sent her up to bed, but kept watching for Richard. He finally got back at a quarter past ten, and headed straight for the bathroom. He'd carried a six-pack of Cokes with him, and said that he'd had enough caffeine to last him a week.

"Well?" I prompted when he came down to the den.

"Well nothing."

"Linwood didn't go anywhere?"

"Oh, he went places, but he didn't set any fires."

"What did he do?"

"Let's start at the beginning, shall we?" He reached into his back pocket and pulled out a notebook. "I got to his house and parked about half a block away. Linwood showed up a few minutes later, stayed in the house long enough to eat dinner, then headed for the car."

"Didn't he see you?"

"Of course not. I'm a trained professional."

I goosed him.

"Okay, I'm an untrained amateur, but so is he. He didn't even look around, just got in and drove away. A few seconds later, I followed."

"Where did he go?"

"Where didn't he go? He couldn't have given me a more thorough tour of Byerly if he'd tried." Richard listed the roads they'd gone down, and I had to agree that Linwood had covered most of the area.

"You're sure he didn't know he was being followed? He could have been trying to shake you."

"He could have lost me if he'd wanted to, but he didn't try. In fact, he made it easy to follow him. He stopped at stop signs, used turn signals, and drove below the speed limit."

"Really? That doesn't sound like Linwood." From the way he usually drove, I'd always suspected that he harbored a secret ambition to become a stock car racer. "Maybe he knew you were there and was leading you on a wild-goose chase."

"Why bother? Why not just go back home if he spotted me? It would have saved a lot of gas. Besides, if the way

he's been acting recently is any indication, he'd have confronted me if he'd known I was following him. At least he'd
have flipped me the bird."

Richard was right. Subtlety had never been Linwood's
style.

He said, "At any rate, at a little after nine, Linwood
drove back to his house, parked, and went inside. I waited
to make sure he wasn't coming back out, but when the lights
in the house went out, I figured he was in for the night."
He leaned forward and rubbed his lower back. "I had no
idea how much work it is to drive around aimlessly."

"Poor baby," I said, and took over the back rub for him.
My wearing panty hose for a few hours hadn't been nearly
as uncomfortable as his night.

"What about you?" he said. "Did Grace break down from
guilt and confess?"

"No such luck," I said, and told him what had happened.
"Burt's supposed to get me Max Wilder's file sometime
tomorrow. I'm just hoping it will do us more good than the
other files we've got stacked up."

"It will," Richard said serenely.

"Do you have a hunch about Max?"

"No, it's just that when you rub my back, I'll agree with
anything you say."

"Is that so? What if I rub someplace else?" I demonstrated.

Richard rubbed some in return, and we decided it was
time to go upstairs. There was nothing like seeing a recent
widow to make me appreciate Richard. A lot of things could
suddenly change, and I didn't want to waste any time with
my husband.

Chapter 28

I was impressed. The doorbell rang at eight-thirty the next morning, and when I went to the door, Ralph Stewart, a security guard from the mill, was standing there with an envelope.

"Hey there, Laurie Anne. Mr. Walters asked me to bring this by for you."

"Thanks, Ralph." I was dying to open it, but didn't want to violate Byerly's code of manners by shutting the door in his face. "Won't you come in and have something to drink?"

"No, thank you. I've got to get back to the mill."

He left, and I started ripping the envelope open before the door was closed. "Burt came through!" I said to Richard.

"How do you suppose he handled the horrendous Hortense Hunsucker?"

"You've been saving up that piece of alliteration, haven't you?"

"Alliteration is an old and honored poetic device. For instance, Shakespeare—"

"Investigation now, alliteration later." I pulled out a typed note, and read it out loud:

Dear Mrs. Fleming,

Please accept the enclosed as payment in full for your consultation in the matter of Marshall Saunders's missing password. I appreciate your effort on the behalf of Walters Mill, and hope this recompenses you adequately for your services.

Burt Walters

"Did he really send a check?"

"Of course not. The letter is just camouflage for getting Miss Hunsucker to send Ralph out here with Max's file." I pulled several folded sheets of paper out of the envelope. "Application form, including references. Insurance application. Tax stuff. Formal offer letter listing salary and benefits. Job appraisals. Work schedule, and actual hours worked. Even a copy of the photo from his employee ID."

"Now what?"

"Now we look at it and see what we can see."

For the better part of an hour, that's just what we did. And we found exactly nothing. I was desperate for there to be something there, but I sure couldn't find anything. I looked hardest at Max's references and the information about his former jobs, but it all looked fine to me. Then again, how would I know if there were something off-kilter?

"Richard, maybe we're going about this the wrong way."

"Meaning what?"

"Meaning that the Saunders's financial information didn't help us because we don't know beans about finances, Marshall's statistics didn't help because we don't know statistics from a hole in the wall, and this stuff isn't going to help because we know next to nothing about human resources."

"An impressive selection of folksiness, and I'm afraid I agree. What's the alternative?"

"Consulting an expert. What do you say I call Cathy at work?" Cathy was GBS's human resources person, and if her complaints were at all accurate, she'd read as many résumés as I'd written lines of code. I just called the number for my office, and a familiar voice answered, "GBS. Can I help you?"

"Michelle? This is Laura."

"Laura! How are you doing? Are you having a good time?"

"Pretty good, but—"

"Is something wrong with Thaddeous?"

"He's fine."

"He hasn't got a new girlfriend, has he?"

"Of course not," I said. "As far as he's concerned, you're the only woman in the world."

"It's not that I don't trust him, but you know it's been a while since I've seen him, and you know what they say. Out of sight, out of mind."

"In your case, it's absence makes the heart grow fonder."

"That's what I want to hear. So, have you found me a job down there?"

"Not yet."

"I tell you, Laura, I'm going crazy up here. Maybe I should just come down and get a job as a waitress to tide me over until I can find something in my line."

"Not on your life! You know Thaddeous won't hear of it, and neither will I." To distract her from the idea, I said, "I need to ask Cathy a question. Is she around?"

"She won't be around for another six weeks. Maternity leave."

"She's not due for two more weeks."

"You know that, and I know that, but the baby didn't know that."

"Rats!"

"Is there a problem?"

"No, I just wanted to ask her a question." Then I thought of something. "You help Cathy weed through résumés, don't you?"

"All the time."

"Then let me ask you. How do you go about checking somebody's job references?"

"It's a piece of cake. You just call the human resources department of the company where they used to work."

"What kinds of things do you ask?"

"The usual stuff. How long did the person work there? Was his or her work satisfactory? Why did the person leave the company?"

"What about personal references?"

"The same thing. You call and ask how long he or she has known the person, and whether they consider the person a reliable worker. Most of the time, they do, of course. Nobody gives a personal reference unless they're sure the person is going to say good things. Why are you asking about this?"

"There's this man whose background we're trying to check out, and—"

"You're on another case, aren't you? Is it another murder?"

Michelle had always taken vicarious pleasure in what she called our cases, and had been even more enthusiastic ever since she had had a chance to help Thaddeous and me in Boston.

I said, "Well, we were looking into something else, but now it looks as if a murder is involved." Before she could ask for details, I added, "I'd tell you more if I could."

"Of course, if you don't trust me . . ." she said, sounding huffy.

"Come on, Michelle, you know I trust you. Heck, you're nearly family. It's just that Richard and I promised to keep it a secret. Once it's all over, I'll tell you everything I can."

"Okay, I can wait."

"Anyway, this guy moved to Byerly a few months ago, and I have a hunch that he's lying about something, but everything in his personnel file looks on the up-and-up."

"You've got a suspect's personnel file? That's unusual."

I had to laugh at that. "They checked everything out when he came to work at the mill, so I guess there's no reason for me to call people back."

"Not necessarily. What I told you before just applies to the people you've got good feelings about. If there's somebody you're not sure about, you dig a little deeper. You know that guy we brought back for a second interview last month? The gorgeous one who applied for accounts payable?"

"Sure, I remember him. I thought we were going to hire him—everybody liked him." Some of the single women had been more than a little disappointed, and one of the male programmers was heartbroken, too.

"We were that close to making him an offer, but I had a funny feeling about him. When Cathy told me to get in touch with him so they could talk money, I stalled her long enough to go over his references again. I'd talked to the human resources department before his interview, but this time I talked to his direct supervisor. It turned out that the supervisor suspected him of setting up phony accounts to pay and pocketing the money, but she couldn't prove it. That meant she couldn't fire him, but since they had a layoff coming up anyway, she got rid of him then. Of course, she were afraid to put anything on paper because of lawsuits, and this being a big company, human resources never knew anything about it. They only told me what was in his folder, not what the supervisor suspected."

"How did you get the supervisor to tell you?"

"First, I spoke to her long enough to figure out she had some sort of reservations about the guy that she didn't want to bring up. Then I started shooting the breeze with her, and eventually I found out that we went to the same church when we were kids, and that we were even confirmed together. Between one thing and another, she decided she didn't want me to get screwed by hiring this guy, so she spilled the beans. Off the record, of course. By spending that extra hour and forty-five minutes on the phone, I saved us I don't know how much money."

"That's amazing." I wasn't looking forward to being on the phone that long, but if that was what it took, I was willing to give it a shot. I reached for a pad and pen, ready to take notes. "Tell me what to do first."

"It depends. You have to find out if you've got anything in common, maybe sports, or TV shows, or music. But don't give an opinion until you know what they like. I mean, you don't want to tell somebody who hates science fiction how much you love *Star Trek*. Be sure to agree with them, but don't make it sound as if you're kissing up. Usually you're better off talking to another woman, but sometimes a man is good. Once she trusts you, you work your way over to what you really want to know. Be subtle, but not so subtle she doesn't know what you're after."

I was furiously writing all this down, then crossing things off as she contradicted herself. "It sounds complicated."

"Are you kidding? It's a piece of cake."

"Uh-huh." I looked at my notes, which were illegible by then. "I guess I'll give it a shot."

"Look, Laura, is this important?"

"It could be."

"Then fax me the file, and let me see what I can do. If there's something there, I'll find it."

I enthusiastically agreed and hung up, but faxing the file wasn't as easy as it sounded. There are a few fax machines in Byerly, of course. The mill had one, and there was probably one at Arthur's dealership and at some of the other businesses around town. What there wasn't was a copy shop with a fax machine on every other corner the way there is in Boston. Even if there were, I'd be reluctant to hand over Wilder's file to somebody who might recognize his name and then casually mention that fact to somebody else in town. So Richard and I headed for a copy shop in Hickory, fairly sure that nobody there would care what we were sending.

After that, we took the morning off, knowing that Michelle would do a better job than we could have. To Richard, taking a morning off means going to bookstores, so we visited the three that Hickory offers. On the way back to Byerly, we stopped at Fork-in-the-Road for barbecue, as I once again tried to decide if they or Pigwick's had better food. This was a long-term research project for me, one I was in no rush to complete.

I heard the phone ringing as we pulled into the driveway at Aunt Maggie's house, and ran to grab it.

"Burnette residence," I said, out of breath.

"Laura, please tell me that they have answering machines in North Carolina," Michelle said.

"Lots of people do," I assured her, "just not Aunt Maggie. She says if it's that important, they'll call back."

"She's right—this is the fourth time I've called."

"Does this mean that you found something?"

"Of course. I told you I would."

"And?"

"And you'd better stay away from this guy. He's not just a phony, he's a con artist. A pro!"

"What are you talking about?" Richard had caught up with me, and I motioned him down to the den so he could pick up on the other extension.

I heard paper flipping, as if Michelle were looking through the pages we had faxed. "Okay, I started with the last place listed on Wilder's application. The woman in human resources said he was a model employee: punctual, reliable, never shirked, even baked cakes for peoples' birthdays. He only left because he was downsized through a lottery, and I got the impression that half of the people in the company broke down in tears when it happened."

"But you said—"

"Just listen. So I called the job before that, and they loved him even more than the first place."

"I don't get it."

"Hear me out. So I'm thinking that this guy is really as wonderful as these people are saying, because I'm not getting the first hint of anything suspicious. Just to be thorough, I decide to try his personal references. Of course I don't expect to find anything, because like I said before, personal references never say anything bad. Only I couldn't get any of them."

"You mean they weren't at home?"

"I mean they don't exist. At least not at those numbers and addresses. This Wilder character, if that's really his name, gave three personal references with phone numbers, and every one of those phone numbers has been disconnected. According to his file, he was only hired in late January, yet all three of his references have moved without leaving forwarding numbers. Do you know what the chances of that are?"

"Astronomical," Richard said from the downstairs phone.

"So I called information for those three people. All of them supposedly lived in Atlanta, but none of them are listed. Then I called my cousin who works at the library in Malden, and got her to check the crisscross."

"The what?"

"It's like a phone book, only it lists people by address instead of by phone number. One of the addresses didn't even exist. There's a street there, but there's no such number. The other addresses were for actual apartments, but those people didn't live there, and the people who do live there have been there for years."

"How could that be?"

"The first thing I thought of was that nobody checked the personal references, just the job experience."

"I'm sure they were checked." Miss Hunsucker might be a pain in the neck, but she was thorough.

"That means Wilder set up phone numbers for the sole purpose of having people available for references. Then, after he got the job at the mill, he disconnected the lines."

Though I was glad to know my suspicions about the man

had been confirmed, I was flabbergasted at the extent of his deception.

Michelle went on. "Needless to say, after not being able to reach the personal references, I called back the job references and asked a few more questions. That's when I got the rest of it."

Michelle paused, obviously waiting to be prompted, and I wasn't about to disappoint her. "Don't stop now."

"I called back the woman at the most recent job, and I could tell she was wondering why I was bothering her again because Max is such a gold mine of an employee. She goes on and on about him, and I just know it can't be true, so I finally ask if she went out with him, because it sounds like she was in love with him or something. She says that's not it at all, that he was like a father to her."

"A father? How old was she?"

"That's the thing. She sounded a lot older than me. Now the picture you faxed me was kind of fuzzy, but there is no way this guy could be my father, let alone hers. So I say that he's awfully young-looking for his age. That's when she says how everybody in the office was shocked when he turned fifty while he was working there."

"Fifty? Michelle, he can't be older than thirty-five."

"That's what I thought. So I said something about maybe a new haircut making him look younger, and she laughed and said he must have gotten a wig, because he was as bald as a billiard ball when he worked there. He didn't have a beard, either."

"I suppose he could be wearing a toupee," I said slowly, though if he was, it was an awfully convincing one. "And he could have grown a beard."

"Did he change colors, too?"

"What?"

"After the bit about the hair and beard, I said maybe we were talking about different guys and described the guy in the picture. She told me there must be some mistake, because her Max Wilder was African-American."

"Are you serious?"

"I'm guessing he found out the real Max Wilder's social security number, and from that he found out everything else he needed to know to impersonate the man, who anybody in his right mind would hire."

I'd hoped that something was wrong about Max, but this was crazy. "Why would he go to so much trouble? Not to mention the money he'd need to spend to set up all those phone lines."

"How do I know? It's your case. But I was thinking that maybe the lines were already there. Maybe he had connections with a boiler room."

"A what?"

"You know, for toner phoners and paper pirates."

Richard sadly intoned, " 'O thou monster Ignorance.' *Love's Labor's Lost*, Act IV, Scene 2."

"You two are such innocents," Michelle said, but I suspected she was relishing the opportunity to educate us. "A toner phoner calls businesses to find out what kind of copiers and printers they have. Then he sends out inferior toner cartridges and invoices the company at outrageous prices. If you've got a big enough company, or if people aren't paying attention, everybody assumes that somebody else ordered the cartridges and accounts payable pays the invoice. Paper pirates work the same deal, only with lousy copy paper instead of lousy toner."

I thought I heard a murmur of "Avast ye hearties" from downstairs. "Isn't that illegal?" I asked.

"Of course it's illegal. Why do you think they set up boiler rooms to do it?"

"You mean they call from the basements of buildings?"

Michelle sighed theatrically, and now I was sure she was enjoying her role as lecturer. "A boiler room is a temporary place of operation. They rent some old building, throw together some desks and chairs, and fill it up with telephone lines for calling all over the country. They hire people for cheap, maybe give them a commission for sales, and put them to work as toner phoners, paper pirates, phony charities—all kinds of scams. At the first hint that the authorities are on to them, they close up shop and move somewhere else."

"How do you know this?"

"How can you *not* know this?" she replied. "The first week I was at GBS, a toner phoner tried to trick me, but I could tell something wasn't right, so I checked with purchasing and found out that a couple of other people in the company had already fallen for it. That's when we started sending all administrative people to seminars to learn what to watch out for. Don't you remember us sending that memo around telling people not to give out information about our equipment over the phone?"

"I guess," I said, trying to remember if I'd ever spilled the beans to an anonymous caller.

"I don't know for sure that this Wilder guy used that kind of setup," Michelle went on, "but it stands to reason that he did something like that. He's not just padding his résumé—he's got to be a full-fledged con artist, Laura."

"Nobody would go to so much trouble just to get a lousy job at Walters Mill." I remembered about how Max had worked shifts in every department, and how the mill had been plagued by equipment breakdowns. Then I thought about Max making himself indispensable in the union. "There are only two reasons I can think of for somebody to do all that: sabotage and industrial espionage." After what Michelle had just told me, I was willing to bet that Max had been busy doing both.

Chapter 29
▼●▼●▼●▼●▼

Before hanging up, I thanked Michelle profusely for her hard work, and again promised to tell her what it all meant as soon as I could. Then, when Richard came back upstairs, I said, "Max has to be in league with somebody."

"The Saunders?"

"Who else would benefit from the problems at the mill, and who else would want inside information? But then who murdered Marshall? What reason would Max have had? And if he did, why stick around afterward?"

"Maybe somebody found out what Saunders was up to and killed him to put a stop to it."

"Why kill him? If I worked at the mill and found out that Marshall was behind the problems, I'd just tell everybody about it, starting with Junior."

"Maybe whoever it was didn't have any proof."

"That wouldn't stop me," I said. "I'd still tell what I suspected, and let somebody else find the proof. Even the appearance of wrongdoing would be enough to stop the buyout."

"Caesar's wife must be beyond reproach."

"*Julius Caesar?*"

"Yes, but the man, not the play."

"Whatever. Anyway, it still wouldn't make sense to kill Marshall."

Richard thought for a minute. "Okay, what if our arsonist is a mill worker, and he finds out Marshall is up to something? He gets angry, and in the heat of the moment, hits Marshall over the head and kills him."

"The autopsy said Marshall died in the fire."

"But our arsonist doesn't realize that. The blow was enough to knock Marshall out, and maybe his breathing is shallow enough that whoever it was *thinks* he's dead."

"Okay," I said, doubtfully.

"So he's just killed a man, and is afraid people will think it was premeditated. Let's assume this guy had been vocally against the buyout, so it's going to look very bad for him. Maybe Marshall had realized he was the arsonist."

"Are you talking about Linwood?"

"Not necessarily. Linwood wasn't the only one yelling insults when Big Bill and Marshall spoke at the cookout."

"True. So the arsonist thinks that he's killed Marshall. Then what?"

"His first impulse is to hide the body, or at least destroy any evidence of his attack. He knows about the old warehouse, so he takes Marshall out there and burns the building and the body."

"Why was Marshall tied up if the arsonist thought he was dead?"

"Camouflage."

"How did the arsonist find out what Marshall was up to without Max being involved, and how did Marshall find out who the arsonist is when even Junior hasn't been able to figure it out?"

"That I don't know."

"I was afraid you'd say that." Then I cheered up. "You know what—it doesn't matter. We've still got Max Wilder to give to Burt Walters. Between his lying about himself and his connection with the Saunders, that should be enough for Burt to stop the buyout. And with that much information, Junior should be able to figure out what happened to Marshall. Right?"

"Shall we call Burt and tell him?"

"You bet." I was feeling pretty happy about it, too. We still had work to do where Linwood was concerned, but at least that much would be done.

Mindful of Burt's wish for secrecy, we drove to a pay phone and Richard made the call to Burt's office. Richard does have a Northern accent, but nothing like the South Boston one he used for the phone call, so I was sure even Miss Hunsucker wouldn't know who was really calling. Richard came up with the phony name himself: Fenway, because we'd talked about baseball when Burt was at our apartment.

Sure enough, Burt came to the phone, and said he'd meet "Mr. Fenway" at the same place as before.

We took that to mean the church parking lot where we'd met before going out to the mill, so as soon as Richard was off the phone, we hightailed it to the Methodist church and drove around to the back of the building, where nobody could see us from the road. Burt was already there in his Cadillac, and motioned for us to get in with him.

"Have you got something?" Burt asked eagerly.

"Yes, we do," I said with more than a little satisfaction. "That file on Max Wilder turned out to be fascinating reading, if you like fiction. He's been lying to you since day one."

"About what?"

"About everything, from his name to his job experience

to his social security number. Heck, if I hadn't heard so much testimony to the contrary, I'd suspect him of lying about being a man." I explained what Michelle had found out about the real Max Wilder, and what this told us about the phony one.

Burt waited until I was done, then said, "I'm not sure how this is going to help me. If Wilder has been acting as a saboteur, how do we know he's not doing it on his own?"

"That's the best part," I said. "Max and Grace Saunders are in collusion." I explained that I'd seen them together the night before.

"That's it?" Burt asked. "You want me to go to my daddy and tell him to cancel a deal as important as this one because you saw two people talking?"

"It was the way they were talking," I insisted. "It was suspicious."

"Suspicious?" he said, rolling his eyes. "I can't wait to hear what Daddy has to say about that."

"Look, if you confront Grace the right way—"

"If I go to Grace Saunders with nothing more than this, she's going to laugh right in my face, and Daddy will, too. Even if all you say about Wilder is true—"

"It is true!" I said.

"Fine, I believe you. But all it's going to prove is that I hired somebody under false pretenses, and that I've let an impostor run loose in my mill. What good do you think that will do me?"

"What I think is that once Junior Norton hears about this, she'll be able to find a connection between Wilder and the Saunders, and she'll probably be able to solve Marshall's murder."

"Maybe, if she heard it, but she's not going to." I started

to speak, but he said, "It's not that I don't appreciate the work you and Richard have done so far, Laurie Anne, but until I can get a connection between Wilder and Grace Saunders—a clear connection, mind you—y'all haven't finished the job."

"We've done as much as anybody could expect," I said stubbornly.

"Y'all haven't finished it," he repeated, "and until it is finished, I still have your word that y'all will keep this information confidential. Right?"

"I suppose," I said through gritted teeth.

"I sure don't want to think about what would happen to your relatives at the mill if you broke your word."

I had to take a deep breath to do it, but I kept my voice calm as I said, "Mr. Walters, I told you this in Boston, but I'll tell you again. Don't you ever threaten my family unless you want me to return the favor!"

At least he had enough sense to back down. "You're right—I apologize. And I do admire all you two have done so far. I mean that sincerely."

My mama always taught me to say 'thank you' when I was complimented, but I just couldn't do it this time.

"When you can make that connection for me, you call me right away—day or night. All right?"

I still didn't trust myself to answer.

"All right," he said, answering himself. "Now I've got to get back to the mill. Daddy and Grace are still stuck on a couple of points, but they're nearly ready to sign on the dotted line. Fortunately, our lawyer is out of town until Monday, so they can't finalize anything until then, but as soon as he gets back, Daddy's going to have him draw up the papers. That means Monday is our deadline. If you can't find anything by then, you may as well not find it at all."

Richard and I got out of the car without saying anything else, and watched as Burt drove away. Then I started kicking our rental car's tires.

"That weasel! That idiot! That low-down scum-sucking snake! That—" Being in a church lot inhibited me from actual cussing, so I had problems coming up with words bad enough.

"That scurvy, old, filthy, scurvy lord?" Richard suggested. "As valiant as the wrathful dove, or most magnanimous mouse? A vicious mole of nature?"

"All of that and more! Who does he think he is?"

"A candle, the better part burnt out? A rank weed, and we must root him out? A very serpent in our way?"

Richard showed every sign of being able to continue indefinitely, and knowing just how many plays Shakespeare had written, I decided not to put it to the test. "Okay, that's enough."

"I've got more."

"I'm sure you do, but it isn't helping us finish the job, as Burt put it."

"Does this mean that you want to keep going?"

"Do we have a choice?" I asked bitterly.

"Of course we have a choice. No matter what Burt Walters thinks, we don't work for him."

"That's part of what infuriates me. I went all the way to Boston to make sure I'd never have to work for the Walters, and then I let myself get trapped this way."

"You are *not* trapped. You are performing a one-time service to get something you want. That's it. And if that service turns out to be too much, we'll stop. So let me ask you again. Do you want to keep going?"

I opened the car, got behind the wheel, and leaned back to think. The thing was, I was sure that there was a link between Max and Grace Saunders. I'd said over and over again that I didn't have an opinion about the mill buyout, but if Grace Saunders was the kind of person who'd hire a con man to do dirty work for her, then I didn't want any Burnettes working for her. It wasn't just a matter of doing a job for Burt Walters anymore. Now I had my family to protect.

"Do you mind driving?" I asked, getting back out of the car. "We're going after Max Wilder, and I need some time to figure out how we're going to do it."

Chapter 30

▼▽▼▽▼▽▼

By the time we got to Aunt Maggie's, I had an idea for how we could get Max. I asked, "Richard, would you say I'm a reasonably attractive woman?"

"I would not."

"You wouldn't?"

"I'd quote Shakespeare's *'Sonnet 18'* and say, 'Shall I compare thee to a summer's day? Thou art more lovely and more temperate.' Or perhaps I'd say, ''Tis beauty truly blent, whose red and white Nature's own sweet and cunning hand laid on.' *Twelfth Night*, Act I, Scene 5. But surely I've made my feelings for you obvious by now. If not, perhaps we should retire upstairs and—"

"You've made them perfectly clear," I said. "I was just thinking that according to the triplets, Max has quite an eye for the ladies."

"Not just an eye, apparently."

"They also told me that he hangs out at Dusty's. What if I go over there and see if he notices me?"

"Don't you think he'll recognize you? You have met him, after all."

"Then it's high time I got a makeover." I reached for the phone and called Aunt Daphine at the beauty parlor, and asked her if she had time to give me a hand. She was awfully curious, especially when I described what I wanted, but either she'd heard Aunt Maggie's directive about us or she was too polite to push.

Aunt Daphine said she didn't have any more appointments that afternoon, so she could leave the shop early to come to the house and do the job in private. She showed up a little while later with a satchel full of supplies, and though Richard was dying to watch, she shooed him off and we went upstairs for her to get to work. It took her right up until four-thirty to get everything fixed to her satisfaction. Of course, it might have gone faster if we hadn't been laughing so much.

To test how successful Aunt Daphine had been, I had her go down to the den to distract Richard while I sneaked outside. Then I rang the doorbell and waited for him to open the door.

"Yes?" he said.

"Hey, there," I said in my phoniest Southern accent. "Did you call for company?"

He blinked a few times, and started to stammer, "I'm afraid you've got—" Then he did a double take, followed by a triple take. "Laura?"

I heard Aunt Daphine coming upstairs, giggling like crazy. "What do you think of Laurie Anne's new look?"

"It's different," was all he could say. Apparently the Bard didn't provide an appropriate quote for this particular situation. Then again, I'm not sure if anybody in Elizabethan England used hair spray the way Aunt Daphine had on me.

My hair was so big that it looked as if I had twice as much as I really did, and she'd used some sort of tint, too, to change it from light brown to reddish brown. Then we'd layered on makeup twice as thick as I'd ever wear it, with bright colors that I never wear. Aunt Daphine said salespeople were always leaving her samples, and she was glad for an excuse to use them all up. The result was pure bimbo, if one could be said to be pure and a bimbo at the same time.

Aunt Daphine gathered up her supplies and left after that, lamenting the fact that she didn't have a camera. I did ask her if there was anything special I should do to keep from smudging my makeup or messing up my hair, but she assured me that I'd have to work at it to destroy the effect she'd created. Then she giggled more, which made me wonder how I was going to get it all off.

"What do you really think?" I asked Richard once she was gone.

"Do you want an honest opinion?"

"I know I look atrocious. I want to know if you think this will fool Max Wilder."

"I'm not sure," he said. "It would definitely fool somebody who gave you a casual glance, but it seems to me that Max takes pains to notice attractive women."

"Why, Mr. Fleming," I said in the ridiculous Southern accent as I batted my eyes, "I didn't realize you found this style so appealing. Maybe I should get Aunt Daphine to fix me up more often."

"That's okay," he said. "And don't think I don't know you're trying to distract me. What are you going to do if Max recognizes you?"

"Maybe he won't care," I said. "He's never hesitated to go after married women before, and since he's not from around here, he's not likely to know that I'm not that kind of girl. He'd have no reason to suspect that I have ulterior motives."

"I don't know about that. He's been here long enough that he might have heard rumors about us," Richard said. "Just in case, you're not going by yourself. I'm going, too."

"I thought you were going to watch Linwood."

"Damn! I forgot. Look, Laura, I don't want you alone with this guy."

"We won't be alone—we'll be in a bar."

"That's not good enough."

I started to argue further, but he did have a point. "What if I get Augustus to help? He can keep an eye on me, and I'll work out a signal to let him know if I need help. Fair enough?"

"Fair enough."

Making arrangements for all of that took the rest of the afternoon. First, I called Augustus to get him in on it. Fortunately, he'd already told Aunt Maggie he wasn't going to that night's auction with her, so he was free. He'd heard about Junior's questioning Linwood, and assumed that this had something to do with helping him. I felt bad about misleading him, but I couldn't say anything different without making it worse. Next, I called Michelle again to get background information to use on Max. And finally, Richard and I arranged to borrow cars. Richard got Aunt Daphine's car because our bright red rental car was too noticeable, and I got Aunt Nora's so I'd have one with North Carolina plates. With all that, Richard and I just barely had enough time to get in position before shift end at the mill. I headed for Dusty's, and Richard went to Linwood's.

Chapter 31

▼◗▼◗▼◗▼◗▼

I'd been to Dusty's once or twice before, but it wasn't my kind of bar. It wasn't much of a bar at all, really, just a place for mill workers to rinse the cotton dust out of their throats before going home. That's where it got the name—there wasn't a Dusty.

It was dark inside, with no windows to let in the afternoon sun. A row of booths ran along one side of the big room, a plain wood bar lined the other, and a few Formica-topped tables were scattered haphazardly in the space between. The only decorations were a collection of neon bar signs, all from American beers, and a few yellowing pictures of the mill. I didn't have to look at the jukebox to know it was stocked with country music and Elvis songs.

I gingerly walked across the sawdust-strewn floor and perched on a barstool. I had to move gingerly. In addition to fixing my makeup and hair, Aunt Daphine had borrowed appropriate clothing from Gladys the manicurist at her shop, meaning that the jeans I was wearing were a size smaller than what I normally wore, and the heels on my gold sandals were an inch higher. As for the hot pink top, it was so tight that I didn't think I'd be able to drink more than a couple of beers without it coming apart at the seams.

The place was nearly empty when I arrived, but a glance at the Budweiser clock behind the bar told me it wouldn't be too long. The bartender must have realized the same thing. After giving me a beer, he started slapping stacks of cardboard coasters all down the bar, then opened up cans of beer and lined them up in preparation for shift change.

Full bowls of peanuts and pretzels were already in place, and I pulled one closer so I could nibble while I waited. Considering the fit of my clothes, it was risky, but not as risky as drinking beer on an empty stomach would have been.

Maybe five minutes after shift end, the first mill workers started coming in the door. Most were men, but there were enough women that I didn't feel too conspicuous. It looked as if most of them were regulars because they took beers from the bar, grabbed coasters, and headed for tables without speaking. I was glad I'd stayed at the bar—I was afraid that if I'd sat in somebody's regular seat, he'd have sat down right on top of me.

The room was already half-filled when Augustus came in, his eyes blinking as he adjusted to the change from outside light. The older Augustus got, the more he favored our grandfather. Like Paw, he was a slight man with light blue eyes, a good chin, and a quick smile.

Augustus knew enough of the routine to come to the bar and get his beer and coaster, and then he stopped to look around. I tried to catch his eye, but he didn't seem to notice me. Not sure if he was that good an actor or not, I smiled at him. That time I knew he saw me, but his only response was a blush.

Finally, he found an empty spot at the bar as far away from me as he could get, and leaned against it while watching the door. I shoved a pretzel into my mouth to keep myself from laughing. He really hadn't recognized me. The problem was, how was he going to keep an eye on me if he didn't know who I was?

Fortunately, he was between me and the bathroom. Leaving my beer and the tiny excuse for a pocketbook Aunt Daphine had provided to save my seat, I tottered toward the ladies' room, keeping close enough to the bar that it didn't look too obvious when I stepped on poor Augustus's foot. Luckily he was wearing work boots, which were almost enough to protect him from my sandal's heel.

"I am so sorry," I said as he jerked his foot back. "Did I hurt you?"

"I'm fine," he said in a strained voice. "Don't you worry about it."

"Are you sure?" I said. "I can't imagine how I could be that clumsy."

"It wasn't your fault," he said gallantly. "It's these big old feet of mine. My mama always tells me I ought not let them hang into the aisle."

I think he was trying to see if there was any blood leaking from his shoe because he sure wasn't looking at me. I said, "I bet you don't always do what your mama says, now do you?"

That got him to look me right in the face, and darned if he didn't have that same expression deer do when caught by a car's headlights. Then his eyes widened. "No, ma'am, I guess I don't. Me and all my *cousins* are always getting ourselves into trouble."

The way he emphasized *cousins* reassured me that he knew who I was. "Well, you be sure and stay out of trouble tonight, you hear?"

"I will if you will."

We grinned at each other, and I went on toward the bathroom, avoiding any stray feet as I went. I didn't need to use the facilities, but I took a few minutes to puff my hair up even more so it wouldn't look odd if anybody was noticing. By the time I got back out into the bar, it was too crowded for anybody to notice much of anything. If I hadn't left the purse on my barstool, my seat would have been long gone.

I looked for Max, but there was no sign of him yet, and I started to think how silly I was going to feel if he didn't show that night. Finally, the door opened and in he came. In retrospect, it made sense that he wouldn't be one of the first to leave work. He wanted to give the impression of being a conscientious worker, not a clock-watcher.

My next worry was that he already had a date, but after he got his beer and coaster, he saw me and smiled warmly. I smiled back in invitation, and he came to lean on the bar next to me.

"Hey," I said. From what I'd heard, I didn't think Max required a sophisticated approach.

"Hey there, little lady. Don't tell me that a pretty thing like you is in here alone."

"I am so far," I said airily.

"We'll have to see what we can do about that." He drank down his beer in one long gulp, and signaled to the bartender. "Can I buy you a fresh one?"

"Not yet." I giggled. "I don't want to get wasted this early."

"Oh honey, nobody's going to waste if I can help it."

We both laughed at his wit, but I was inwardly longing for something from Shakespeare.

He said, "I suppose I ought to introduce myself. I'm Max Wilder."

"I bet you're wilder than most," I quipped, so we could laugh at my wit. "I'm Lori Yadon." Lori was close enough to my name that maybe I wouldn't get confused, and Yadon was the name of a boy I'd known in elementary school. Since he and his folks had moved away from Byerly, I thought it would be a safe name to use.

"Are you from around here, Lori?"

"Nope, just in town a few days visiting my aunt. Where are you from?"

"Oh, I live here. I work at the mill down the road."

"Really? I'm surprised."

"Why's that?"

"I'd have pegged you as somebody on his way else-where."

"Like where?"

I looked around the room. "Like anyplace other than here. No offense."

"None taken." He leaned a little closer. "Maybe I should have said that I'm living here for now."

As Max and I made small talk, I noticed how changed he seemed from when I'd met him at the cookout. Before, his speech had been polite, almost courtly, but he'd changed into a good ole boy, and his jokes were just this side of vulgar. Even his mannerisms were different. Unlike me, Max hadn't needed a makeover to become somebody differ-ent, and I wondered if either persona was the real one.

The bar started emptying out as mill workers headed home for dinner, but leaving enough people around that Augustus didn't stick out. By then he was watching the news on television, but I saw him looking our way every once in a while.

One thing about Max, he could put away the beers, so I didn't even try to keep up. I just acted more and more buzzed, complete with giggles and spilling beer on the bar. Eventually he got around to asking what I did for a living, which was what I'd been waiting for.

"I'm between jobs right now," I said with a hiccup. "My old place got closed down, but there's a new boiler—" I paused long enough to make sure that he'd noticed my phony slip of the tongue. "I mean, I've got a lead on a new company opening up down in Florida."

Max nodded knowingly. "Would this be something along the line of phone solicitations?"

I opened my eyes wide, and looked around as if nervous that we'd be overheard.

He put his arm around my shoulders. "Don't worry, honey, I've worked a few 'phone solicitation' jobs myself."

I tried to look relieved. According to the class Michelle had taken, con artists like being part of a group of insiders, folks in the know as opposed to their marks. So it made sense for Max the con man to enjoy meeting fellow con artist Lori, and vice versa. At least, that's what I was hoping.

"Is that right?" I almost purred. "Like I said, you don't seem like a local yokel." Lowering my voice, I said, "Are you into something now?"

"A little bit of this, a little bit of that. Nothing I could cut you in on, if that's what you want to know."

"That's not why I was asking. I told you I've got something starting up in Florida soon. It's just that I've been thinking of trying something new once I get a stake together, and if this Florida job works out the way I think it will, I'll be able to put it together. I could use some help, but most of the other people in the boiler— Most phone solicitors don't have the imagination I need. I just have a hunch that you might be exactly the kind of man I'm looking for, but if you're already committed ..."

"Only for a little while longer," Max assured me. "Once this job's over, my dance card is yours to fill. If the plan is worthwhile, that is."

"Oh, it is," I said. "I've got a few more details to work out, but I think it's going to be big." I looked around the room and made a face. "Big enough to buy this place."

"The bar?" Max said with amusement.

"The bar? I'm talking about enough money to buy the whole damned town." I thought I had him hooked, but he was doing a good job of playing it cool, so I said, "Of course, if you're not interested ..."

"I might be interested, but I'd have to know a whole lot more before I could say for sure."

"Well, I've come up with a twist on rent skimming." My using the phrase was just to get Max's attention, but Michelle had fed me enough details that I thought I could fool him into thinking I knew what I was talking about. She'd even come up with a scheme using crooked contractors that sounded as if it could work. The plan was for me to get Max to trust me by pretending to trust him. Then maybe he'd talk more about what he was doing in Byerly. "Of course, I can't go into details here."

"Maybe we should go someplace a little more private."

I gave him a look. "Would that be for business or for pleasure?"

"Honey, I always mix business with pleasure."

The bar's phone had been ringing on and off all night,

but this time, after the bartender answered, he called out, "Is there a Lori Yadon in here?"

I looked up, surprised. Richard was the only one other than Max that I'd given that name to. "That's me," I said and took the portable phone from the bartender. "Hello?"

"Laura?" Richard said. "There's a fire at Aunt Maggie's place."

Half a dozen questions were on the tip of my tongue, but I couldn't ask any of them in front of Max. All I said was, "I'm on the way." I broke the connection and laid the phone on the bar. "Max, I'm sorry, but I've got to go. My aunt fell and hurt her hip. She's afraid it might be broken, so I've got to get her to the hospital."

"Is she going to be all right?" he asked, sounding sincere.

"I don't know. I've got to get over there." I grabbed my purse and started digging around for money.

"I'll cover the beer," he said. "You want me to drive you over there?"

"No, thanks. I'll be fine. I'll be in touch about . . . About that other thing. You're in the book, right? Bye!" I rushed out the door, risking breaking my ankles with those heels. I started the car, rolled down the window, and waited for Augustus, who came out a minute later.

"What's wrong?" he asked.

"There's trouble at Aunt Maggie's. Have you got your truck?"

He nodded.

"Then I'll see you there." I drove off, leaving him to follow.

Chapter 32
▼◎▼◎▼◎▼

Byerly isn't a big town—unless the traffic or weather is bad, it doesn't take but a few minutes to cross from one border to another. So I don't know why it seemed to take hours for me to drive to the Burnette home place. When I got to the right street, I saw Byerly's ladder truck partially blocking the way, and the road was lined with cars that had sirens stuck on their dashboards to identify them as belonging to volunteer firemen. One of Byerly's police cruisers was parked sideways to stop cars from going farther.

I parked as close as I could and saw Augustus pulling up behind me. Going as fast as I could in those damned shoes, I jumped out of the car and ran the rest of the way to the house. Augustus caught up with me, and helped me push my way through the crowd of neighbors standing around to watch.

Finally, I got close enough to see that the house was still standing, and a weight I hadn't known was there lifted from my chest. I know it's only a house, but there's a reason we call it the home place. No matter where we Burnettes end up living, that old farmhouse is home to all of us.

There had been damage. The living-room window was shattered and smoke was still seeping out, and the front porch was blackened with soot. Water streamed every-where, making rivers of ash that ran down the street. The stench was the worst, a nasty, acrid smell that made me want to breathe through my mouth.

In the glare of the flashing lights from the fire trucks, I saw Richard standing with Linwood and Junior in the driveway, and I tried to make my way over there without stepping on any of the glass from the windows.

"Is Aunt Maggie all right?" I demanded as soon as we were close enough to be heard.

Richard said, "She's fine—she was still at the auction when it started."

"What about Bobbin?"

"She's with Aunt Maggie."

I took a deep breath, more relieved than I could have said. "Thank goodness. What in the Sam Hill happened?"

"That's what I'm trying to find out," Junior said.

"I already told you what happened," Linwood said, his face red. I wasn't sure if it was from anger or exertion, but I suspected it was from both. "I was driving by and saw the fire, so I jumped out and got the hose to try and put it out."

"You just happened to be driving by?" Junior said with more than a trace of skepticism.

"Why shouldn't I drive by my own family's house?"

Before Junior could answer, Richard said, "That must have been about the time I got back. I didn't see Linwood, just the fire, so I went to a neighbor's house and called 911, and then Laura. After that, I came over, saw Linwood with the hose, and tried to help him as best I could."

"I was doing fine without him," Linwood said ungraciously.

"Quite a coincidence that y'all both showed up right then," Junior said.

Richard said, "What can I tell you, Junior? We were lucky."

"Lucky that nobody was home, either," she said. "Isn't that your rental car in the driveway, Richard? How come neither you nor Laura were driving it?"

Luckily, before we had to come up with an explanation for my being in Aunt Nora's car while Richard was driving Aunt Daphine's, Tavis Montgomery came up, dressed in his fire gear. "It's all over but the cleanup," he said. "Good work there, Randolph. The rest of us might as well have stayed home."

I could almost see Linwood's head swell, but I wouldn't have begrudged it if I hadn't remembered that some rage arsonists get a special kick out of saving the places they set fire to.

"Any idea how it started, Tavis?" Junior asked him.

"You should probably get the investigators from Hickory out here, but I'd guess it was arson again."

I stiffened, and Richard put his arm around me. I didn't dare look at Linwood for fear I'd jump him right in front of Junior.

"Same as the others?" Junior said.

Tavis shook his head. "A little different this time. In the other cases, the accelerant was poured on the building and then set on fire. This time, it looks as if a flaming projectile was thrown through the window."

"A flaming projectile?" Junior said. "Are you talking about a Molotov cocktail?"

"That's what they call them."

Junior looked thoughtful, and I thought I knew why.

Most criminals stick with a particular method for their crimes—surely arsonists were the same. She turned to Linwood. "I don't suppose you saw anybody prowling around the house when you got here."

"Don't you think I'd have told you if I had?" he said.

Just then, we heard a loud voice saying, "Lord love a duck!"

Aunt Maggie had arrived, and over the next few minutes, she was followed by all the available aunts, uncles, and cousins. Even Vasti showed up, complaining about her swollen feet the whole time. Somewhere in the midst of all the questions, hugs, and tears, Junior realized that she wasn't going to be able to get any useful information out of anybody. Just before she slipped away, she gave me a funny look that I guiltily attributed to her knowing that I was up to something. Later on, I realized she was probably trying to figure out why I was dressed the way I was. I was just grateful the family was so agitated that nobody else noticed.

We must have milled around for an hour or more, drinking coffee supplied by the neighbors as we waited for the arson investigator to arrive, go through the house, and take a passel of pictures. Finally, we were given permission to go inside and see the damage for ourselves. I think we were all afraid of what the glare of our flashlights would reveal.

The Molotov cocktail had landed in the living room, so that room had sustained most of the damage. All of the furniture and the carpet were ruined, and the aunts started crying when they saw the remains of their mama's china cabinet and the figurines she'd loved so much. Then everybody cheered when Aunt Maggie rummaged around and triumphantly produced a geisha girl and Scottie dog that had somehow escaped destruction. We cheered again when

Willis, who knew about carpentry, announced that the house itself was structurally intact, and that most of the damage was only cosmetic.

The general opinion was that it wasn't as bad as it could have been. Planks and tools appeared from somewhere, and the broken window was neatly boarded up. Mops and rags showed up just as mysteriously, and everybody went to work sopping up water and wiping off soot. Somebody even produced cans of air spray and we roamed through the house spraying. The awful smoky smell pervaded everything, but at least there was an overlay of pine trees and spring flowers.

The fear I'd felt when I saw the smoke seeping from the home place had shaken me, making me realize how much that ridiculous collection of boards and nails meant to me. When Burt had come to see Richard and me in Boston, he'd told us that passing Walters Mill on to his nephew was important to him. Now I thought I knew how he felt. Maybe the Burnette home place wasn't as impressive a legacy as the mill, but I still wanted it to be there for the next generation.

Of course, the most important thing was that nobody had been hurt. No house, even the home place, was as important as my family. The rest of the Burnettes must have realized that, too, because at some point in all the commotion, I noticed that nobody was feuding anymore. Aunt Maggie was talking to the triplets, and Uncle Buddy was speaking to Uncle Ruben, and everybody was speaking to Linwood. In fact, Linwood got so many pats on the back for nearly putting out the fire single-handedly that he must have been sore the next day. I know Richard was, and he didn't get nearly as much attention as Linwood did.

Odd that it had taken the near loss of the family home to glue the family back together again.

Chapter 33
▼●▼●▼●▼●▼

I think the only thing that kept us from starting on more serious repairs to the house right then and there was the fact that the power had been turned off, and had to remain that way until the electric department checked things out. As it was, it was well into the wee hours of the morning before people started drifting away. Aunt Nora and Aunt Daphine were among the last to go.

Aunt Nora asked, "Aunt Maggie, are you feeling up to driving yourself to my house or do you want to ride with me?"

"Nora, I was thinking Aunt Maggie could come stay at my place," Aunt Daphine said. "And Laura and Richard, too, of course."

"Now Daphine, my house is bigger than yours."

"But with Augustus back home, you don't have as much space. You let them come stay with me—as late as it is, I don't want you up at the crack of dawn fixing them a big breakfast."

"What about the shop? You've got to be there early to open up."

"I'm not going in tomorrow. Gladys can open up for me."

I don't know what Aunt Nora's counter-argument would

have been, because Aunt Maggie said, "What are you two fussing about? The fire was in the living room, not the bedroom. I'm not going anywhere."

"But Aunt Maggie," Aunt Nora said, "it's not safe here tonight."

"That's why I'm staying. The last thing I need is a bunch of looters coming around while the place is empty." I'd never heard of looters in Byerly, and Aunt Maggie probably hadn't either, because she added, "It's bad enough that somebody tried to burn my house down—I'm not about to let him chase me out of it."

"There's no lights," Aunt Daphine pointed out.

"I'm going to bed—I don't need any lights. If I do, I've got a flashlight. And before you say anything else, I don't need heat or air-conditioning, either. If I get too hot, I'll open a window, and if I get cold, I'll put on a blanket." Her tone made it plain that she'd made up her mind, and there wasn't anything that was going to change it.

Aunt Nora must have known that, but she couldn't resist making one more attempt. "What about Laurie Anne and Richard? You don't expect them to stay here, do you?"

"They can suit themselves."

"Then you two can come to my house," Aunt Daphine said.

I was sorely tempted. Even though I'd just realized how much the house meant to me, right about then a well-lit room that didn't smell of smoke sounded like the height of luxury. I wasn't worried about looters, and I knew Junior would be keeping an eye on the place, so I wasn't even concerned that the arsonist would try again. But I just couldn't leave a seventysomething-year-old woman in that house by herself after the night we'd had.

Of course, there was no reason Richard had to put up with the primitive conditions. I looked up at his face, as smudged and streaked with sweat as my own was, and started to say, "Richard, why don't you—?"

"Laura and I are staying, too," Richard said, using the same tone that Aunt Maggie had.

I stood on my toes to kiss his dirty cheek. It tasted like soot, but he deserved it.

Of course, Aunt Nora and Aunt Daphine tried to change our minds, but eventually they conceded defeat.

After everybody else had gone, Aunt Maggie said, "You could have gone to Daphine's. It wouldn't have hurt my feelings any."

"I just didn't want to have to pack up my stuff," I said as if it were no big deal.

"Uh-huh," she said, meaning that she didn't believe me. "Well, I can't offer you anything to eat or drink, and we can't watch TV, so we might as well go to bed."

"That's the best idea I've heard all night," I said. With the help of flashlights, we stumbled our way upstairs, and darned if habit didn't push me to flip the light switch as Richard and I went into our bedroom.

"I don't think that's going to help, Laurie Anne," Aunt Maggie said, and I didn't have to see her face to know she was grinning.

"You'd have done the same thing if I hadn't messed up first," I retorted.

She just chuckled and closed her door behind her.

Richard had already thrown himself across our bed, sooty clothes and all.

"Oh no, you don't," I said. "No sleep until you tell me

what happened tonight. What you told Junior sure as heck wasn't the whole story. I want a report!"

He moaned and groaned a few times for effect, but knew better than to argue with me. So as we stripped off our clothes and tried unsuccessfully to find something to sleep in that didn't smell of smoke, he started.

"Using the same methods as last time, I set up the stake-out outside the subject's dwelling well before his usual time for returning home, disguising myself with a newspaper to avoid his notice when he arrived. After three-quarters of an hour inside his domicile, during which time I deduced that the subject was eating dinner, he returned to his car and—"

"Richard, what are you doing?"

"You wanted a report," he said far too innocently.

"You know, it's not so dark in this house that I can't find you."

"Is that a threat?"

"Yes."

"I find that positive reinforcement is more effective than threats."

"Okay, if you'll quit talking like Joe Friday, I will give you a back rub while you tell me what happened."

"Now *that's* positive reinforcement." He sat near the edge of the bed so I could work on him while he went on. "The first part of the night was a repeat performance of last night. I think I've now seen more of Byerly than most natives."

"Then what?" I asked.

"Then I lost him," he said, sounding embarrassed. "A woman cut me off, and while she was between us, Linwood turned off without my seeing it. When I couldn't find him again, I thought I might as well come back here, and that's when I saw the fire. From that point on, what I told Junior was true. I knocked on somebody's door and asked to use the phone, then ran to the house."

"That reminds me—I never told you how proud I am of you." I hugged him tightly.

"I didn't do very much," he said. "Linwood was already spraying down the front of the house, and he told me what to do to help. Which I did until the fire brigade arrived."

"You were wonderful," I insisted. I expressed my admiration for a few minutes, and even though I hadn't done anything to put out the fire, he kindly returned the favor. I would like to have kindled a different kind of blaze, but I was too distracted. "Richard, how long was Linwood out of your sight?"

"You mean, was it long enough for him to have started the fire?"

I nodded, knowing he could feel the gesture even if he couldn't see it.

He didn't try to sugarcoat his answer. "I'm afraid it was. I looked for him for twenty minutes or so, and then spent about ten minutes driving here. From the point Linwood got away from me, he could have driven directly here in less than five minutes."

"Damn."

"Setting the family home on fire does fit the pattern," Richard said gently. "Linwood could be sure to be the first one here, and by putting it out, he's made himself a hero again. Especially with the other Burnettes."

"I know," I said, thinking of how everybody had been hugging onto him, just the kind of attention a firebug craved. Linwood's saving the family home place wasn't something any of them were ever going to forget. The house wasn't just important to me—it was important to all of us. The way we'd all come running and worked so hard to make repairs proved it. That's what made me say, "He didn't do it, Richard."

"I know you want to believe that, but how can you be sure?"

As I explained it to Richard, it made more and more sense to me. "Look at the kind of person Linwood is. His father Loman died, and nobody in the family but Linwood was sad to see him go."

"I sure as hell wasn't," Richard muttered.

"In fact, Thaddeous and I have been congratulated for what happened, which has got to hurt Linwood. And since this is Byerly, everybody in town knows the whole story. That's why Linwood got into trouble at the mill. He was trying to defend his father's memory."

"True," Richard said, and I knew he was wondering where I was going with all this.

"Now if this had been you, wouldn't you have left town? I left Byerly, and I didn't have nearly that good an excuse."

"That was different," Richard objected. "You weren't running away—you were just looking for something different."

"I know, but you see my point. Despite everything, Linwood stuck it out and stayed. Why? His house isn't that great, and I feel sure Sue would go with him wherever he wanted to go. At one point, he didn't even have a job. Why did he stay in Byerly?"

"Stubbornness?"

"Partially," I conceded. "There's a strong streak of ornery in all the Burnettes."

"I hadn't noticed," Richard said dryly.

"The only thing Linwood had going for him in Byerly was his family," I said, ignoring his comment. "And he is devoted to this family. He comes to all the family gatherings—he even came to those right after his father died, knowing he was going to run into Thaddeous and me, the people he blamed for his father's death."

"Are you sure he doesn't come just to make you two uncomfortable?"

"It's been years. Don't you think he'd have given up if that were his only motive? It's more than that. Being a Burnette means a lot to Linwood."

"So he's devoted to the family. 'Those precious motives, those strong knots of love.' *Macbeth*, Act IV, Scene 3. Why would this mean that he didn't start the fire tonight? As we both noticed, this has made him popular in the family in a way he's never been before. Doesn't that make it more likely that he did it?"

"If the target had been any other house in town, yes, it would. But not *this* house. All of Aunt Maggie's generation was born here, and all of the aunts. When my cousins and I were born, this is the first place our parents brought us after we left the hospital, and this is where most of the Christmases and Thanksgivings and birthdays have been celebrated. Not to mention funerals. It doesn't matter where everybody lives now. Those are just houses and apartments. *This* is our home place—it's Linwood's home place. I think he'd sooner burn his own hand off as to set this house on fire."

Richard was quiet for a while, and I wasn't sure he understood what I was trying to tell him. His parents had a lovely house in Gloucester, but they'd only been there twenty years or so, and none of his grandparents lived where they'd been when he was growing up. His mother's parents had a condo, and his father's had bought a house on the Cape when they retired. Could he understand?

Finally, he said, "Okay, let's look at the other suspects."

I kissed him soundly. "We'll look at them tomorrow. You're worn-out, and so am I."

He didn't argue, and in fact, there wouldn't have been time for even the most civilized argument before Richard fell asleep. I snuggled next to him, trying to follow suit, but my mind was working too hard. After what seemed like hours, I took my pillow, sneaked out of bed, and crept into the hall. Not wanting to go down into the ruined living room, I only went halfway down the stairs, to the point where the stairs end at a little landing before turning a corner to continue to the first floor.

I sat down in the corner and leaned against my pillow. Part of the reason I'd picked there to sit was the streetlamp right outside the landing's tiny window that gave me a little light to see by, but the main reason was that it had been my favorite spot to sit when I was growing up. I'd read countless books there, planned more adventures than one person could ever survive, and even written love letters to Richard. It was a comforting place to be, and with the uncomfortable thoughts I was thinking, I needed a fair amount of comforting.

First off, there was the rental car. To make sure neither Max nor Linwood would recognize what we were driving, we'd borrowed cars that night, leaving the rental car parked in Aunt Maggie's driveway. Second, because we'd been in a hurry, we'd left lights on in the house, something Aunt Maggie never does. In other words, it had looked as if Richard and I were there when that Molotov cocktail came crashing through the front window.

Up until then, the arsonist had targeted abandoned buildings—this was the first time he'd gone for one where people actually lived, where somebody could have been hurt. I didn't think that was a coincidence. Whoever it was knew Richard and I were after him, and he was trying to get to us first.

Had Linwood and Richard not shown up when they had, there's no telling how much more of the house would have been destroyed. Aunt Maggie didn't have smoke alarms, so if Richard and I had been asleep, we might not have woken up in time to get out of the house.

The question was, had he just meant to scare us off, or was he trying to kill us? Maybe he hadn't even cared, which was even more frightening.

I couldn't imagine a worse way to die than burning to death, and I should have been scared as I sat there in the dark, but mostly I was angry. It wasn't just that somebody had tried to kill Richard and me, though that was part of it. I was livid that the bastard had nearly burned down my home! I decided right then and there that Richard and I were going to get that son of a bitch if it was the last thing we did.

Then I sighed. It was easy enough to make that declaration, like Scarlett O'Hara railing against poverty. The tough part was carrying through and finding the arsonist. Richard and I were so far away from being able to do that that I wondered why he'd even bothered to make a move.

That was encouraging, in a way. If we were that much of a threat to him, we had to be on the right track, even if we didn't know it yet. So what did we know?

We'd found out that Max Wilder was a con man and was up to something. Since I'd inadvertently provided him with an ironclad alibi, obviously he couldn't have set the fire that night, but that didn't mean he wasn't involved with the murderer.

Could somebody have discovered that we'd been checking up on Max? Michelle had only tracked it all down that morning, and surely that was too soon for anybody to have connected her with us. Even if Max had seen through my disguise at Dusty's immediately, I didn't think he'd had the opportunity to call and warn anybody about me. Besides, anybody he would have called would have then known I was with him, and not in the house.

I wasn't ready to cross Max off of our list, but whatever the murderer was afraid of, it wasn't what we'd found out about him.

Then I thought back to how we'd become suspicious of Max in the first place. I didn't think Grace or Max had seen me the night I saw the two of them together, but what if one of them had? Max was in the clear, but Grace wasn't.

Even though Grace wasn't from Byerly, she could have heard enough about me and Richard to be worried that we might be taking an interest in her plots, especially since we'd had a chance to look at Marshall's files. It was hard to imagine her getting her hands dirty with a Molotov cocktail, but that didn't mean she couldn't have done it. I've done plenty of things that people have trouble imagining.

There was no way to check Grace's whereabouts right then, but I put that at the top of my mental list of things to do.

What else did we have? All I could think of were Marshall's computer files. Sure, I'd looked at them before without finding anything, but that didn't mean there wasn't something there. I'm a computer geek, not a statistics geek. Maybe if I looked at them hard enough, I could figure it out.

My eyes must have gotten used to the dark because I was able to tiptoe into the bedroom and get my laptop and the stack of paper files without stubbing a toe. Then I went back to my spot on the stairs and booted up, glad that I'd recently recharged the battery. I had three to four hours of power—the battery would probably last longer than I would.

At it turned out, it was a close call. The first discovery came quickly because I knew more than I had when I looked at the files before. This time I knew Max Wilder was up to something. In a set of productivity graphs, Marshall had documented the mill's equipment failures. The pattern of those failures correlated with a graph of sick time used, and that graph correlated neatly with the overtime hours listed in Max's file. In other words, I had circumstantial evidence that while dear, sweet Max substituted for others, he had committed sabotage.

Oddly enough, Marshall had left himself a note attached to the graph of sick time used, wondering if the illnesses had led to the equipment failures, reasoning that sick workers might make mistakes that healthy ones wouldn't. Was that camouflage in case somebody else saw the file, or did it mean that he hadn't known what Max was up to? Could Grace have set it up without her husband knowing? If she did, wouldn't that make her a better suspect for his murder?

I nearly shut down after finding that, but I wasn't ready to quit. Though I'd found evidence that Max was a saboteur, it wasn't anything I hadn't already known, and it wasn't enough to help me convince Burt Walters to get off his duff. There had to be something more.

In the short time that I'd spoken to Marshall, he'd been most enthusiastic when talking about graphs and statistics, and it was graphs that Grace had been trying to access when she ran into password problems. So I went through the graphs of Walters Mill data over and over again, trying to find anything that looked odd. I recalculated figures, switched to show numbers in different scales, converted bar charts to pie charts and back again, even changed the colors used. In short, I tried every trick to disguise statistics that I'd ever heard of.

Finally, after the warning light had begun blinking to tell me battery power was getting low, I found what I was looking for. Only then did I shut the computer down and crawl into bed beside Richard. Dawn was already starting to creep through the sky, so I didn't have much time to sleep, but I knew that I'd need every bit I could get.

Chapter 34

I'd have thought my nose would be numb from smelling smoke all night, but somehow the smell of hot bacon, eggs, and biscuits roused me. Richard was still out cold, but I heard voices from downstairs. A stop in the bathroom reminded me that I hadn't gotten all of "Lori's" makeup and hair spray off the night before, so I gritted my teeth long enough to take a shower without the benefit of hot water. Then I dressed and went to see what was going on.

True to Aunt Daphine's prediction, Aunt Nora had gotten up early to put together the breakfast she'd spread all over the kitchen counter. She, Aunt Daphine, and Aunt Maggie were lingering over coffee while Uncle Ruben, Augustus, and Willis conferred, apparently trying to decide what lumber they needed to make repairs.

"Good morning," Aunt Daphine said. "Come get something to eat before it gets cold."

"Are the eggs cold already?" Aunt Nora fussed. "I can run back home and fix a fresh batch, or I can—"

"I'm sure the eggs are fine," I said quickly. "As hungry as I am, I could eat them if they were still in the shells." I fixed myself a plate of eggs scrambled with cheddar cheese, grits, biscuits with strawberry preserves, and enough bacon to clog every artery in my body. Then I poured a glass of orange juice, so I could pretend I was eating healthy.

As I ate, I asked, "How does the mess look in the daylight?"

"Still soggy, and there's soot that I'd swear wasn't there last night," Aunt Maggie said, "but it's not so bad that we can't fix it. If that crew over there can figure out what they're doing, that is." Though she'd raised her voice on the last part, the menfolk pretended that they hadn't heard her.

"Is Richard handy with tools?" Aunt Daphine asked.

"He's built sets," I said, "but he's not going to have time to help out today. We've got plans." At least, I did. "Has Junior been by?"

"Just long enough to make sure we're all right and grab a biscuit," Aunt Daphine said. "She doesn't know anything more about who did this, but she said she's going to talk to the neighbors and see if she can find out anything."

"That's a waste of time," Aunt Maggie said. "If anybody around here had seen anything, they'd have come forward by now."

I nodded in agreement. "Is the phone working?"

"Not yet, but you can go to my house if you want to call somebody," Aunt Daphine said.

"That would be great. I've got a bunch of calls to make."

After that I concentrated on eating. Even though I could see that all three of the aunts were dying to know what I had in mind, somehow they resisted asking. I had to wonder what Aunt Maggie had told the others. I'd dared her to trust that Richard and I were doing the right thing, and clearly she was taking me at my word. I only hoped that my plan would work and that she'd be satisfied with the outcome.

I started to clean off my plate once I was finished eating,

but Aunt Nora took it away from me to wash it herself and sent me upstairs to wake Richard. I knew he would have liked to sleep longer, but we had a lot to do, and I didn't want to waste any time.

I had to to pry him out of the bed and shove him into the shower, but after a few minutes of chilly water running over him, Richard was awake enough for me to explain what I'd found in Marshall's graphs and outline my plan.

Richard suggested a few enhancements, then went downstairs to eat breakfast while I made a list of things to do. Next I took Aunt Daphine aside to ask her assistance for that afternoon, and Richard enlisted Augustus and Willis to help out later that evening. All we had to do was tell them that we thought we could catch the person who'd set the home place on fire, and they were more than willing to do whatever we wanted.

I would rather have told everybody the whole story, but I couldn't think of a way to do so without bringing Burt Walters into the picture. Besides, I didn't want to spend the time it would have taken to explain it all.

With the first pieces in place, we headed for Aunt Daphine's house to make a slew of phone calls to put the other pieces together. It took longer than I'd expected to make the calls and run the necessary errands, but by the time the day shift at the mill ended, "Lori" was back on her barstool at Dusty's.

The crowd was larger and more boisterous this time, probably because it was Friday night, but Max spotted me as soon as he came in and made his way to the stool I'd saved for him.

"I was hoping you'd be back," he said.

"I owed you one after running out on you last night," I said, and gestured for the bartender to bring him a beer.

"How's your aunt?"

"Better. It turns out she didn't break her hip after all. It's only bruised, but her pain medicine makes her so sleepy she said I might as well go out because she was going to bed early."

"There are worse places to spend Friday evening," Max said with a leer.

"You are *so* bad," I said.

We continued to flirt, saying nothing in particular. In fact, I don't know that it's possible to both flirt and say anything meaningful. After several beers for Max, and two slowly nursed ones for me, I finally brought up what I wanted to talk about.

"Max, there's something I'd like to ask you."

"Honey, no matter what the question is, the answer is yes."

I giggled dutifully. "Seriously, did you mean it when you said you'd be done with this town soon?"

"I don't have a specific timetable, but it sure looks that way. Why come?"

"It looks as if I'm going to be able to get my project going right much sooner than I thought. After I got my aunt back home from the emergency room last night, she started talking about how much she'd always liked me and how she really wanted to help me get ahead. She never had any kids of her own, and I'm the only one of her nieces and nephews who ever pays her any attention. My late uncle left her pretty well off, and she said she wants to put her money someplace where it could help me."

"Good Lord, Lori, what kind of drugs did you pump into that old lady?"

I made a face. "It's not like that, Max. She just wants to see me make good. The problem is, I know darned well that my cousins want to get their hands on her money, and if they get wind of what she's aiming to do, they'll try to talk her out of it. That means I've got to move quickly and get everything set up."

"Can't you just get her to write a check now?"

I shook my head. "She won't just give it to me—she wants to invest it, keep it businesslike."

"Which means that you have to set up a business toot sweet."

"That's right—I need a good pencil and oh, all the usual things." Michelle had told me that a *pencil* was the front man for an operation, frequently a lawyer or at least somebody who could sound like a lawyer. "I was wondering if you're going to be available soon enough for us to work together."

"When would you need me?"

I pretended I was thinking. "We've got a family reunion in June, and it will have to be before then because I know she'll spill the beans once she's around everybody. I need a couple of weeks to make the arrangements, and of course, I'll have to get some more people ... Will you be free in three weeks?"

Max took a long drink of his beer. "I'd be real darned surprised if I wasn't. What do you say we get down to brass tacks? Tell me exactly what you've got planned."

I looked around nervously. "I don't want to talk about it in here."

"Then let's go to my place."

"Are you sure we'll just be talking business?"

"Honey, like I told you last night, I always mix pleasure with my business."

Over Max's halfhearted objections, I paid for our beers to make sure he hadn't noticed how little I'd been drinking. Then I let him talk me into riding with him. Though he was almost certainly over the legal limit, he acted sober enough, and I knew it wasn't far to his house.

Max had rented the old Husey place, not too far from Walters Lake. It was isolated, but the triplets had speculated that he preferred it that way so none of his girlfriends would run into any of his other girlfriends. Knowing what I knew about him, I figured he had other reasons for wanting privacy.

Though the yard was haphazardly maintained, inside the place was immaculate. At first I was surprised Max was such a good housekeeper, but it made sense. If one of his girlfriends saw somebody else's cigarettes in the ashtray or a glass smeared with the wrong shade of lipstick, it would be that much harder for him to hide his tracks.

The living room looked like it belonged to somebody who wasn't planning to stay long. The couch, easy chair, and coffee table were nice enough, but showed none of Max's personality, and the only decorating he'd done was to put up a couple of dime-store art prints.

"This is nice," I said.

"It looks a whole lot nicer with you here," he said as he stepped closer to me.

"Business first," I said. "Otherwise, I won't be able to keep the details straight."

"I guess you're right," he said, "but I think better when I've got something to drink. You want a beer?"

"I think I need to visit the little girls' room first."

"First door on the left," he said, heading for the kitchen.

I went into the bathroom and locked the door. Though I really did want to use the facilities, my real reason for going in there was to stall. So after I was done, I killed time by poking in the medicine chest, checking to see if there was anything hidden in the linen cabinet, and feeling around the back of the toilet to see if Max had taped anything interesting back there. A college friend once told me a toilet was a wonderful hiding place, especially if you didn't clean it often, because nobody wants to look there. It was lucky for me that Max kept his clean, because I'd have been more annoyed at coming up empty if I'd gotten my hands dirty.

Maybe five minutes later, I heard enough noise that I figured it was safe to come out. When I got to the living room, Max was sitting on the side chair, looking both angry and nervous. Thaddeous, Augustus, and Richard were standing around him, staring at him ominously with their arms crossed for maximum effect. The room was small as it was— with the three of them surrounding Max, it was downright cramped.

"It's about time y'all got here," I said.

"You know them?" Max squeaked.

"Of course. I'm sure you recognize Thaddeous from the mill, and this is his brother Augustus and my husband Richard."

"Your husband?"

"Don't you remember meeting us?" I asked. "I'm hurt."

He looked at me closely and thought for a minute. "Fleming. Laurie Anne and Richard Fleming."

"Very good," I said approvingly.

"The Holt sisters are your cousins."

"Right again. And so are Thaddeous and Augustus."

"What the hell's going on here?"

"Like I said at Dusty's, I wanted to talk to you in private." Augustus had again watched Max and me from a safe distance at Dusty's, while Richard and Thaddeous waited in the parking lot. Then they'd followed us to Max's house. Though we didn't think Max was the type to grab a hostage, they'd given me enough time to get out of harm's way before knocking on the door and pushing their way inside.

I took a seat on the couch and smiled pleasantly at Max. We'd arranged for me to do most of the talking—Richard thought the men would be more threatening if they didn't speak.

"What's all this about?" Max said, trying to sound tough.

"It's about industrial espionage and sabotage."

Max was a pro, all right. He didn't even blink. "What's that supposed to mean?"

I reached out, and Richard put a file folder into my hand so I could pull out a faxed photo to hold in front of Max. "Does this look familiar?"

"Should it?" he asked, still trying to bluff.

"Oh, yes. This is the real Max Wilder." I'd had Michelle get back in touch with Wilder's former employer and fax us a picture from his going-away party. "Not much of a resemblance, is there?"

"Okay, I used a phony name to get a job. I didn't mean any harm by it—do you know how hard it is to get work when you've got a record?"

"Nice try, but that doesn't explain how you know Grace Saunders."

"Of course I know her—she's been hanging around the mill all week."

"I've got a witness who saw you two together, and overheard some of your plans." Actually, I hadn't heard a word, but if he could bluff, so could I. "And there's the little fact that over seventy percent of the mill's equipment failures in recent months took place either on your shift, or were discovered during the very next shift." From the file folder, I pulled out a graph that showed it.

"Just a coincidence," he said. "You can't prove anything different."

"Nope, I probably can't."

He looked surprised, and then suspicious.

"I don't care about proving it. Quite honestly, Max or whatever your name is, I don't care about you. All I care about is Grace Saunders."

I could almost see the wheels moving in his head. "Are you saying that we can make a deal?" he said.

"That's right. We're perfectly willing to let you pack up and get out of here just as soon as you do two little jobs." I reached into the folder again. "First, I want you to sign this."

I handed him a piece of paper, and watched as he read it. It was a confession that detailed how he'd been hired by Marshall and Grace Saunders to get a job at Walters Mill under false pretenses in order to get inside information about the mill's workings and to commit sabotage to bring the asking price down.

"How do I know you won't use this in court?" he asked.

"Because it won't be legal—your name isn't Max Wilder, is it?"

He hesitated, but said, "Okay, I'll sign it. But one thing in here is wrong. Marshall just thought I was snooping around. The sabotage was Grace's idea."

Though I didn't say anything as I scratched Marshall's name out and had Max initial the change, I was glad that I hadn't completely misjudged Marshall.

Max signed the paper with a flourish, and handed it back to me. "What else?"

"In a little while, my cousin Willis is going to get sick at work, and he's going to call and ask you to work the rest of his shift for him. You're going to say yes, and Thaddeous and Augustus are going to escort you to the mill. Then they're going to sit outside the gate and make sure you don't try to sneak out. Once you get inside, I want you to show this around." I pulled another one of Marshall's printouts from the folder.

"What's that?" he said.

"It's the thing that got Marshall Saunders killed."

He blinked a few times, but took the printout. "Productivity by shift? Saunders was killed over a bunch of statistics?"

"That's right." I'd looked at the graph I don't know how many times before finally realizing what it meant. Marshall had input productivity data for the past five years, and had then broken it down by shift. Even though the number of workers and the number of socks produced was roughly the same on both the day and night shifts, productivity was much lower on the night shift. The difference was in the number of imperfect socks, or "seconds." Far more socks flunked inspection at night than during the day.

Of course, that didn't necessarily mean anything shady was going on, so I'd tried to consider innocent explanations first. Maybe the day shift's inspectors weren't thorough enough. Since the triplets sometimes worked in the inspection room, I'd called and asked them, but they assured me that the supervisor was as strict as could be. Or maybe the night shift's inspectors were too thorough, but that didn't seem likely either. Working in inspection was tedious work, particularly at night, and the folks on night shift tended to nod off. Carlelle said she'd seen more than one inspector facedown in a pile of tube socks.

The only reasonable explanation I'd come up with was that somebody who had access to the inspection room had been stealing socks for at least the five years that Marshall had graphed. Stealing socks didn't sound like a big deal to me, but from the numbers on Marshall's graph, it would have added up to quite a bit of money. Maybe it wouldn't have been enough to make most people kill, but that didn't mean that it wouldn't be enough for somebody.

According to the triplets, most people don't want to work the night shift, which meant that the turnover rate was high. Without going through employment records, they'd only come up with three people who'd had access to the inspection department for as long as five years: Floyd Cabiniss, the night supervisor in inspection; Tavis Montgomery, night shift supervisor for the whole mill; and Burt's secretary Miss Hunsucker, even though she didn't work at night, because she was in charge of tracking production.

I was guessing that Marshall had figured out that one of those three was stealing, and had confronted him or her that night he went to work at the mill. In the case of Miss Hunsucker, he might have called her. Somehow the thief had convinced Marshall to go to the old warehouse, and once they were there, he or she had murdered him.

I'd also asked the triplets if they could find out whether Floyd or Tavis had been absent from the mill long enough on the night Marshall died to have killed him, but unfortunately, they said there was no way to be sure. Both of the men's jobs required a fair amount of moving around the mill, meaning that there was no way to verify where either of them had been. And Miss Hunsucker lived alone, so she had even less of an alibi.

If Junior and I'd been on better terms, I'd have given her those three names and let her take over, but I didn't think she'd listen to me. She'd just assume that I was still grasping at straws to prove Linwood innocent. Maybe she would have investigated, but I was afraid she'd move too slowly to stop the buyout and, more importantly, too slowly to keep the killer from coming after Richard and me again.

Max was still looking over the graph. "I have to flash this around the whole mill?"

"Not the whole mill, just the inspection department. There are only a couple of dozen people in there—you should be able to get to all of them." Though Montgomery, Cabiniss, and Miss Hunsucker were our chief suspects, we didn't want to assume that in case there was a veteran inspector that the triplets had forgotten. And, of course, Miss Hunsucker wouldn't be there at night, but I reasoned that if Max eliminated everybody who was there, we'd know she was the one.

"Then what?"

"If we're right, the killer will recognize that graph and what it means. It shouldn't be too hard for you to tell which one is upset by seeing it."

"How am I supposed to figure that out? When he comes after me?"

"I imagine a man with your experience with human nature will be able to spot it."

"What if I can't?"

"Then we turn you in to the police." He started to object, but I said, "I know, we can't prove anything. But if there's any evidence out there, Junior Norton will find it. Not to mention the fact that I wouldn't be at all surprised to find out that you've been involved in other shady schemes. You can change your name, but you can't change your finger-prints."

That was another bluff. We wouldn't involve Junior with-out Burt's approval, and I didn't think he'd give it. But Max didn't know that.

"You could be putting me into a dangerous situation," he said, his voice quavering.

"Tell that to the people working with the mill equipment you sabotaged."

"Hey, nobody got hurt."

"No thanks to you," I shot back. Several of the incidents could have cost people fingers or hands, or even worse. I felt some guilt for using Max as a stalking horse, but not as much as I'd have felt if I'd sent in Thaddeous or Willis or the triplets. The killer knew they were my family, so would suspect anything coming from them as a trap and react accordingly. Max had no connection to us, which should pro-tect him.

Max thought it over. "It sounds like I don't have a choice."

"I'm afraid not," I said cheerfully. Goodness knows Rich-ard and I had done our best to come up with a situation in which he wouldn't.

"What do y'all get out of this?"

"Never you mind about that." I wasn't about to tell him about Richard and my deal with Burt. I checked my watch, and said, "Willis should be calling in five minutes or so, in case you want to change clothes or anything."

"With these three watching?" he said. "No thanks."

"Suit yourself."

For the next few minutes, we all stayed where we were without speaking. Richard, Augustus, and Thaddeous kept looking threatening, and Max looked as if he was trying to come up with a way out. It was a relief when the phone rang.

I grabbed it. "Willis?"

"Hey, Max. You busy? I don't feel so good."

Willis, like his father, keeps his words to a minimum. That was as many words as Willis usually said all day, and I appreciated his effort. "Max is on the way. You can go on, just the way we planned."

"Thanks," he said, and hung up.

"You're on," I said to Max. "Once you get what we want, my cousins will bring you back here—you don't even have to work out the shift. You get a free pass out of Byerly and a guarantee that nobody will come after you. But if you try anything funny, we go straight to Junior." Thaddeous and Augustus, still wearing their poker faces, started to escort him out, but I stuck out my hand. "I think I'll hold on to your car keys."

Max didn't like it, but he gave them to me. I didn't think he'd be able to get away from my cousins, but if he did, he'd have to do it on foot.

Richard watched as the three of them drove away, then turned to me with a look of relief. "I had no idea how hard it is to look mean."

"But you did it so well."

"Thanks. I think."

"It's a tribute to your acting ability," I assured him.

"What do we do now?"

"We wait." Max might find the killer right away, or it might take him most of the night.

At least I could finally wash my face and brush the worst of Aunt Daphine's handiwork out of my hair. I only wished I'd brought along a change of clothes—my feet hurt and I'd much rather have been wearing a pair of jeans loose enough to sit down in comfortably.

Then we spent an hour or so searching the house. We'd hoped to find something else to link Max to Grace Saunders, but either he was too smart to keep anything around or he'd hidden it too well for us to find it. We did find a stash of driver's licenses and credit cards made out in a variety of different names, but had no idea which of them, if any, gave Max's real name. I would have liked to cut them up and flush them down the toilet, but Richard thought that might be going back on our deal.

After that, there was nothing to do but sit and watch television. After a while, the events of the past few days caught up with me, and as Richard kept watch, I dozed on the couch.

It was around midnight when Richard nudged me awake. "They're back," he said.

From outside we heard three car doors slam, and a minute later, Max, Augustus, and Thaddeous came in.

"Well?" I asked.

"I made him, all right," Max said with a smirk. "The second he saw me with that printout, he turned white as a sheet. He tried to get me to go off alone with him, too, but I was too smart for that."

"Who?"

He looked around, as if a thought had just occurred to

him. "You know, I'm going to miss payday next week—a little cash sure would come in handy."

Without hesitating, I said, "Richard, call Junior."

"Wait a minute!" Max said. "I just remembered I put a few bucks away for just such an occasion."

"That's a surprise," I said sarcastically. "Now give—who is it?"

"Would you believe Mr. Politics himself? Tavis Montgomery."

"Tavis Montgomery," I said slowly. I don't know that he'd have been my first choice, but it did make sense. As head of the fire brigade, he'd have known just how to set the fire that killed Marshall, while his position as night shift supervisor would have given him plenty of opportunity to play games in the inspection room. His goal of becoming a mover and shaker would cost money—probably more than he could earn legally at the mill—and that same goal provided the motive. If his thefts had come to light, he could have kissed his plans goodbye.

"Now that you've got what you want, are we square?" Max asked.

"You're sure it's Tavis?" I said.

"He couldn't have been more obvious if he'd tried. Now if you'll hand over my car keys, I'll be getting out of here." I fished the keys out of my purse and gave them to him, and as he headed for the door, he said, "I won't say it was a pleasure, but it was educational. If you ever decide to change lines of work . . ."

"Aren't you going to pack?" I asked him.

"Nothing here worth packing," he said.

I thought about reminding him of the phony IDs he was

leaving, but decided it was no skin off my nose if he didn't take them.

Thaddeous and Augustus were between Max and the door, but after I nodded, they moved out of the way and he opened the door. Only he didn't get all the way out. He backed into the room, his hands held at shoulder height, as Floyd Cabiniss stepped inside, a pistol aimed at him.

Chapter 35

"I was just on my way out," Max said as he backed farther into the room, obviously trying to get somebody between him and Floyd's gun.

"Not yet, son," Floyd said.

"You weren't supposed to come in until I was gone," Max said, sounding outraged.

"I'm afraid I need you to help me out. Now, all of you step back. I may be old, but I can still shoot."

Thaddeous and Augustus did as he said, but unlike Max, they were trying to get between Floyd and me. Richard was tensed, too, and I was afraid somebody was going to try to jump the old man, getting shot in the process.

"You son of a bitch!" I said to Max as a distraction. "You set us up!"

"It's just business—nothing personal."

"That's right," Floyd said. "There's nothing personal about any of this. I'm mighty sorry about what I've got to do, but y'all haven't left me any choice."

I said, "I suppose you didn't have any choice last night when you tried to burn down our house with Richard and me in it."

Floyd shook his head, and darned if he didn't look sorry.

"If y'all hadn't come to town right now, everything would have been all right. I wasn't too worried about Junior, but you two . . . Everybody in Byerly knows that once y'all start snooping around, nobody's secrets are safe."

I'd have felt more complimented if it weren't for the gun. As it was, I would have preferred a less sterling reputation. "How long have you been stealing socks to sell at the flea market, anyway? Were they worth killing Marshall? Are they worth killing us?"

"It ain't the socks. It's my life we're talking about. I've given nearly thirty years to that mill, but if Burt Walters found out about those socks now, he'd yank my pension away. I've got plans—I didn't work all those years to be left with nothing."

I thought about the Winnebago Aunt Maggie had told me about, and how Floyd wanted to see the country. No, it wasn't just a bunch of socks to him.

"Max," Floyd said, "I need you to tie these folks up." As he spoke, I noticed the coil of nylon rope Floyd was carrying—it's funny how having a gun aimed at you makes you miss details. The awful part was realizing that it was the same rope that had been used to tie up Marshall Saunders.

"You said I wouldn't have to get involved," Max whined.

"You're already involved, whether you like it or not," Floyd said matter-of-factly as he handed Max the rope. "Augustus, you sit down in that easy chair."

"Mr. Cabiniss, you don't want to go doing this," Augustus said.

"I don't have a choice," he said again, and aimed the gun at me. "Now sit down, or I'll shoot her."

Floyd was smart. Augustus might have risked getting shot himself, and Thaddeous and Richard would have, too.

But neither of them would risk my life. As for me, Richard had my arm held so tightly I knew I couldn't move quickly enough to do any of us any good, especially not when I was still wearing those stupid high-heel shoes. It wouldn't have even done any good to yell for help—Max's house was too far from anywhere for anybody to hear us.

After Max trussed Augustus to the chair, Floyd had him pull out a kitchen chair for Thaddeous. Then he tied Richard and me together and tethered us to the couch. I don't know if Max learned to tie knots as a Boy Scout or in con-man school, but he knew what he was doing. I could barely move a muscle.

"That's all of them," Max said when he was done.

"I'm afraid not," Floyd said, sounding more sorrowful than ever. "You'd better sit down, too."

"Hey!" Max said. "We had a deal!"

"I'm as sorry as I can be, but I can't take the chance. You're going to have to stay here with the others."

"Listen, old man—"

"Sit down!" Floyd said, his voice filled with steel. "With what I'm fixing to do to people I've known all their lives, do you really think I'd hesitate to shoot you?"

Max sat.

I was hoping that Floyd would let down his guard while tying Max, but he had it planned. He made a loop with the rope while out of Max's reach, then lassoed him from a few steps away and tightened the bonds enough that he could safely move in closer and finish the job. In no time at all, Max was as tightly tied as the rest of us.

Floyd stepped toward the door. "I'm afraid I'm not going to be able to knock y'all out first the way I did with Mr. Saunders. There's too many of you and I don't have time.

I'd like to at least use a bullet to make it easier for y'all, but I'm afraid somebody would hear, even as far as we are from anybody. It's funny how the sound of a gunshot carries at night, and besides, the police can do a lot with ballistics these days. I am sorry."

"We appreciate your concern," I said scathingly, and gave him a look that I think Aunt Maggie would have been impressed by.

Floyd shook his head again, and went outside. A few minutes later, we heard splashing and caught a whiff of gasoline as liquid seeped in under the door.

"Jesus, he's going to burn us alive," Max said, thrashing in his chair.

"Wiggling around is just making the line tighter," Augustus remarked.

"You'll cut off your circulation if you keep it up," Thaddeous added.

"What's the matter with you people?" Max cried. "Don't you know what's happening? He's setting the place on fire!"

"Of course he is," I snapped. "You're the one who was stupid enough to make a deal with an arsonist."

"How did I know he'd double-cross me?" Max said, still struggling.

"Why wouldn't he? You double-crossed us."

"That's different. Cabiniss and I want the same thing— to get out of town. I don't know what y'all want, and without knowing that, I couldn't trust you."

It hadn't occurred to me that Max would be that distrustful of our motives, but I guess a con man has to be paranoid. I only wished he'd been a little more paranoid with Floyd.

"I don't suppose you left any slack in our ropes, did you?" I said.

He just kept struggling, which was as much of an answer as I needed. Idly I wondered if he'd even bother to let any of the rest of us go if he did break free.

The gas fumes kept getting stronger, and Max's movements were getting more and more frenzied. I leaned up against Richard as much as the ropes would allow, and closed my eyes, wishing I was somewhere else. Then I heard tires screeching, and opened my eyes to see blue-and-red lights flashing through the curtains. There were shouts, and a moment later, gunshots.

Floyd was right. The sound of gunshots carries awfully well at night.

Chapter 36

Max's eyes were wide with shock, but I just felt relieved.
A minute later we heard water swooshing over the front of
the house, and then the door was kicked open. Willis burst
in, and asked, "You okay?"

"Just fine, little brother," Augustus said.

"You cut it pretty fine there, didn't you?" Thaddeous
pointed out.

Willis moved aside as Junior Norton came in.

"Hey there, Laurie Anne," Junior said. "It looks like
you've had some trouble here."

"Not as much as we would have had if you hadn't shown
up."

"You knew the cops were out there?" Max sputtered.

"I hoped they were," I corrected him. We hadn't trusted
Max any more than he'd trusted us. "Willis didn't go home
when he left the mill. He was hiding, keeping an eye on
his brothers. When y'all headed back here, he saw Floyd
following y'all and knew something was wrong. So he called
Junior. Isn't that right, Willis?"

Willis nodded, and pulled out a pocketknife to saw at
Augustus's ropes. Once that brother was free, he went to
work on Thaddeous. Meanwhile, Junior got out her knife to

take care of me and Richard, and then Max. As the five of us were massaging away the marks of the ropes, Tavis Montgomery came in.

"I think we've washed most of the gasoline away," he said, "but if I were you, I wouldn't smoke any cigarettes around here for a while. Floyd was mighty thorough, and he was about to light a book of matches when we got here. Another five minutes and this place would have been gone."

I shivered, which was ironic, considering what could have happened. "Where is he now?" I asked.

"Outside," was all Junior said, but I saw the look on her face, so I wasn't surprised to see somebody zipping up a body bag as we left the house. Floyd had said it was his life he was talking about, and it had turned out to be true.

"You folks feel up to telling me what went on tonight?" Junior said. Though she'd phrased it politely, we knew it wasn't really a question. She split us up so she and her deputies could question us separately, saving me for last. I didn't mind waiting because it gave me time to figure out how much I wanted to tell her. Not that I intended to lie, but I didn't intend to tell her everything, either. The downside was wondering what tales everybody else had told. I knew I didn't have to worry about Richard or my cousins, but Max was a wild card.

When Junior came to get me, she handed me a Coke and said, "All right, Laurie Anne, let's hear it."

It was tricky, but I managed to explain what I'd done to trap Floyd without mentioning Burt Walters. I told her that copying the files from Marshall's hard disk had been my own idea, which was true enough—though Burt had obviously had the same idea, he'd never said so explicitly.

I had to leave out what I'd found out about Max, since

it was Burt who'd given me his file, which meant I couldn't say that I'd blackmailed him into helping us. Instead I implied that he'd volunteered to help us once we told him that it would have been too dangerous for any of the Burnettes to confront Floyd directly. Junior looked skeptical, but since she didn't question it, my story must have matched Max's.

"Did you suspect Floyd all along?" Junior asked once I'd finished.

"No, all I knew was that it had to be somebody in the inspection room or who had easy access to it. This just seemed to be the quickest way of figuring out who."

"I probably could have done it another way, if you'd told me about it."

"I didn't think you'd believe me, considering how our last conversation ended."

"You've got a point there," she conceded. "I wasn't a hundred percent sure Linwood had killed Marshall, but it did seem likely. Floyd does fit the arsonist profile, but not nearly as closely as Linwood does. I've never known anybody else to act so much like a firebug as he does."

"I know. You were right the other day—if Linwood weren't my cousin, I'd have thought it was him, too." I didn't enjoy admitting that, but I owed her that much.

Junior shook her head ruefully. "I wish I had listened to you. That way, Floyd might still be alive."

"I doubt it, Junior. From the way he talked tonight, I don't think he'd have given himself up no matter what." Maybe I should have felt bad about the man being dead, but it was mighty hard to feel sympathy for somebody who'd tried to burn me and Richard to death twice, not to mention

Augustus and Thaddeous. And he had killed Marshall Saunders.

"I guess that's it, then. Of course, y'all will have to come down to the station sometime and sign statements, but that should cover it. And I'm afraid you're going to have to find somebody else to help you next time around—your friend Wilder says he's leaving town."

"Is that right?" I said. "I guess he wouldn't be too happy living here after what happened tonight."

"Yeah," Junior said dryly, "that must be the reason. So, do you suppose any of this hullabaloo will have any effect on the mill buyout?"

"Who knows?" I said, trying to sound innocent. Then I saw a familiar white Cadillac drive up. "Isn't that Burt Walters's car? Maybe he can tell you."

"Knowing Burt, he'll be more interested in asking than in telling," she grumbled.

I left her to him, and went to find Richard. He was being enthusiastically interviewed by Hank Parker, who was pleased to be getting the story in plenty of time for Sunday's paper. I added a few quotes and we posed for pictures, then Hank went looking for Max, saying he hadn't got a shot of him yet. I didn't think he'd have much luck. I had a hunch Max wouldn't want his picture in the paper.

"Did you call Burt?" I asked Richard.

"You bet. I borrowed Hank's cell phone."

"He didn't hear who you were calling, did he?"

"You wound me," he said. "I got Thaddeous and Augustus to distract him by demonstrating how they'd been tied up."

"Aunt Nora is going to love seeing that in the paper."

"I called her, too, and I expect her to arrive any minute."

In fact, a fair number of Burnettes arrived over the next few minutes, all of them wanting to make sure we were all right. Then there were discussions about Floyd Cabiniss, ranging from, "I'd never have thought he could do such a thing," to, "I never did like Floyd—just didn't trust him."

Aunt Edna cried so hard after she hugged Richard and me that Aunt Daphine had to drive her back home. Most of the Burnettes thought her concern for us was awfully sweet, but I think Aunt Maggie knew there was more to it than that. She actually gave us both a peck on the cheek and said we'd done good.

Finally things calmed down enough that we were about ready to leave, but then Burt Walters came up to us.

"Here are our heroes now," he said loudly. "I've just got to hear the whole story from the horse's mouth. Why don't I give you two a ride home?"

I looked at Richard, who shrugged. We'd ridden with Thaddeous, and since Aunt Maggie had already left, somebody was going to have to drop us off anyway. If Burt was willing to take the chance of blowing our cover after all this, it was his call.

"That would be real nice," I said, and he grandly escorted us to his car.

Burt kept smiling as we drove away, but once the doors were shut, he said, "What happened?"

"Didn't Junior tell you about Floyd Cabiniss?" I said.

"Of course, and I'm glad Marshall's murderer is out of the way, and I'm shocked to hear about Floyd's pilfering, but y'all know that's not my main concern right now. What about the buyout?"

"We were right," I said smugly. "Max Wilder was working with the Saunders. Or at least with Grace."

"Can you prove it?"

In answer, I pulled out Max's signed confession. He couldn't read it all the way through while driving, but he saw enough.

"Damn!" he said happily. "If this doesn't do it, nothing will."

"We did have to make some concessions to get this," I warned him. "You can't take any action against Wilder—he gets to leave town and never hear anything else about this."

"Wilder is the least of my worries. That paper doesn't say anything about his faking his way into the mill, does it?"

"Not a word. So your father doesn't have to know about that—just that he was working secretly for the Saunders."

"Then the mill still belongs to me!"

"Don't forget your end of the deal," Richard said. He was talking about our "payment" for the job. Concern for family jobs had been part of what motivated us to come down, but the other part was wanting to help Thaddeous and Michelle. We'd made Burt promise that if we did what we wanted him to, then he'd give Michelle a job commensurate with her experience and pay her a decent salary.

"Don't worry!" Burt said. "Your friend can have her pick of jobs—anything that's available and almost anything that's not. I'll create a job for her if I have to."

"Wonderful," I said. Michelle and Thaddeous would be ecstatic. At least, they would be as long the mill was still around. The question was, how long would that be? Grace and Max may have aggravated the problems there, but they didn't cause them.

"You must be gratified to know the problems at the mill

weren't your fault after all," I said carefully. "Max Wilder was causing the equipment failures, and Floyd Cabiniss was making productivity look worse than it really was."

"That's right," Burt said, sounding far too pleased with himself.

"It's just a shame there weren't any procedures in place to track the situation sooner."

Burt looked over at me. "Laurie Anne, I may not be the brightest bulb on the chandelier, but I know there are problems at the mill, and that I still have my work cut out for me to keep Daddy from selling the place out from under me."

"Of course, now you've got the benefit of knowing what Marshall and Grace Saunders had planned. You did say they had some good ideas, didn't you?"

He didn't answer, and I didn't need Richard nudging me from the backseat to know that I'd said as much as I dared. Burt was a Walters, after all, and the Walters didn't accept advice gladly. All I could do was cross my fingers that he'd take the next step on his own. Finally, just as we pulled into Aunt Maggie's driveway, Burt said, "Do you still have those files you copied from Marshall's computer?"

"Yes, sir."

"Would you mind copying them for me? I'd like to take another look at those plans the Saunders came up with."

"I'll get them to you before we leave town."

"I'd appreciate that." He actually got out of the car to open my door, shook both our hands, and thanked us.

As we watched him drive away, I said, "I think there's hope for him after all."

Chapter 37

▼◉▼◉▼◉▼◉▼

Richard and I had hoped to sleep late the next morning in triumph, but it didn't happen. Not only did the phone keep ringing, but at eight o'clock, family members started showing up to continue repairing the house. By ten–thirty, most of my relatives were hard at work, while Aunt Maggie stayed busy making sure everything was done to her liking.

Somebody had gotten the power turned back on and, after indulgently long, hot showers, Richard and I joined the repair crew. At least, Richard did. As for me, I'm better with a keyboard than with a hammer, so the best I could do was fetch tools, deliver drinks, and answer endless questions about the previous night.

I was taking lunch orders for a run to Pigwick's when Alton Brown called to tell us that he'd heard that the mill buyout was off, and that Grace Saunders was leaving town immediately. The official story was that finding out that a mill employee had killed her husband had soured Grace on the deal. The unofficial version was that Big Bill had gotten something on the Saunders, but specifics were sketchy. That's when Alton paused, no doubt hoping I'd fill him in. Instead I asked him how he'd done in the betting, but his only answer was a pleased chuckle. I made a mental note to tell Earl that if he'd been wanting to ask his father for any expensive gifts, now would be a good time to do it.

After I hung up, I called Burt for more details. I didn't know if he'd be able to talk or not, but as it turned out, he was so happy at the way things had worked out that he didn't bother to suggest calling me from a pay phone or meeting at midnight under an old oak tree. He didn't even whisper.

Burt had given Big Bill the information about Max's sabotage right away, and Big Bill had confronted Grace with it over breakfast. Not surprisingly, she hadn't folded all at once. First she tried to deny it, but Big Bill didn't buy that for a second. Then she suggested that Max had done it on his own, as a favor to her because he was her cousin. That explained how Grace had known him, something I'd wondered about. Businesswomen, even unscrupulous ones, didn't usually have con men in their Rolodexes. It turned out that Max was from Massachusetts, too, meaning that his Georgia accent was as phony as everything else about him. At any rate, when Big Bill wouldn't swallow any of her excuses, Grace gave up and Big Bill ordered her out of his house.

Just for a minute, I felt sorry for her. She'd come so close to succeeding. Even though she was dishonest, some of her ideas really had been good. If she hadn't stooped to sabotage, Big Bill probably would have sold the mill to her, but it was like Aunt Maggie had said—Grace had wanted it too much.

I asked Burt how Big Bill was taking it, he said Big Bill's chagrin at having been fooled by Grace was balanced out by his relief at having found out in time. It didn't hurt that nothing had been made public. Big Bill hated being wrong, but he hated people knowing he was wrong even more. As it was, he was mighty impressed that Burt had saved him embarrassment, and though he wouldn't swear not to try to sell the mill later, he did seem more willing to let Burt have another chance to bring things up to speed.

After Burt thanked me again and I hung up, I went to spread the news. I was a little leery at first, considering how divisive the buyout had been, but I knew people would find out soon enough anyway. As it turned out, once folks heard the unofficial version of why Grace was gone, they agreed it was for the best. I think the general feeling was that if they were going to be stuck with owners who were less than honest, it might as well be the Walters.

When I got back with lunch, I found out that Aunt Nora had decided to throw a family party that night, and was already hard at work cooking. She claimed that she wanted to celebrate getting the home place put back together, but everybody knew that what she really wanted to celebrate was the family being back together. So later that afternoon, we all piled into cars and headed for Aunt Nora's place. We got a nice surprise when we got there, too. There'd been a mix-up with the Ramblers' schedule, so Aunt Ruby Lee and her crew were back in town for the weekend. Aunt Nora was so happy to see us all in one place again that she was teary-eyed all through dinner.

We were starting in on Aunt Daphine's apple pie when Vasti said, "I don't know about the rest of y'all, but I'd like to hear more about what went on last night."

"Are you serious?" Augustus said. "We haven't talked about anything but what happened last night!"

Everybody laughed, but Vasti said, "Oh, I know about

the trap you set for Floyd and all that, but what I don't know is why."

"Why what?" I asked. "Why did I suspect somebody at the mill?"

"No, I mean that Marshall Saunders wasn't killed until after you and Richard got to town, and y'all were up to something before then. So why did y'all come home in the first place?"

"Good Lord, Vasti," Aunt Maggie said, "don't you trust your own cousin?"

I appreciated the defense, especially when Aunt Maggie had been more than a little distrustful herself a few days back.

But Vasti persisted. "Now, Aunt Maggie, I know you didn't want anybody bothering Laurie Anne and Richard while they were doing their investigating, but now that it's all over, I want to know. Was it the fires that got y'all suspicious?"

I didn't dare look at Aunt Edna when Vasti asked that.

"Vasti, why don't you leave Laurie Anne alone?" Aunt Maggie said.

"It's all right, Aunt Maggie," I said. "I don't blame her for being curious. I imagine y'all are all curious. It's just kind of complicated." Under the table, Richard reached for my hand and squeezed it. "The truth is, we came down because of the buyout. We were hired to see what we could find out about the Saunders."

"Hired? By who?" Vasti asked.

"I can't tell you. It was somebody who didn't trust them, who wanted us to find out something bad about them to stop the buyout."

"Then you were against it all along?" Thaddeous asked.

"No, but I was concerned. An awful lot of us Burnettes depend on the mill. So Richard and I decided to come down and see if there was anything to worry about. I'd have been just as happy if the Saunders had turned out to be honest, but if they weren't ... Well, I wanted to know that, too. When Marshall was murdered, we thought it had to be connected somehow, and we started trying to find out who killed him." I went into more detail about what we'd done, leaving out only what I had to in order to keep the secrets I'd promised to keep. Then I waited to see if anybody was going to blast me for interfering, or for sticking my nose in where it wasn't wanted.

I was more relieved than I could say when Vasti said, "I figured it was something like that." As she and everybody else went back to eating their apple pie, she muttered, "I bet that Grace Saunders probably didn't know anything about running a debutante ball anyway."

Though I was glad my explanation had gone over so well, I didn't have any illusions that my next conversation would go as smoothly. I also knew I couldn't put it off, so after Aunt Nora refused my offer of help cleaning up, I hunted Linwood down and asked if he'd come outside with me for a minute. Richard and I had agreed that there were things that needed to be said to him, and since he was my cousin, I ought to be the one to say them.

Linwood didn't look thrilled, but he followed me out to a quiet corner of the backyard, lit up a cigarette, and said, "I suppose you're waiting for me to thank you for catching Marshall Saunders's real killer and getting me off the hook."

"Don't bother," I said. "We both know I did it for your mama, not for you."

"That's what I figured. So what do you want?"

"I want to talk about the fires."

"What about them?"

"You set them, didn't you?"

"Are you crazy? You know it was Floyd Cabiniss who set them—you proved it yourself!"

"I'm not talking about the fire that killed Marshall Saunders, Linwood, or the fire at the home place. I know Floyd set those. I'm talking about the one in the old Woolworth's building, and Drew Wiley's chicken coop, and all the others. You set those fires."

"You're full of shit!" he said, but he wouldn't meet my eyes.

"Then why were you the first on the scene for two of the fires? Why weren't you at home when any of them were set? How did you go through all those cans of gasoline when your lawn hasn't been mowed in months? Why have you been spending so much time driving around Byerly if you weren't looking for other places to burn down?"

I was nervous about that last question because I figured Linwood would realize that we'd been keeping tabs on him, but either he didn't care or he already knew.

"You can't prove anything," he said.

"I don't have to prove anything. I know I'm right. Linwood, it's got to stop."

"What are you going to do? Tell Mama? Or Sue?"

"Why bother? They already know, whether either of them will admit it or not."

He didn't answer me, just furiously sucked on his cigarette.

"What I am going to do is keep my ears open. If there's one more fire set in Byerly, or anywhere near Byerly, I'll find out about it. And then I'm going to tell Junior. She suspected you of being the arsonist all along, but she knows you didn't kill Marshall, and if the fires stop, she won't investigate any further. But if the fires start up again ..."

"There ain't going to be any more fires," he said, looking down at the ground.

"I'm sorry, Linwood, but your just saying that isn't good enough. I've read a little about people who set fires. It's a compulsion. People don't stop just because they want to."

He sneered. "Since when are you a head-shrinker?"

"I don't have to be a psychiatrist to know that Alton Brown couldn't stop gambling on a bet, or that Augustus wouldn't have quit smoking pot without his support group. You're in the same boat."

"Are you saying you don't think I'm man enough to quit?"

"Of course you're man enough—you're a Burnette," I said firmly. "But you can't quit alone. You need help."

"Don't you start talking about Reverend Glass. Mama's been after me to go see him, and I'm not going to do it."

"That's fine, but there are other people who can help. I wrote down a list of counselors for you." With the help of some phone calls that afternoon, I'd found the names of several psychologists and psychiatrists, plus a group session. "Most of these are in Hickory, but there's one in Statesville if you'd rather go somewhere farther from Byerly." I knew that getting psychological help was considered a sign of weakness by some folks, so I thought it would be easier if Linwood didn't have to worry about seeing anybody he knew.

He took the list from me, but said, "How the hell am I supposed to get time off to drive all the way to Statesville? Not to mention paying for it."

"You just tell Burt Walters when you need the time off.

Either take it as sick time, or make it up later. I've already set it up with him, but don't worry. He doesn't know why." Burt had been curious when I talked to him, but he was still so happy about the mill staying in the family that he was willing to stay blissfully ignorant. "As for paying, your insurance from the mill should pay for part of it. When that runs out, just have them send me the bills."

"Are you serious?"

I nodded. Knowing how tight Linwood and Sue's finances were, I'd worried about that part. It was Richard who'd said that we'd take care of it, and if I hadn't known before, I'd have known then that he was the perfect husband. As for Linwood, putting my money where my mouth was probably convinced him that I meant what I said quicker than anything else could have.

Linwood looked at the list. "I guess this might be a good idea."

I hated to antagonize him again, but I said, "That's not all I want you to do."

"What else?" he said suspiciously.

"You've got to pay back all those people whose buildings you burned down just as soon as you can swing it. If you send it in cash, they won't know where it came from, but they've got to be paid back."

"None of them buildings were worth more than two cents."

"Then send them two cents. No matter how much they were worth, it's not right that the owners should be out the money."

He nodded, but still sounded hostile when he asked, "What else?"

I took a deep breath, knowing that this was going to be

the hardest piece for Linwood to swallow. "I think you should start being nicer to Caleb."

"The hell—"

Raising my voice enough to talk over him, I said, "Caleb loves your mama, Linwood, and anybody with two eyes can see how much happier she is with him around. It's not right for you to come between them. How would you have liked it if Aunt Edna had tried to keep you and Sue apart? A lot of women would have. They'd have said it was Sue's fault she got pregnant and done their best to make sure you never saw her again. Sue's own mother was all for her having an abortion, but Aunt Edna talked her out of it. She welcomed Sue into the family and helped throw you a nice wedding, and has never said a word against Sue. Isn't that right?"

"That's different," he muttered.

"Why?"

"Because I didn't have a wife—Mama had a husband."

"Linwood, your father has been dead for four years," I said gently. "That's a decent interval for a widow to wait in anybody's book. Aunt Edna was so lonely before she started seeing Caleb. You know she needs somebody in her life."

"But I don't need another daddy!" he said defiantly, as if daring me to argue the point.

I knew better than to even try. "Caleb doesn't want to be your father. He just wants to be Aunt Edna's husband. He treats her well, and they love each other. I don't think you could pick a better man for her. Do you want her to spend the rest of her life alone?"

He thought about it, but finally said grudgingly, "I guess not."

"Well, she will if you make her choose between you and

Caleb. If it comes to that, even if it breaks her heart, she'll choose you. Caleb knows it, too, which is one reason he's been working so hard to get you to like him. He doesn't want to lose her any more than you do."

Linwood didn't say anything for a long while, and I wished I knew what he was thinking, but I'd said as much as I could safely say. The decision had to be his. Maybe if he still wasn't convinced, whatever counselor he ended up with would be able to do what I hadn't been able to.

"I'll have to think on it," was all he would say. Then he hesitated for a couple of seconds, as if there was something else he wanted to tell me, but what came out was, "You want a beer?"

I said, "That sounds good." Heck, getting offered a beer from Linwood was as good as getting a hug from anybody else.

Chapter 38

Richard and I headed back for Boston the next day, after an enthusiastic send-off from the whole family. Thaddeous was probably the happiest—now that Michelle had a job lined up, she would be able to move down in just a few weeks. It looked as if she was going to replace Miss Hunsucker, who'd suddenly handed in her resignation the day before. It seemed that she was one of Max Wilder's many conquests at the mill, which explained how his credentials had passed muster. When he left town without saying a word to her, she realized how she'd been used by him and decided she was too humiliated to work at the mill anymore. I was sorry for the woman, but I was also glad that Michelle was going to be in a position where she could really make a difference at the mill. If anybody could drag Burt Walters into the twentieth century before it ended, it was Michelle.

Despite all the fond farewells, and knowing that things were going to be all right in Byerly, I still found myself brooding on the plane. Richard being Richard, he noticed it almost before I did.

"What's wrong?" he asked.

"I'm not sure. Maybe I'm just worried about whether or not we did the right thing."

"How so? Linwood is going to be in therapy, Marshall's death is avenged, the mill is safe, the family feud has ended, and Michelle has a job so she and Thaddeous can be together. As you-know-who said, 'All's well that ends well.' "

"Did I really have the right to interfere so much?"

"Burt Walters asked you to interfere, and so did Aunt Edna."

"They didn't ask me to let Linwood get away with arson, or to let Max Wilder get away with what he did," I pointed out. "They certainly didn't ask me to get Floyd Cabiniss killed."

"Cabiniss got himself killed," Richard said. "As for the rest, they did just what you wanted Aunt Maggie to do. They trusted you to do the right thing. Which you did."

"Are you sure?"

"The important question is, are you sure?"

I considered it. "I think so. I just keep worrying about how awful it would have been if something had gone wrong. And there's still so much that can go wrong. What if Max Wilder graduates to something more dangerous than monkey-wrenching and con games? What if Linwood goes back to setting fires and somebody gets hurt? What if Burt runs the mill into the ground, and everybody loses their jobs and their pensions—"

"Laura, you're borrowing trouble. None of those things is going to happen."

"Probably not," I agreed, "but they could."

"Is there anything you could have done differently? Or did you do everything you could think of to protect your family?"

"I guess I did," I said doubtfully. "It just seems like I've taken on a lot of responsibility."

"I don't have as much family as you do, so it's hard for me to judge, but isn't taking responsibility part and parcel of being in a family? Maybe even the most important part."

"I guess you're right." I'd done a lot for the family before, from finding out who'd murdered Paw to helping Aunt Maggie when she needed to clear her conscience, but it had always been at somebody else's request, and I'd mentally laid the responsibility for any consequences on them. Maybe it was time to accept a few consequences myself. And more responsibility, too.

"Richard," I said, "would you like a larger family?"

He took my hand in his. "Are you asking what I think you're asking?"

I nodded. "I want to have a baby. If you want to, I mean."

The kisses he gave me were answer enough, even without a quote from Shakespeare.

All the way back to Boston, we daydreamed about what it would be like to have a child, but I couldn't help wondering how my family was going to react. They'd accepted my marrying a Northerner, but what would they say when they found out that a Burnette was going to give birth to a damn Yankee?